The Legend of V

Book 2
Triangle Corruption

by Varak Kaloustian

CONTENTS

Chapter 1

The Mysterious Threat

All right, round two.

The Unbound Evil will not get near my family again. This time, I'm ready for It. But I don't know what's going on with Vizor. He woke up momentarily, asked who I was, then slipped out of consciousness again. Is he still remembering his treacherous past?

Oh, here comes my best friend, Griff. He's wearing his favorite orange T-shirt with a star on it. Despite his pale skin and light-brown hair, the color looks good on him. Just shy of 14 years old, we're both about 5'10", even though my fluffy brown Afro makes me look taller.

"Enjoying the view of the Golden Gate Bridge, V?" He takes out a Ghirardelli milk-chocolate square from his trademark backpack.

"Yeah. It's been a while. This is the only place I'd want to be after an apocalyptic battle for the entire galaxy." The view from my house is fantastic; a cliff overlooking the bay, best to look at during sunset because of the way the sunlight bounces off the water. It makes my eyes feel like they're glowing. "So anything from Vizor?"

"Not yet. I can't believe he's been out since we brought him here."

Oh, that's right, I never told him what I saw with my dad. "That's not exactly the case."

"What do you mean? Did he ever awaken?"

"Well…" I tell Griff everything, including how my dad and I got inside Vizor's head and saw his younger brother, X.

"Really?"

"I'm not sure how the Unbound Evil got inside X, but that is what we saw."

"Huh? It's crazy, isn't it?"

"What is? The Unbound Evil?"

"Yes and no. I meant this whole adventure. It's awesome how bit by bit we're tying all of these loose ends together. And, best of all, I'm doing it with you, V."

I can't help but smile. I know it's a bit corny, but moments like this make me happy. "Griff, don't forget Rodger. He's helped us out a ton. In fact, if it weren't for Rodger and his team of officers, we would've been toast back in Alexandria."

Griff's eyes widen, exactly like the first time he saw Vizor.

"What is it? Did you remember something?"

"We've had so much going on that we completely forgot about Azilez!"

Azilez… the reason we didn't take her with us to Egypt is that we didn't want her to be in harm's way. She has probably tried to contact us, and is worried sick that we never got back to her.

"I hope she's OK…"

"Hold up. Let me get the keys to her house."

I head toward the entrance, but then think – *There's a faster way.* Using the Speed Prophecy's power, I leap over the main room of the tree house, and then use the roof of that room to leap to mine. I sneak through the window, grab the keys to Azilez's house, and jet back down to where Griff is.

"Ha. Show off."

"Funny. Let's go."

Azilez's house isn't very far from ours to begin with, and, with our speed, the trip is that much shorter.

"You do the honors, V."

"Thank you, my good man." I try to place the key in its slot. But on the slightest impact, the door makes a cringing, creaking sound, breaks apart from its hinges, and falls to the ground. A cloud of dust ensues because of all the debris on the floor of the house. My eyes tear and

I cough to get rid of that awful, fibrous taste in my mouth. I signal Griff to follow me. Inside the house, he's as surprised as I am.

"Unbound Evil again?"

"I didn't expect It to strike so soon."

"Hey, who's that over there?" We notice someone buried under a pile of broken wood. We totter toward the body, careful to avoid the debris. It's Azilez's mom. She's not moving. I scramble to find her jugular, and, when I do, am relieved to find a pulse. The burning in my face abates as I exhale.

"Are you all right?"

No answer.

"Griff, go get some cold water or ice from the kitchen. That might bring her back to consciousness."

"I'm on it." He scrambles into the kitchen while I keep my eye on Azilez's mom. "The pipes are all busted."

"Ugh, I was afraid of that."

– V, you feel it too, do you not?

– Wha…? Oh, right, Dark Spirit. It's been a while since You've talked. Have You been snoozing inside me?

The Dark Spirit is a divine life force created by God, initially as the Light Spirit. But then it was tainted with darkness. It has been waiting a long time to help me fulfill my legacy, The Legend of V. When the Earth first formed, my ancestors tried creating a utopia, during the Great War. They were stopped by a threat created by the Devil, called the Unbound Evil, who wanted Its own utopia, from which It and It alone would rule the universe. That's why Griff and I are on a hunt for the Unbound Evil. Eons later, the Unbound Evil is back.

The Dark Spirit doesn't find snoozing questions amusing, so I remain on topic…

– I do feel something. And it's upstairs. But first I want to make sure Azilez's mom is all right.

– V, did you forget about My powers? I can easily heal her.

I think this is a new record for me. I wonder how much I've forgotten over the last few days. Of course the Dark Spirit can heal her. I place my hands on her shoulders to let the magic begin.

– *Have a go at it, Buddy.*

The Dark Spirit leaves my body and enters Azilez's mom. Within seconds, the Dark Spirit flows through her entire body and reenters mine.

"Griff, she's starting to wake up!" I yell so he could hear me in the kitchen.

"Mmrrff… urgh… wha…? Who is this?"

"You mean you don't recognize your daughter's best pal?"

"Griff?"

"… The other one."

"Oh, V, is that you?" Excitedly, she jumps to her feet. Azilez's mom looks pretty decent for having just been tackled by wood. She has the same crystal-brown eyes as her daughter, along with the same flowing brown hair. Her smile is similar, definitely genuine, but not as radiant as Azilez's beaming grin. The emotion of her mom's smile just feels different.

"Can you tell me what happened to your home?"

"What are you…?" She looks around, and, as she starts to remember, her polite smile turns into a furious expression.

"Oh," Griff comes out of the kitchen with a cookie jar, "you're awake."

"Shhh. Not now, Griff. She's remembering how her house got ransacked."

"It was Azilez! V, I can't believe it. She did this. All of it, including knocking me out."

– *Suspicious?*

– *I'd say. All these years you've known Azilez: I don't think you can believe she'd hurt anyone, especially her own mother.*

– *Exactly right, Dark Spirit. Azilez is too sweet.*

"Are you sure it was her?"

"Positive. When I get my hands on that girl… She's in big, big, monumental trouble. V, do you know where she could've gone?"

– *Uh-oh. She's mad, and we need to see Azilez in private, sooo…*

"Uh… yeah! She went to the pier."

"WHICH ONE?"

"Uuhhh… I think she said 39." I've never seen her so angry. Who could blame her? She gets into her car and races off at a clearly illegal speed.

"Let me take a wild guess, V. She's upstairs."

"Read me like a book. Yup, she's up there, Griff. The Dark Spirit and I both feel her presence. I'm assuming you can too?"

"I guess that's one way to put it. I can't really explain it myself, but I knew she was up there the minute we walked in. Let's go see her."

We tiptoe up the ramshackle stairs, trying to step on only those boards that feel solid enough, in order to safely advance to the second floor. Then, suddenly, Griff slips behind me.

"Are you all right? Griff?" Wait… where'd he go?

– I felt it, V. That was definitely Azilez.

– That was awfully fast. I sort of missed her. Maybe our premonition was on the money.

– It's highly likely…

– One way to find out.

I make it to the next floor in one piece. Azilez's room is just down this mess of a hall. Her door is the only one in the house that hasn't been torn down or smashed. The walls on the sides of the hall have broken pieces of art, Azilez's works. Azilez is very talented. I'd even call her a master. The drawings on the walls range from cartoons to figurative works and even… demons? I don't remember seeing that one on her wall. It's been drawn right over her illustration of Griff, herself, and me.

– OK, yeah. She's totally possessed. She'd sacrifice her life to save this wall. She wouldn't just blow it to pieces.

I approach the door, shaking. Could the Unbound Evil have really done this? And, more importantly, why? What could It gain beside trying to crush me? Regardless, I press on. I grab the doorknob and gently open it to make sure it doesn't fall down. The door is fine. Azilez's room is also perfectly fine. Nothing is too out of the ordinary. In fact, she's standing right in front of me, wearing jeans shorts and a tie-dye tank top, painting away on her canvas.

The second I try to walk toward her to see if her head's screwed on right, she drops her brush to the ground.

"I never thought you'd show up again, V."

Why is she crying?

"Where's Griff? What did you do to him?"

"How about you focus on me for a change!" She confronts me so fast I nearly fall. Her eyes are filled with pure hate. And they're not their normal color. Both eyes have one red dot where the pupil should be. They're like white voids with a drop of blood at their center. She isn't possessed though; I don't sense the Unbound Evil.

– I was certain the Unbound Evil would be here.

– Me too, Dark Spirit. But if it wasn't the Unbound Evil, what's wrong with Azilez?

– I can't even say. I've never felt this before.

"V, run! She's ruthless!"

"Griff?" I can't even keep up. I'm so confused…

"Come join your friend, you FIEND!"

What…? That statement shoots at my very core. The friend who has shown me inexhaustible kindness and literally given me my life back now wants to tear it down. But maybe it's not like that. It *can't* be like that. The real Azilez would never do this. I'm going to set her free of whomever, or *whatever*, is controlling her mind.

"Come here, V." She grabs her brush and shoots out spear-like, dark-purple stalactites. I fuse with the Dark spirit, transform into Dark V, and go through the ground to dodge it.

"Where'd you go?"

"What's wrong? Not so confident anymore?" I retort.

Dark V has awesome powers and looks intimidating with his red eyes and spiked hair. I really do miss this transformation. I touch the back of Azilez's head to see just what's going on in there. All I find is Azilez herself. There's nothing else.

– How is that possible?

– You seriously have no idea why she's like this?

– No, I've… A flying dark crystal to the face cuts us off. I crash

into the wall.

– Why can't I move? V… Ugh…

– Dark Spirit? Dark Spirit!

The Dark V transformation slowly wears off.

"Grrrrrr!" Azilez walks up to me with a nasty frown on her face. She looks just about ready to kill me.

"What's gotten into you, girl? It's me, V!"

"That's exactly why I've…" Her facial expression suddenly, completely changes from a savage killer's to a surprised friend's. But before I could ask her anything, she faints.

"Wow, that was certainly an interesting sequence of events. Griff, help me out."

"I would. Except I'm stuck, just like you."

"Where exactly are you?"

"In the closet. How are we going to get out?"

– Dark Spirit? It's knocked out inside of me. Azilez must have hit a sweet spot or something. "Maybe there's a way…"

"Sometime today would help, V."

"Hmm… I got it! Brace yourself, Griff."

"Braced."

I close my eyes and visualize the five Solar Prophecies inside me: Wisdom, Speed, Power, Chaos, and Solar… They unite to light my soul on fire! BOOM! A fiery blast breaks Griff and me free of the stalactites that had imprisoned us.

Since we're free now…

"Azilez, are you all right?" I lay her head down on my lap and check her pulse. Still beating. Whew. "She's going to be all right. Thank goodness."

"What's your plan now, V?"

– Dark Spirit, can You hear me?

– Ngh… hmm? Oh yes, I hear you.

– Ok, nice! I was starting to worry. Are you ready?

– Yes. Let's revive your friend.

"Stand back! Doctor V is in the building."

– Seriously? Doctor V?

I place my hand on Azilez's head. "All done," the Dark Spirit proudly announces.

"It's been a while. Where've You been all this time?" asks Griff, placing his hand on the side of his face.

"Sleeping. Inside V."

"That last adventure was strenuous on You. A well-deserved break."

"Much appreciated, Griff."

"Hey, look! Azilez is waking up!"

"Mrrggh… uggghhh… wh… wha…? Where am I?" Ahhh… The sight of her real eyes is so refreshing that it melts my soul. It's almost like I'm meeting her all over again. Then she realizes who both of us are.

"V? Griff? Is it really you?"

"Yeah, we're back."

SMACK! The second she gets up, she slaps Griff and me. Dazed, we fall over.

"YOU TWO WENT AND SAVED THE GALAXY FROM IMME-NENT DOOM, AND YOU DIDN'T EVEN INVITE ME?" After a few seconds of absolute silence, Azilez helps us back up. "Get a grip, you two! I WANT AN ANSWER."

We shake our heads and try to stand up straight. "All right, Azilez. Jeez. What exactly do you want to know?"

"How about… oh… I don't know…" she starts in a caustic tone, "WHY YOU TWO WERE GONE FOR WEEKS?"

"As long as it doesn't mean our faces getting leveled again by your backhand."

She takes a deep breath and calms down. "Deal. Now, tell me everything."

Griff and I take turns explaining the grand adventure that had recently transpired. We tell her about the Solar Prophecies -- the five prophetic rocks that helped me discover my inner strength, the Great War, how we encountered both the Devil and God, King Tut's chamber, Melok, Zapzoid, King Electrox the Third, the Cave of Destiny, the massive palace of the Solar Prophecies underneath King Tut's tomb, the master prophecy inside said chamber, the Dark Spirit, and Vizor with his set of Shadow Prophecies. I don't know how long we talked — perhaps hours.

"WHAT? God? And the Devil? AND you lived to tell about it? I'm not quite sure I believe you two. But if it's true, that's quite a trip you guys just had. By the way, where's Rodger? Is he just looking out for himself now?"

"Rodger will never ONLY be looking after himself. He is too kind a soul. He's looking after the community, serving again as a police officer. We were lucky to have had him as our legal guardian. He will always have a special place in our hearts."

"Well, that's not to say he won't visit us every now and then."

"Of course, Griff. We're practically family, and are forever grateful to Rodger. He's done more for us than we could've ever imagined. He was basically our dad all those years." I get a little teary-eyed remembering the day that Rodger came to our aid. It was the same day our families were ripped away from us. Our families… Azilez has never met them. "Ready to meet everyone, Azilez?"

"I've always wondered what your families were like. I'm dying to meet them! Let's go! Oh, wait. I almost forgot. I can't go out like this." She runs into her closet and grabs a waist-cut leather jacket and fingerless biker gloves. She looks like a rainbow with a black outline. "How do I look?"

"Awesome!"

"Wait…" Griff suddenly turns solemn. "I still have a few questions for you. First, how did you know we saved the galaxy?"

Azilez scratches her chin, thinks long and hard, but in the end can't come up with an explanation. "It's weird. I just know. I'm not sure how. It's like part of my memory has been wiped."

"The Unbound Evil's been here," Griff knowingly exclaims as he glances my way.

"Let me explain. Azilez, the Unbound Evil has many special powers. Many of which we still don't even know yet. But we do know that whenever It possesses someone, the host body has no memory of what happens until the Unbound Evil is lifted."

"Oh..." Azilez shivers. "Do you think I could've been possessed?"

"Maybe, but I can't say for certain. The Dark Spirit and I didn't sense It, which is confusing because you definitely were not yourself when this happened — your eyes were blood-red. And your house has been ransacked, which we thought for certain was the Unbound Evil's doing."

Azilez is stoic — which is never a good thing. She glances around and sees the holes in her walls. I open her room door. Azilez runs outside and stares at the painted walls that she both created and destroyed. She drops to her knees, turns away from us, and starts to cry.

"How could I have let this happen? Who else could I have hurt?"

Griff and I look at each other and decide not to tell Azilez about her mom. Wait, her brush! If it was shooting out sharp crystals earlier when Azilez was evil, then maybe it still has powers now that she's herself? I wonder...

"Azilez, try waving this around." I grab her brush. As soon as I do, I feel warm and fuzzy inside.

– Ahh... Are you taking a bubble bath, V?

– Nope. It's this brush. Notice anything about it?

– It's teeming with energy! See if you can release some of it.

I wave it around, but nothing happens. I can feel the energy, but can't use it.

"Azilez, catch!" I wink and give her a "V" sign. She picks up the brush and her heart-melting smile breaks out.

"Wow! What am I feeling?"

"On my previous adventure, I learned that everyone has a special ability. It's no different for you. Azilez, this is your power. This is the energy you radiate, and it's unique to you. No one can take it from you. Now try waving it around."

Azilez closes her eyes and takes a deep breath. She reopens her eyes to paint the canvas that is the world around her. The second she makes a stroke, a rainbow flies out of her brush and her face glows with excitement. But the rainbow is just sitting there in front of her. It's not really doing anything. "It's so pretty, but what's it supposed to do? If it's my power, then…" She flicks her brush toward the paintings and the pulsing energy of the rainbow cleans up the demon-infested wall.

"That's awesome, Azilez! I've never seen anything like that."

"Ha, this is so cool! And only I could use this, right?"

"That's right. We all have something unique to us. We're a team. And we use our combined strength to fight the evil threat we face."

"Come on, Griff, let's go home. Azilez, I probably already know the answer to this, but do you want to come with us on our next adventure?"

"I wouldn't miss it for anything! I appreciate you trying to protect me by not telling me anything the first time around and not getting me involved… Actually, I don't know why I'm trying to be polite… No, I don't. And it looks like this Unbound Evil is going to take some girl power to finish off. And no one lays a finger on my best friends without having to answer to me! Got that?"

We run and give her a great big hug. "Welcome aboard, Azilez."

Our group hug breaks and Griff asks, "Uhh… V, what IS our next adventure?"

– That's the question of the day.

– Tell me about it. I'm curious about Vizor's home world, but I really don't know where to start.

– Yes, well, why don't we regroup at your place and let Azilez meet your family and Griff's family first? Afterwards, when we've gathered everyone who wants to go, we'll brainstorm.

– Sounds good. Oh, and one more thing. Dark Spirit?

– Yes?

– Come out and introduce Yourself to Azilez. She hasn't met You yet.

– Oh, that's right! Where are My manners?

The Dark Spirit jumps out of my body and materializes into a shadow figure that looks just like me.

"Azilez. This is the legendary Dark Spirit. Dark Spirit, Azilez."

"A pleasure to meet you. You are quite the lovely young lady."

"Why thank You!" Azilez tries to shake the Dark Spirit's hand, but feels embarrassed as it goes right through the Dark Spirit.

"Well, should we all get going? Come on back, Dark Spirit. Wouldn't want anyone seeing a shadow doppelganger of me wandering around, would we?" The Dark Spirit breaks down into the form of a purple puddle, then flies back into my body.

"That is one of the coolest things I've ever seen!"

"Wait till you meet the Solar Prophecies, Azilez. Come on!"

Azilez grabs her new, wonderful paintbrush and all of us run out the door. As we get closer to our tree house, Griff and I are alarmed to see it has been attacked.

"Oh, no, our families!" With one giant leap, we land onto the floor of what was the living room. We search through the rubble, and find Z and D.

"Guys! What happened?"

"Vi… Vizor… ugh…" D tries to mutter, but collapses.

"Did Vizor do this? Where could he have gone?"

"Did you guys seriously already forget about me?" Azilez crawls up the ladder. "Yikes! V, are your brothers OK?" She points at Z and D. Griff had finished dragging them out of the rubble. They are both unconscious.

"Do your thing, V."

"With pleasure, Griff."

– *Dark Spirit?*

– *I'm always ready.*

"Clear." I place my hands on them. First, the Dark Spirit works on D. Then It slithers into Z and heals him too. Within a matter of seconds, my brothers regain full consciousness, as if nothing had happened. "Are you two OK now?"

"Never better. Thanks, V."

"But… but…" D is frightened. I think he wants to tell me how this happened, and maybe, once he stops shaking, he can even tell us where Vizor has gone.

"Calm down, D, calm. Can you tell me how Vizor did this?"

"I think we should let him get a grip." Z holds my shoulder. "He's still taking it all in. It happened pretty quickly."

"Then you tell me. How did Vizor wreck this place?"

"I can't remember too clearly either. But Vizor didn't seem normal. His eyes were pitch-black."

"Pitch-black? That can't be a good sign."

Z looks over to my friend who just spoke and realizes I'm too preoccupied to make the introduction. "Azilez, was it?"

"Yup. That's my name! How did you know? I don't think we've met..."

"The Unbound Evil showed you to us once or twice. I can't remember very clearly. But then again, I don't want to remember how I was kidnapped, trapped, and then thrown into a castle for half my life."

"And you are...?"

"Z. V's older brother. Nice to meet you."

"And the little one is D, right? He's so adorable! I want to squeeze his cheeks. Come here!" D is hesitant, but Azilez is way too eager and hugs him anyway. Eventually D pushes away.

"What's wrong?" It's like he wants to say something, but isn't. "Come on, I'm your brother's best friend. You can tell me."

D is never good with first encounters, especially with total strangers. But he soon comes around and whispers into Azilez's ear.

"WHAT?"

D gets scared and hides in a blanket in the ruined corner.

"What? What is it, Azilez?" Griff is impatient to find out.

"One single red dot in the pupils, just like how I looked when I was on a rampage. You guys said the rest of my eyes were white. His looked black and soulless, according to D."

"I wonder what that means." I close my eyes and twirl my hair.

– *What do you think, Dark Spirit?*

– *Well, it seems the force that controlled Azilez and Vizor is similar. But I can't make the connection. We should find Vizor.*

– *Yes, and ask him how he got up. Maybe a memory was triggered in his mind?*

– *That's a possibility. Or the Unbound Evil...*

– Aww, not so soon. I was hoping for some lazy days of Smash Bros. and SpongeBob.

– Not happening, sadly.

"Z, any idea where Vizor could've gone?"

"Nah. He bolted without a word. So I'm clueless."

There's a TV in the rubble. It still looks functional. If Vizor is out and about, maybe the news spotted him. "Z, does the TV still work?"

"I don't know. Does it look like I've been watching TV?"

"Not the best time for sarcasm. Guys, inspect the other rooms to make sure that everyone else is still alive and well."

"On it. C'mon, D." Z holds D's hand as they walk up the stairs to the remaining rooms.

After hitting the TV enough times, it turns on. We find the news.

"Good. It works." There's a live report. "Guys, get a load of this..." Azilez and Griff huddle around the TV.

"A mysterious man who looks like San Francisco's hero is on top of the burning Ghirardelli building. He seems to have five hostages. Could that savage really be V? And if it is, why has he dyed his hair blue? It looks awful!"

"MOM?" Azilez grabs hold of the TV.

"Not our families again!" Griff punches the nearest piece of wood he can find.

"Argh! The Ghirardelli Factory?" He's adding insult to injury. "He's taken our families again! And now our favorite chocolate too. Vizor's going to be sorry he messed with us... again. C'mon, Azilez. You'll get to meet our families, I promise."

We head to the blazing factory.

Griff, Azilez, and I dash off as fast as possible. In the middle of Fisherman's Wharf, Azilez stops dead in her tracks with her head facing down.

"Hold on, Griff. Griff!" It's no good. He can't hear me since he has disappeared into the next street corner. I walk back to see if Azilez is OK.

"Why do you keep ignoring me?" she says, crying. Azilez is much sadder than I would've thought.

It's at that moment that I realize how much I've hurt her. "You've been feeling this way for a few weeks, haven't you?"

"Well, yeah. V… I… I'm…" I hug her before she finishes her thought. I know she has every right to feel mad. She probably tried to contact us during our adventure. And when she couldn't, she must've felt that we had abandoned her. How could I have done that? I should've at least let her know why we were going to Egypt. As for the rest, well, there was no way we could've foreseen any of that.

I cup her face in the palms of my hands and wipe her tears with my thumbs. "No, Azilez. I'm sorry. I haven't been a good friend lately. Would you forgive me?"

At long last, she lifts her head up, smiles, and says: "Of course." We continue to hug, and everything seems right again, until I snap back to reality.

"Azilez! Griff is fighting Vizor alone. Come on, let's get to Ghirardelli." We always feel a sense of urgency when we run from the Wharf to Ghirardelli Square, but this time it's not because of the heavenly chocolate. I start to run, but since I'm a lot faster than Azilez now, thanks to the prophecies' influences, I head right back to her.

"I'm not… *huff, huff*… quite as fast… as you, V."

"You want me to carry you? I will." Although I know she is too strong, independent, and stubborn to accept such an offer.

"Wait, WAIT! I've got an idea." She pulls out her paintbrush from her back pocket.

"What are you going to do with that?"

She spins around once, and waits for the rainbow to close in on itself. Then she stands on top of it. "What do you think?"

"Love it, Azilez. I'd expect nothing less from you. Come on, let's go." Azilez can fly on that board, so she easily keeps up with me. Watch out, Vizor, here come V and Azilez with flying colors!

Literally.

Chapter 2
A Legendary Rekindling

Azilez and I make it to the burning factory in no time. At the base of the building, there lay half-burnt plastic bowls and gallons upon gallons of ice cream. The charred snowflakes pierce through my nose and make me cough. The sight of my favorite dream palace with its creamy, chocolate river burning away makes me livid.

"This is horrible! How am I ever going to eat an Earthquake now?" Azilez is almost brought to tears.

We look up and see that all our parents are tied to poles with thick rope. Vizor is next to them and is wearing a backpack. Wait, that's Griff's backpack! Vizor looks happy to see me. Suspiciously, way too happy. "GWAHAHAHAHAHAHA! Looks like I've finally lured my catch."

"UNHAND OUR FAMILIES! Especially Azilez's mom. She has nothing to do with this."

"Oh, but she does. Now that Azilez has that magic brush in her possession."

Azilez gasps. We haven't told anyone about her brush. But then again, she did use it to fly through San Francisco.

"How do you know about this, Vizor?"

"I think what matters now is how I know THAT YOU TWO ARE DEAD!" He points to our left, and we notice our buddy lying unconscious in the rubble.

"Griff!" I rush to his aid. "Umph!" I'm blocked by a force field. It's most likely Vizor's doing.

"Wait awhile, V. Watch the blood seep out of his forehead for a few minutes. THEN LET'S SEE WHERE HE'S GOING! HAHAHAHA!"

What? I'd ask questions, but Griff could die any second now. I've got to beat Vizor, and quickly.

"Freeze!"

That voice. I'd recognize it anywhere...

"Put your hands in the air, and let V get to Griff."

It's Rodger! He's got a gun. But is it enough?

"Come at me, Rodger! LET'S SEE YOU TRY!"

Rodger's got something up his sleeve. I know it. He's oozing confidence right now. He shoots at Vizor, but the shot is off-target —too far off to be an accident.

Vizor whips out his hair blades and attempts to rush Rodger. But Rodger's "bullet" creates an electromagnetic pulse that radiates onto Vizor's blades and electrocutes him.

"AAAARRRRGGGGHHHH!"

The force field around me wears off. Without a word, I rush to Griff. I immediately transfer the Dark Spirit into his forehead, and his wound heals. But he doesn't wake up.

"Griff...?" No! He can't be!

"GRIFF!" Azilez grabs him by the shoulders.

"Looks like you two are too late!"

We get hit from behind and fall over.

It can't be! Griff can't be dead. Can the Dark Spirit even do anything about this now? No! No!

Ugh...! What was that? Something just grasped a hold of me in my spirit. It hurts! Arrrghh! What am I doing? Vizor's got the upper hand now. To make matters worse, the fire inside the building is seething out and rising to the roof.

The cards are stacked squarely against me right now. It's been like this since I was a little kid. However, my last adventure helped me find the answer. And it lies within me.

As the fire from the factory gathers around me, I feel a deep inner spirit light ablaze. Whatever was bothering me a few seconds ago has been burned up. My body emits high amounts of solar energy, as if I'm the sun itself. There's so much energy around me that I feel my hair fly around. Time for Extreme V.

Everyone surrounding the Ghirardelli Factory starts to levitate. Seconds later, BOOOOOOOOMMM! Vizor goes flying and hits the giant Ghirardelli sign that overlooks the square. Now it reads "hirardelli". I place everyone gently onto a nearby road. Azilez has her hands in front of her face. Her brush spawns a rainbow shield and helps her absorb the blast.

"Nice. You're getting the hang of this, Azilez."

Her eyes suddenly twinkle, and her jaw drops. She's looking at me kind of funny.

"Your hair and eyes… They look like the color of the sun. Are you even V anymore?"

"This is what the prophecies helped me achieve, Azilez."

"It's so… so… COOL! I mean, hot. Duh! You know what I mean!" She looks like she's in deep thought. I hope she understands the power of the prophecies — miracle-working tablets that help people become conscious of their inner strength. Now it is clear to me that Azilez is fully aware of it. So aware that I feel the energy rising in her. It's so different. Yet it has kindled because she has felt my fire. That's the beauty of inner strength. It can't be copied, not for anything. Strength is your essence first, then everything you are second.

Azilez's hair flies up on its own, almost as though by psychokinesis. The tip of her brush spews fire, her eyes glow a blazing orange, and her power starts to radiate.

"Vizor…THIS CHARADE ENDS HERE!" Azilez says as we point at Vizor. With our combined powers, we enclose just the three of us in a cage of fire. Stand by. This is going to get ugly.

Chapter 3

A Plague of Evil

Vizor, Azilez, and I are in a triangle formation. Any one of us can rush at any second. Before getting extreme, I try to see what's going through Vizor's head. Maybe he can explain why his eyes are like that.

"Vizor, what are you doing? Why would you kill Griff like that?"

"My mission is to gather the Solar Prophecies. I need them to obliterate this world. Anyone who dares stand in my way will be eternally punished!"

"That's horrible!" Azilez prepares her brush. "What kind of mission is that?"

Vizor smirks. He grasps his blades and thrusts both into the ground with authority. The resulting earthquake knocks Azilez and me to the ground and makes all of the nearby buildings quiver. "I'm not through with you two just yet!" He takes out his grappling hook from his hair and attaches his hair blades to both ends. Now he has a weapon that resembles a nunchuk.

If those buildings fall over, then everyone in the surrounding area will…

"EVACUATE! EVERYONE! NOW!"

"No one leaves until I…" Vizor locks eyes with me. Just then, he collapses like Azilez did back at her house. Did he realize something like Azilez had?

"Azilez, help me tie him up!"

"Right. One sec." She materializes a rainbow rope and we get to work.

As I am tying Vizor, I can't help but think of Griff. I never checked his pulse. Is he really dead? Were we really too late this time? I feel the sweat trickle down my neck. My eyes feel swollen in their sockets. I'm not even sure the Dark Spirit can help him this time. The only way the Dark Spirit can heal him is if he's still alive. Could Griff really be gone? I don't know what I'd do without him…

"Secure enough?"

"Huh? Oh, yeah, I'd say so. Let's leave him on that bench over there."

After we drop off Vizor, we fly up to get a better view. "Do you see where everyone evacuated to?"

"Yeah! Right there. Come look!"

Everyone is huddled around a hospital about five blocks from the fire. As urgently as I want to see Griff, I know we should try and put the fire out first. But how do I beat fire with fire? I've never tried this in my extreme form before.

"Azilez, let's see what we can do about this burnt block."

"Rodger!"

"What about him?"

"Oh no, I meant… Roger as in 'I understand'."

"Ha!" I wonder if that pun was intentional. Well played, Azilez.

We land in the midst of the flames and Azilez looks around, but my eyes are locked on one place, the Ghirardelli Factory. "That was my favorite…"

"Oh, that's right. Well, we can't really do anything about it now, right? It's almost completely gone."

"Maybe we can. Did you already forget about your brush?"

"Oh, yeah!" She fires a rainbow toward the flame, but it dissolves right into it.

"So we have to quell the flames first. Hmm… Oh! Let me see if I can absorb them." I lift up my right hand and concentrate on the inferno. The flames fly into my hand. Eventually the fire subsides, but the damage has been done. That's where Azilez comes in. "You're up."

"I'll make it quick. We've gotta hurry to Griff!" She flies on a rainbow, rematerializing what was lost in the fire, even the Ghirardelli Factory. It takes longer than we'd like due to the extent of the damage, but afterwards it seems like the city block was never touched.

"Amazing! V saves us again! And… Ms. Flying Colors?"

Azilez flies down and comes face to face with the reporter. Her hands are on her hips and her shoulders hunched. "I HAVE A NAME, YOU KNOW! IT'S AZILEZ!"

"How long have you been standing there?" I ask the reporter.

"Well, we had to rush over here after that fire started. Not only that, but that HUGE explosion! Do you know who caused it? What could've caused it? And who was that man who looked just like you?"

"Look, I'd love to stay and chat, but I'm worried about my friend. He needs my help!"

"Another scoop! Well, folks, you heard it here first. V's friend is in dire need of help."

I hate the news media. I guess it's my own fault. I should've seen this coming. I shouldn't have said anything at all.

Regardless, Azilez and I fly to the hospital.

"V, you don't really think Griff is dead, right?"

"I hope not. I gave him the Dark Spirit. It was all I could do at that point because Vizor wouldn't let me do anything else."

"So the Dark Spirit has the ability to heal ANYTHING?"

"Most things, yes. Mainly physical. It's a miracle how helpful It's been to us."

"I wanna hear all about it!"

"Sure. But when we get Griff out of here, alive."

We revert back to normal, and go to the front desk in the main lobby. "Hello, miss. We're here to see our friend. His name is Griff."

"The one that was rushed in here a few minutes ago?"

"Yes, that one!"

"I believe he's in critical condition right now. No one will be allowed…" Just then, the alarm goes off.

The door leading to the elevators bursts open and everyone panics. "He's mad! The patient's gone MAD! He's taken out all the security."

Griff? He's alive? That's awesome! But… he's taken out all of the security? Oh, no. Was Vizor's energy contagious?

As everyone is running to the door, the police barge in. The crowd outside the hospital disperses. Meanwhile, the reporter is caught in the middle of everything.

"I'm not certain exactly what is going on here. But according to my sources, the patient who was in critical condition just a second ago is now on a mad frenzy!"

Mad frenzy? This has to be the same energy that consumed Azilez and Vizor. Hold on, Griff. We're coming!

"Not so fast, you two. This area is extremely dangerous!" a random policeman cries out. "Evacuate the premises immediately!"

"V? Azilez?" Out of the storming line of officers, a familiar face jumps out.

"Rodger!" I run to give him a hug.

"How've you been, V? Hopefully no more destroyed neighborhoods?"

"Don't worry. That'll never happen again. Not on our watch. Right, Azilez?"

"Oh, yeah! That evil is gonna pay!"

"Sir! You know these two?"

"Of course! This one with the big hair was the one I adopted for seven years. And the lovely lady next to him is his best friend. Well, one of them."

"What difference does it make? You two should leave, now!"

"I think not! You two are coming with me."

"But, sir…!"

"And that's an order!"

"Yes, sir!" We put our hands on our foreheads as if we're saluting. The three of us go up the stairs to see if Griff is in his room. To our surprise, he actually is, but not by his free will. At least ten policemen are pinning him down, and it looks like Griff could still shake them all off. When I look into his eyes, I see it: the exact same stare Azilez had shot when she nearly killed us.

"About time you two got here."

"Griff? What's wrong with you?"

"You should know, Azilez. You've had this sensation before. AND NOW I'LL USE IT TO ACTUALLY KILL BOTH OF YOU!"

– *V!*

– *Dark Spirit?*

Damn! I forgot I gave It to Griff so he could heal. This is not good...

– *I can't move about My own will! You have to knock Griff unconscious!*

– *But, Griff...?*

– *He's just like Azilez from before. Left unchecked, and he'll destroy everything! HURRY!*

What's going on? Why do my best friends suddenly feel the need to attack me?

Griff lets out a cloak of dark purple that ensures the police's absence, including Rodger's.

"AAAAHHH!"

"Rodger! NO!"

"Too late, V! There's no helping him now. It's just us three... well, four, if you count IT."

"Why you little...!"

"V, calm down! Griff is still somewhere inside. All we have to do is drag him out." Azilez holds my shoulder.

I take a deep breath. "You're right. Sorry, I just don't know what to think right now..." This is Griff we're talking about. I can't just fight him. Though it's like the Dark Spirit said: – *Left unchecked, and he'll destroy everything! HURRY!* I guess I don't have a choice. I've got to do this...

Arrgghh! It's that burning pain from last time. Why does it keep doing that? It's as if it acts up only when I feel sadness or grief... What is it? I can't think about that now. I've got to stay strong and focus on getting Griff back.

"What's the matter, V? Scared?"

Azilez launches a rainbow at Griff's forehead, thinking it'll get him to stop acting evil, but it's futile. Griff brushes it off like it's nothing.

"You two can't touch me! NOT WHEN I HAVE THIS!"

"We'll see about that!" I haphazardly throw a punch. I stumble right through Griff and pass out.

"Pathetic. I'll end your miserable life now, V. V…"

– *V!*

– *Unnngghh… wha…? Griff?*

– *Listen to me! Whatever's going through your mind right now, forget it! I don't have much time. Teach this fake a lesson.*

– *But I'd be hurting you in the end…*

– *Better that than letting that abomination run free! You can heal me after the fact. Remember?*

– *I just… I don't know… this feeling in my head… ugh…*

– *V!*

I completely lose consciousness.

"You monster!" Azilez yells.

"That's not very nice, now is it?"

"I'll tell you what's not very nice! Putting V in a position like that one! Who are you? 'Cause you're certainly not Griff!"

"It doesn't matter who I am! What matters is that you… ARE UNDONE!"

"Bring it, you sleaze ball!"

This ought to be interesting: a fight between best friends. I hope Azilez is wary of the Dark Spirit. Otherwise this is over before it starts.

Griff uses the Dark Spirit's power to hide inside the floor. Suddenly, Griff fires a bolt of purple at Azilez and she falls over, dropping her brush. Just like that, she's unconscious.

But when it seems as though Griff is about to finish off both of us, Azilez's brush rolls and hits my cheek. Ah, that warm, bubbly feeling again. My headache… It's gone! Time for what Griff wanted me to do.

"I don't know who you are, but you are going to kindly leave my best bud's body, if you know what's good for you!"

"Oh, trust me, I do. And what you just said FILLS ME with energy! FILLS ME!"

"Well," I get up and reveal my eyes — my sun-colored, Extreme V eyes. "At least I don't steal others' strength. Dark Spirit! Your home is with me."

"NO! You shouldn't be in your extreme form. I'm Griff! Your best…"

"Save it for the Hell I'm about to kick you back to!" I create a diversion with a fireball strike to "Griff's" feet and pick up Azilez. I fly out of the building and place her on a bench, with her brush.

"I couldn't have revived without you… Thanks, girl."

SLAM! Griff rocks the street below my feet and storms to me. "YOU THINK THAT WEAK ATTEMPT AT A FIREBALL WILL STOP ME?"

"No, of course not."

"Well, then, what do you plan to… AAAARRRGGHHHHH!" He's being electrocuted! That can only be…

My hunch is true. It's Rodger yet again! But because of his fragile state, he immediately collapses.

– *Finally! I'm free! V… I…*

– *No! Don't enter me. First, go and heal Azilez, then help Rodger!*

– *As you wish.*

The Dark Spirit gets right to work, but Griff somehow targets It and rushes to absorb Its power.

"YOU CAN'T ESCAPE ME THAT EASILY!"

While lit ablaze, I body-slam Griff so he can't harm the Dark Spirit. "It can with this firewall in the way."

"Then I'll just KNOCK IT DOWN."

"Try me."

There's no mistaking it. Griff is not in command of his own body right now. I'll be happy to bring him back, even if it means roughing his body up a bit.

Griff lunges at me, but falls over and tries to disappear into the street. Of course, without the Dark Spirit's influence, he just falls face first on the pavement. However, he is unfazed. He flies underground.

"Didn't expect that, did you, V?"

I go near the giant Griff-shaped hole in the ground and launch fire into it. The flames rage down, following Griff.

And about five seconds later…

"AAHHHH! HOT! HOT! HOOOOTTTT!"

"Enjoying your bath, 'Griff'?" The flames force him back above the ground. "'Cause it's your last one!" I firmly grasp the back of his head and burn away the force controlling him.

"AAARRRGGGGGHHHHHHH! YOU… NOOOOOOOOOOO!" And with that, Griff collapses, unconscious.

With that taken care of, I rush into the Ghirardelli Factory, grab some ice cream, and return to Griff, Azilez, and Rodger.

Chapter 4

Tribulations of the Past

Ahh… that's refreshing. This ice cream hits the spot — with the decadent chocolate syrup covering a creamy core that's melting just the right amount to swim wondrously in my mouth. Even with this scoop of heaven in my hand, I try keeping an eye on Rodger, Griff, and Azilez. I see Griff right in front of me, but where are…

"Peek-a-boo!" Azilez reveals herself.

"WOAH!" I'm startled and drop my ice cream cone. "No! I've been waiting all day for that!"

"C'mon! We can get another one later. But this can't wait!" She leaps and gives me a great, big hug. "Thanks for saving my skin back there."

"Are you kidding? I should be thanking you. Without you, I'd be dead by now."

"Well, that's true. OK, I'll take an ice cream as a thank-you."

Really?

"I've got to thank you too, V." Rodger appears from the rubble of the street, clearly under the influence of the Dark Spirit. "You've contained the menace and helped me revitalize. Mind if I use the Dark Spirit to do the same with my crew? I'd be mighty grateful."

"Knock yourself out."

– I'm already close to that. V, give me a break… Last time for the day after the squad and Griff. Promise?

– I wish I could. With what's been going on today, I can't guarantee anything anymore.

The Dark Spirit reluctantly nods and heads off to heal everyone. Though, whether that nod was for a "Yes" or if It was about to fall asleep, I'm not really sure.

"Rodger, can you keep an eye on Griff too for a second?"

"Sure. Why?"

"I want to get a certain someone some ice cream." Azilez starts whistling and rolling her eyes, pretending not to know I'm hinting at her. "I owe her a huge thank-you after all."

"Go ahead. Take as long as you need. Griff shouldn't wake up until the Dark Spirit gets to him, so you should be fine, assuming you have nothing else to do."

"Hmm… do I? Oh, Vizor! We left him at the bench near Fisherman's Wharf. We've got to interrogate him."

"My squad and I would love to help with that. We'll bring him in and make sure he gives all the answers you want, no questions asked."

"Awesome! But first…"

"Come on, V. Ghirardelli awaits!"

"Right behind you!" We dash to the chocolate factory for scoops of ice cream. We reach the front door. As we enter, we both extend our arms out, tilt our heads back, close our eyes, and take a whiff.

"That smells fantastic!" We say so much in unison that we start laughing.

"So what'll you treat me to, V?"

"Only the biggest thank-you ever!"

"Welcome. May I take your order?" The cashier puts on a smile like nothing has gone disastrous today.

"One EARTHQUAKE, please."

"No way! Are you sure we can handle it?"

The Earthquake is the king of ice creams here. Eight scoops, each topped with gooey strawberry or chocolate syrup, then topped with fluffy whipped cream, chocolate chips just recently made from the chocolate river flowing through the back of the store, and a cherry on top. For the final touch, half a banana splits each scoop. You can even add more to it if you want, but eight scoops should be enough for now.

"What we don't finish, we'll take home."

"Don't you mean your home?"

"Well, it's your home too now. Yours is, well, wrecked."

"But I can fix it with this brush!"

"Think about it, Azilez, you're a part of this adventure team now. Wouldn't it be awesome to live with your partners, especially if they're your best friends? It's only a suggestion, but I like the sound of it."

"I don't know… I like my house."

"Hey, don't worry. You can fix up your house and stay there if you want. I just like the idea of living with my best pals, especially if they're going to help save the universe from evil."

"Can we just eat now? I'm starved. Fighting evil gets me HUN-GRY!"

"Sure. But think about it."

"'K." We plunge our faces, stomachs, and souls into devouring the Earthquake. As Azilez had predicted, we can't do it. It's just too much for only two people, but boy, does she look happy with her stomach full like that.

"Ah, I needed that. Thanks a bunch, V."

"Anytime. You ready to go back to Vizor, Griff, and Rodger?"

"As I always am."

I help her get on her feet, and we're out of there in a flash. Of course, Rodger has kept everything in order, just like he said he would. Griff and the entire crew have been reawakened and they all look ready to help with Vizor… except the Dark Spirit.

"*Huff*… *huff*… *huff*…" I see the purple haze panting on the pavement.

"You haven't done anything like this before, Dark Spirit?"

"Well… yes, I have. But I'm, as you humans say, out of shape. Without constantly doing it, I can't keep my energy flowing. Since our adventure, I've been hibernating inside you."

"Then allow me to help You up. Come here." I place my hand down on the warm pavement and the Dark Spirit crawls into my arm. As soon as I lift It back up, I feel It drop into my body and begin sleeping.

– Sleep well, Buddy. You deserve it.

– Zzzzz… zzzzz… zzzzz…

"That Thing is actually using you as a bed?" Rodger raises an eyebrow.

"Weird, right? But with my hair as a pillow, can you blame It?"

"Point well made."

"Is Vizor still out?"

"Men!"

"Sir, yes, sir!"

"Bring the rain-bowed here!" Rodger commands.

"Really? Rain-bowed?" Azilez buries her face in her palm.

"What? I thought it was clever."

"…"

"OK. Maybe it sounded better in my head."

"I thought it was unique, to say the least."

"Huh? Who said that? Griff?"

"That wasn't me," Griff says from the front of the line.

"It was me, actually."

We turn to see whoever thought "rain-bowed" was clever. To our utter shock, it was the one who actually IS rain-bowed… Vizor! Rodger was right. That sounds a LOT better in your head.

"Hello! Pleased to meet you all. I'm Vizor."

"Why are you so happy? You tried killing us a few minutes ago!"

"What? I did? I don't remember that…"

"What's the last thing you DO remember?" Griff inquires.

"Wait… this isn't home. Where am I? Who are you? Are you the forbidden one?"

"Uhh… chosen one is more accurate."

"What are you talking about? Forbidden one? You have a LOT of talking to do, mister!" Rodger snaps.

"Yeah! Like those soulless, dark eyes."

"Dark eyes…?"

"Save it for the interrogation. You have a plethora of questions to answer."

"I do?"

I don't think he has any idea what he's done to deserve this. Worst of all, he can't remember any of it.

"What are you going to do to me? I'm so confused…" Vizor actually sounds scared.

Yeah, so am I. About many things that you're going to have to answer, Vizor. If we're going to stop the Unbound Evil from accomplishing Its ultimate task, we need to hear what Vizor remembers. This is going to be a grind.

Everyone gets taken to a dark room. All you can hear is Vizor's breathing, sadness, and struggle. "WHERE AM I? WHO ARE ALL OF YOU? DID YOU HURT MY FAMILY? HOW CAN I TRUST YOU?" He is tied to a chair and can't move.

Suddenly, blinding lights flash, enough to make Vizor squint.

"Well, if you can't trust them, then can you trust us?" I appear from a side door. Azilez and Griff are already in the room, looking quite stern.

"Uhh…" Vizor has an uncertain look on his face.

"V, where have you been?" Azilez whispers over to me.

"Making sure of two things. One, that our families are OK, and two…"

"OHHH!"

"Shhh!"

"Sorry! I just forgot! How are they?"

So much for whispering…

"They seem to be OK. They were just used as bait by Vizor."

"Is mine OK too?" Griff chimes in.

"Yeah, Griff. Don't worry. That applied to your parents too."

"Whew! Thank goodness…"

"Well, what was number two? I cut you off."

"This." I reveal the backpack that Vizor had atop the Ghirardelli Factory. Its contents? The five legendary Solar Prophecies: Wisdom, Speed, Power, Chaos, and Solar.

– *V! Let us out, man!* The Speed Prophecy is shaking around inside.

– Ouch! Brother, seize your squirming! The Wisdom Prophecy gets hit.

– Come on! You can take a bigger hit than that! The Power Prophecy acts all tough.

– Really, guys? He's going to let us out, right? the Solar Prophecy asks.

– Yeah, one sec. I unzip the bag, and out fly the prophecies.

"Finally! Air!"

"You never needed it, Speedy…" the Chaos Prophecy points out.

"Oh, yeah…"

"WOW! What are those?" Azilez asks.

"I was about to ask," Vizor remarks.

"Vizor, Azilez, police officers… the Solar Prophecies!"

– Wait… Vizor doesn't recognize us? The Wisdom Prophecy is confused.

– Apparently not. It's confusing to me too. We're about to question him. Mind helping us?

– Not at all! I haven't done anything in a few days.

– Well, you WERE stuck in a cave, just waiting to aid me for countless millennia. What's a few days?

– Point taken, V. Let's do this!

"Vizor." I walk closer to him.

"Wh… what are you going to do to me?"

"Nothing. Nothing. I just want to make sure I'm close enough so I can hear you clearly."

"What's the very last thing you remember?"

"Something hitting me… really hard."

"Do you remember what it was that hit you?"

"No. Not in particular. I do remember I couldn't move though."

"Because you were paralyzed with fear?"

"No, like, I couldn't physically move. I was strapped tightly somewhere."

– Huh? That's odd.

– Why?

– That contradicts what I saw in his memories a few days ago.

– Do tell.

– The last thing that I saw hit him was the Unbound Evil. Do you think his memory is still fuzzy? Or is he lying?

– Not from what I can detect. He seems to be telling the truth.

– Then that means he was either struck sometime before or after the Unbound Evil encounter.

– That seems to be the case.

"Well, do you two have any questions?"

"I do." Griff steps up. "Where do you think you are?"

"I would assume Treah."

"Treah?"

"My home planet. You guys ARE Omoh sapiens, right?"

"Afraid not. We're humans."

"HUMANS?"

Uh-oh, I hope he doesn't try and kill us again…

"I'VE WANTED TO MEET SOME ALL MY LIFE!"

– WHAT?

– THAT was unexpected. But, again, he's not lying. This is all true!

– HOW DOES THAT EXPLAIN, WELL… EVERYTHING THEN?

– Remember, he was possessed to the point where he had no real rational thought of his own. Even in his fits of "free will" he wasn't totally free.

– I guess so. We'll leave it at that for now. Nothing else could've possessed him, right?

– Other than the Devil. But Its grasp is far more powerful than anyone else's. No one has ever been set free from Its grasp until It lets go.

– That's scary…

– Well, what did you expect?

– Wisdom, I live in a world where I have talking rocks as friends. Anything is possible.

"Well, here we are… humans. In the flesh." Griff pounds his fist against his chest.

"NO WAY! Is… is my dad here?"

"Your dad? No, why?"

"Considering what he thought of you guys, I doubt it."

"What'd he think of us?"

"He despises all of you. I've always wanted to see humans, but he'd never let me. Every time I brought it up, he'd be meaner than usual."

"Than usual? What was usual?"

"Omoh sapiens are direct opposites of Homo sapiens, you guys."

"As the name implies. But does that mean that Omoh sapiens are naturally nasty beings?" Azilez asks.

"I'm afraid so. You know how most people look toward lightness and goodness? Omoh sapiens always look for darkness, hatred, ruin, and destruction. They naturally just… hate."

"But you seem so nice!" Azilez rebuts. "How is that possible?"

"That's where my dad comes in. He says I'm 'special' in a bad way. He always tried to whip me into shape by trying to make me a meaner person, but, for some reason, something inside me has screamed resistance. I couldn't ignore that."

"So did your dad ever physically hurt you? Was that the last thing you remember?"

"Again, I'm not exactly sure what hit me. All I know is that it was hard and I couldn't physically resist. My memory draws a blank after that."

That's really interesting… and creepy. To think there's a race out there that acts the exact opposite of us humans. But are they really our opposites? Humans, too, sometimes look for hatred and destruction.

"So, where IS your home planet, exactly? Do you know?" I ask.

"Gosh, if I knew, I would've raced back there by now. Actually, wait… Would I?"

"What do you mean?"

"I mean I hated my life at home. But my family… I just want to see them. I can't even remember the last time I did see them." Vizor actually gets a little teary-eyed. Is this his true nature? If it is, I'm glad he's finally able to show it without chains and shackles on his heart.

"So do you have ANY idea where your home could be?"

"Hmm… It was sucked into a portal of some kind. I can't say where it was leading to, but there was something really scary behind the portal. It was HUGE!"

— *Truth again, V. Before you ask.*

— *You beat me to it.*

"Hmm…" I try to recall Vizor's flashback, the memories my dad and I saw inside of Vizor's head. I didn't notice anything like that… something HUGE? How could I have missed it? Wait! I have an idea of what it might've been!

"What did this 'HUGE' thing look like?"

"The thing had horns. And enormous wings."

"I knew it…"

"What? Do you know what it was?"

"The Devil! And that portal most likely led to Hell."

"WWWWHHHAAAAATTT?"

"V? Are you sure?" Azilez asks.

"I think the Unbound Evil vaguely mentioned something about that." Griff scratches his chin.

"If that's the case, then how do we find Hell? Do we have to die in order to help Vizor?"

"There's got to be another way." The Chaos Prophecy joins in. "I know! How about the master temple? In Egypt. There's bound to be an answer there."

"Oh, Egypt!" Azilez gets a tad jumpy with excitement. "Are we going now?"

"We're in the middle of an interrogation," I point out.

"Aw! Don't be a party pooper. Besides, we can take Vizor with us. If we do find Treah, shouldn't we have a guide to help us navigate?"

"That's always handy in a foreign land… sure. Why not? This Vizor seems a lot nicer, anyway."

"Wait… what do you mean 'this' Vizor?"

"You may not have ever known it, but remember how just now you said Omoh sapiens are nasty?"

"Yeah. What about it?"

"I just thought you lived up to those expectations." I'm trying to put this as delicately as possible.

"What did I do?"

There's no avoiding it now… "Vizor. You were truly vicious. You ripped Griff's family and mine away from us for seven years!"

"You're… you're lying, right?"

"Does it sound like I am?"

"I'd never do THHHHAAAAATTTTT!" He bursts into tears, dazed and confused.

– This isn't an act, V. And based on what he's told us, he hasn't been able to act this way for a long time.

– Poor Vizor… to be abused by his father like that.

"Vizor, there's a way you can make up for all that."

"Yeah! Death penalty!" One of the guards' voice echoes from a speaker.

"NO ONE ASKED YOU! Listen, Vizor, we could really use your help on our quest to stop the Unbound Evil and Its horrid, horrid plan for universal reformation. Are you with us?"

"That THING? It got to you too?"

He has NO idea. "What do you mean?"

"My family has always told me the Unbound Evil is to be trusted and respected. I always knew they were lying. Somewhere inside me, I just knew."

I can feel the chains of his heart breaking free. This is truly Vizor. His spirit is finally saying what it wants to.

"What do you want to do, Vizor?" Azilez walks right up to him, almost about to give him a hug.

"No… stop." Vizor stops her dead in her tracks. He starts to shiver. "It's OK. I know what I've done. I know what you're saying is true. I can barely live with myself. Knowing that I… I ripped your life away, and nearly succeeded. All the memories… they're being unleashed. I see it now… me with a despicable, malicious smirk on my face. In a house, with a big sphere, and someone bawling in front of me… V… I… I… AAARRRRRGGGGHHHH!"

"That's enough!" Azilez leaps and gives him a big hug.

Just then, I get a flashback. It's so similar… the day she and I met.

She did the same thing for me. Vizor and I may be opposites in terms of physical structure, but are we as different than we think?

– This is very hard on him, V. What are you going to do?

– What am I going to do? The only thing I can think of right now.

"Hey, Vizor?"

"What's your wish, V?" Even just mentioning my name makes him cringe now.

"Just now, you said you could BARELY live with yourself, right?"

"Yeah… Why?"

"How about putting that last bit of faith in us? Because there IS one way you can help overturn this dastardly deed."

"Come with you guys, right?" *Sniff*"

"Mmhmm. We really need your help on our quest in hunting down the Unbound Evil and foiling Its plot of universal depletion and reformation."

"How can you guys ever trust me?"

"I think when you sat here today," Griff steps up, "you really showed your true colors. You poured yourself onto the floor like a bucket of water, both literally and metaphorically. It takes true strength to admit the faults of your past, let alone face them."

"You… you really think so?" Vizor gets a grip, finally.

"Think so? We know so. In fact, if it weren't for you, we would've never known that."

I know it sounds pretty bizarre to slyly thank him for nearly destroying our lives, but our experience with Vizor actually taught us something important: always stay on track and never lose sight of who you are, even when gripped by doubt. That's real faith.

"Think of it this way, Vizor," I suggest, adding to Griff's statement. "It's very true that you did something almost no one would ever forgive, but if that had never happened, I probably would've never met two very special people: Rodger and Azilez."

"But two people don't replace six, do they?"

"What do you mean?" Griff asks.

"I took six people away from you guys, and you try to make me feel better by saying you met two new ones? Look, I appreciate it, but it's too late. I've strayed on this path for too long, and I'm not sure which way to turn…"

"Then let all three of us hold your hand all the way there. We're more than willing to do it. I'm pretty sure the prophecies feel the same way."

"Of course." The Wisdom Prophecy finally speaks out loud.

"Your inner strength is admirable," the Prophecy of Power compliments.

"A true crossroads… where you'll need friends. All you have to do is take their hands," the Chaos Prophecy adds.

"Let the fire of your soul burn!" the Solar Prophecy concludes.

"Allow me to affirm your statements, Vizor. I can detect lies and impurities. But during this entire conversation, I have not detected anything that isn't pure of heart and soul. Vizor, give yourself a second chance in life. Everyone deserves one."

"I dunno. He still seems fishy to me…" Speedy abruptly mouths in a sarcastic tone.

"Really, Speedy? And while Wisdom was being… well… wise." The Power Prophecy gives him a nudge.

Vizor chuckles at the sarcastic prophecy. Eventually he bursts out laughing. He laughs for quite a long time, and then begins to cry. Though this time they're tears of joy, tears of relief. He's finally realizing that he shouldn't live with this burden in his head — even so, he's not done apologizing. "V, Griff, take my blade."

"Which one? In your hair?" Griff is startled.

"Why?"

"Just… let me do something."

"OK." We remove the golden, "V"-shaped blade in his hair and each take a piece.

"Now, untie me."

"You're not going to attempt to kill us, are you?" I look into his eyes.

"If you're so skeptical…." He shakes his hair and removes the grappling hook he keeps handy in there. "Take it. I'm unarmed now, helpless."

"What exactly are you doing?"

"Again, just let me do this." Griff and I glance at each other and merely shrug.

What exactly *is* Vizor doing by completely unarming himself and handing us all of his weaponry? Griff and I brace ourselves for the worst possible scenario. As he gets up, he merely takes a knee in front of us and closes his eyes. We all stay there, silently staring at him. Everything is tense, like that feeling when you *really* have to go to the bathroom. I, especially, am waiting for him to do something. But… no. He continues to stay in that exact spot until his hair does something I didn't know it could do. It grows another golden, "V"-shaped blade.

"Whoa…! Wha…?" Azilez sounds shocked.

"Thanks, everyone. But now, the desert sun of Egypt awaits us. Right?"

The four of us smile. Griff and I toss the blades aside, and we all come in for one big group hug, with the sound of the San Francisco Police Department applauding in the background. And yes, Rodger bursts into tears of happiness.

Chapter 5

Delayed Journey

Vizor, Azilez, Griff, and I head back to our tree house and see if everything and everyone is OK there, especially Z and D. Since Vizor was here, nothing really could've gotten to them, right? Right? Right.

Still, the tree house technically isn't all ours yet.

"Azilez?"

"Huh? What is it, V?"

"About the whole living-in-the-tree-house thing…"

"Oh, right. Look, I've given it some thought. I really have. But am I just gonna move into the tree house like that?"

"Oh, trust me, you will! IF YOU WANNA ESCAPE ME, THAT IS!"

Woah! What was that? "Vizor! Not funny!"

"That wasn't me. I swear!"

"Then who…?"

"AM I THAT INVISIBLE?"

"MOM! Let me go!"

Azilez's mom has grabbed Azilez by her jacket.

"NOT UNTIL YOU CLEAN UP THAT MESS YOU MADE BACK AT THE HOUSE! AND AS FOR YOU, V! VERY CLEVER OF YOU TO SEND ME OFF TO PIER 39 JUST TO GET AZILEZ OUT OF TROUBLE!"

– I mean, hey. You DID fall for it.

*– … *Yawn*… what is that ear-grating scream?*

– Oh, ignore it, Dark Spirit. It's just Azilez's mom, Candice.

– If you say so… zzz…

"IT'S STRAIGHT TO THE HOUSE WITH YOU! NO WAY YOU'RE

GETTING OUT OF IT THIS TIME!"

Azilez looks back and winks at me as she's being carried off. I don't think her mom knows how easily she's going to fix their house.

"Shall we go see Picasso at work?"

"Picasso?" Vizor scratches his blade.

"You'll see."

"Front-row seats for me!" Griff runs out the door.

Vizor chases after him, even though he's not as quick as Griff. Still, I want to see who gets there first. That means I've got to beat both of them. I'll take the rooftop shortcut.

I get to Azilez's place, but remain hidden because I'm pretty sure her mom doesn't want to see me after scolding me like that. I peer through the window and notice the house is still in ruins. The two are arguing in front of the house. Uh-oh… this can't end well, especially with their quick tempers. Here comes Griff. And there's Vizor coming in second. Griff spots me, and I give him a signal to keep my presence hidden. I'll leave the rest to him. He can do it. I'll just nap next to this bush for a few minutes. It's been a long day. Zzz…

"What's going on?" Griff cuts into the parent-child argument.

"Griff, help me out here. She took my brush!"

"Well, as punishment, yeah. I get that. You're lucky if that's all she did."

"And I have to fix the house without it."

– Ohhhhhh… I see the problem. Wow, how are we going to explain that?

Azilez's mom, Candice, stomps outside alongside her daughter. "ALL YOU'LL DO WITH THIS BRUSH IS STALL MORE. TELL YOU WHAT, IF YOU SUBMIT TO PUNISHMENT RIGHT NOW, I'LL ONLY MAKE YOU CLEAN UP THE FALLEN WOOD AND I'LL CALL IN THE ENGINEERS AND CONSTRUCTION WORKERS TO FIX THE WALLS."

– She was going to make Azilez fix the walls? It would be impossible for Azilez to pull it off by herself! Wait! Unless she has…

"Ms. Candice, there's a way for Azilez to do all of that."

"I HOPE YOU'RE NOT ABOUT TO SAY…"

"I'm pretty sure Azilez has told you this already, but she can use her brush to do some crazy things. One of which is to fix buildings."

"Look, I get that you think Azilez is especially gifted with art 'n all…"

– *Whew… she calmed down… finally.*

"BUT THAT DOESN'T MEAN SHE CAN SPONTANEOUSLY FIX THIS AWFUL DAMAGE. YOU TWO ARE INSANE!"

– *Hmm… there's gotta be a way to get that brush!*

"What's happening here?"

"Vizor! Maybe you can help me."

"What do you need?"

"See that brush in that woman's hand?"

"Yes? What of it?"

"I was hoping you can swipe it from her somehow, stealthily. Undetected."

"Say no more. I'll get it done." Vizor squeezes himself really hard. His body dematerializes into a puddle. He moves across the ground behind Candice. Once there, he easily hops up and grabs the brush out of her hand. She's so enthralled by her argument with Azilez that she doesn't even notice the brush was swiped. Vizor returns to Griff and becomes whole again. "So, what do you need this for?"

"You'll see." Griff grasps the brush in his hands. – *Wow… the energy emanating from this is like nothing I've ever felt! It feels harmonic, like lying in a hammock!* "Are you missing something, Ms. Candice?"

"What do you…? Where'd it go? The brush is gone!"

Azilez's eyes widen and she stares at her mom, in a panic to find the brush.

"Did you lose it already?"

"Watch it!"

"Guys! Calm down. I have the brush." Griff attempts to hand the brush over to Azilez.

"Finally! Thank you! I'll fix the house now, mom."

"Ha! I'd love to see you try."

Griff and Azilez wink at each other. Azilez walks closer to her house and waves her brush around. The colors of the rainbow are released, and Azilez's mom nearly faints from the sight of it.

"WHHHAAAATTT?"

"Now let's put this to work!" Azilez runs around her entire house, repairing all the damage that was done. Minute by minute, her house starts to look as good as new. "Mom, remember how you wanted the outside of the house a darker shade of blue?"

"Y-Yeah…?"

Azilez whips out that perfect shade and literally slaps it onto the house's exterior.

"UN-BE-LIEVABLE! You actually did it!"

– *OK, NOW she's finally calmed down.* Griff reassures.

"Teehee! Pretty cool, huh, mom?"

"Azilez, I'm speechless. I'm SO SORRY for not believing you earlier. Thanks for knocking that bit of sense into me."

– *Can we even call flying colors logical? Griff wonders. Wait 'till she hears the story of how V, Rodger, and I were gone! But that's a story for another day.*

"*Yaaaaawwwwwwnnnn*… Ahh! I needed that." I finally show myself from behind the bush.

"V, how long have you been there?" Candice is startled.

"10-20 minutes. I took a power nap." – *Speaking of which…are you still sleeping, Dark Spirit?*

– *Zzzz… zzzz… zzzz…*

– *Got it.*

"By the way, V, Griff, Vizor, and I have to go to Egypt for a little while. You mind, mom?"

Azilez doesn't get a reply right away. Her mom is still gushing over the new house. "Oh, sure, do whatever you need to."

"Thanks! See you in a week or two!" That's about when Candice snaps back to reality.

"Wait, WHAT? Egypt? Why?"

– *Seems like that unbelievable story is going to be told sooner than I thought…*

Griff explains all of it to her the best he can: why we were gone, how Azilez reacted when we came back, the result of said reaction, the Dark Spirit, the Unbound Evil, who Vizor is, the Solar and Shadow Prophecies, and The Legend of V.

"What? Am I dreaming?"

"I thought I was too, at first." Griff realizes how unbelievable it all sounds.

"By the way, Griff, aren't the prophecies supposed to be here? Floating?"

"Oh, yeah, about that… I had to stuff them back in here." He reveals the backpack.

"Why?"

"The Speed Prophecy was causing trouble, and I didn't want any-one to get lost."

"Way to go, Speedy!"

"Come now, Power, relax. Be at ease with yourself."

"Wisdom's right. It's not that bad in here."

"Well, when Speed's calm, anyways."

"Can you guys make me feel any worse?" Speed tries to shrug them off.

"I think we should all be asking you that," the Chaos Prophecy redirects.

"I guess that's a yes…"

"Come on, guys!" Griff barks. "Cut it out!"

"So yeah, we need to find out more about Vizor's home world to ultimately thwart the Unbound Evil in Its plan for total conquest, and Azilez wants to help."

"Well, that sounds kinda dangerous…"

"But I'll be fine, mom. They already went on an adventure, and look at them. They're fine. Besides, I can protect myself with this brush now. You saw me fix the house with it. C'mon! Pleeeaasse!" She sounds like a five-year-old who just saw the most amazing toy ever and is beg-ging her mom to buy it.

"Well, I guess so. Plus, V and Griff coming back does reassure that the journey ahead isn't as dangerous as it sounds."

I'm not even going to mention how many times we cheated death…

"Well, OK. But be safe. I don't want A SINGLE SCRATCH on you when you get home!"

"YAAAAYYY! Thanks, mom!" Azilez gives her a kiss on the cheek. "Bye-bye now."

We walk back to the tree house to prepare for the journey ahead. Look out, Treah, here comes The Legend of V!

Chapter 6

The Most Annoying Person on the Planet

My main concern now is whether Z and D are all right —especially D. He's still terrified of the world around him, thanks to the Unbound Evil. I'm going to stop that Thing! I will!

"Huh. The tree house is still like this?" Azilez says.

"How did this happen?"

"You don't know, Vizor?"

"It was me, wasn't it…?"

"Yup. You guessed it."

"*Sigh*… Are you sure you guys want me here?"

"I don't think we'd have it any other way," Griff replies. "Your whole life has been nothing but unanswered questions. We want to help you find the answers. That's when you'll start being truly happy."

"It still amazes me how you guys could ever even consider bringing along the guy who you once thought ruined your lives…"

"Like Griff said," I add, "there were still unanswered questions in that scenario. We found out that the Unbound Evil possessed you, and that you had to obey It. The kidnapping of our families was not your fault."

"I'm still in your debt, guys. Thanks."

"No worries. All you have to do is be a friend now."

"I've wanted to be a true friend to someone for a long, long time."

"Well, let's go check on Z and D. They're coming too, aren't they?"

– I know Z is, but D? He might not ever want to go out of the house again.

*– *Yaaawwwnnn*… I really needed that.*

– Oh, so You're awake now?

– And fully energized. I'm at your command, V.

– Good to hear. We're going to Egypt, again.

– Why?

– The prophecies say there might be a clue there to help us find Vizor's world. Remember the master temple?

– I do indeed. Hmm… I want to say that there IS something important there. But it's so vast.

– Well, if You remember, let me know.

– Will do.

We run up to the main entrance of the tree house and walk inside. "Z! D! Are you guys here?"

"V, we're up here."

Griff gets ahead of me. I follow and find Z and D inside a bedroom. D is fast asleep.

"Awwww, he's so adorable! I want to pinch his cheeks!" Azilez gushes over D.

"Shush. You'll wake him up."

"Why is he asleep, Z? Was he just tired?"

"I guess so. I have no idea. A guy sleeps when he wants to sleep, you know?"

"Yeah. You're right."

"V, are you gonna ask him if…?" Azilez reminds me why we came back here.

"Right. We're on our way to Egypt. You want to come with us?"

"I wouldn't miss it for anything!" Z instantaneously bursts out.

D screams as he wakes up. "Z, what was that?"

"Sorry, buddy. That was me."

"We're going to Egypt, D! Wanna come?" Azilez makes it sound like she's inviting him to go to Disneyland.

D looks around and spots Vizor. He curls under the sheets, shivering with fear.

"What is he doing?" Vizor asks.

"Well…" Vizor is one of D's biggest fears, next to the Unbound Evil. I think of the gentlest way to break the news to Vizor. But then, D peeks out of the sheets and steadily looks at Vizor, who smiles at D. At that moment, D knows it's all right. Even so, he shocks me with what he does next. D gets out of the bed, walks up to Vizor, and hugs him.

"Still. So. CUUTTE!" Azilez can't get enough of D. Can't blame her. He is pretty adorable. It's almost like a spell of his.

"Guys…" D looks at all of us. He nods his head. "I'm… I'm ready!"

"Good to hear, D! Come here!" I carry him and give him a hug too. His spell gets to me. I can't resist. Such bravery too… he just got back home.

"But, V?"

"Yeah?"

"Where's mama? And baba?"

"They're all right. They're all still at the police station, but they should be back any…"

"There you guys are!"

What timing.

"Hi, mom! Dad!"

"Looks like the gang is all here! What are you guys up to?" Dad has a smirk on his face.

"We're heading back to Egypt, baba!" D hops with excitement.

"But you guys just got back here! Stay awhile!"

"Sorry, but no time, sir." Griff stands up. "There's no telling when the Unbound Evil will be back. We need all the help we can get to defeat It. That, and we all need to find out some things about Vizor's world, Treah. We need to go now."

"I get it. Well, try to stay out of trouble guys, OK?"

"Understood, mom."

"On another note, this house is a wreck. I'll spend the entire time you're gone cleaning up."

"Allow me, miss!" Azilez picks up her brush and immediately gets to work. She looks so happy doing it too. Her eyes light up. It's awesome: that feeling you get when you know someone is really passionate about something. I get that, and a lot more, from her. "All done!"

"How? What?" My parents are wonderstruck.

"Yeah. She's been doing it all day." A sound emanates from Griff's backpack.

"Speedy, is that you?" Griff turns to face the bag.

"Why is it that if anyone in this backpack makes a comment, it's automatically me?"

"Actually, that time, it was me," the Power Prophecy admits.

"Why do I carry you guys around again?"

"Because you're a kind soul, Griff."

"Thanks for the reassurance."

"What are we waiting for? Let's go, guys!" Azilez darts toward the entrance.

"Mrs. Lara and Mr. Kal, are my parents here too?"

"Yes, Griff, they're on the other side of the tree house, so go and give them a big hug."

"Of course!" Griff bolts out.

"Z, V, and D?"

"Yeah?"

"Be careful. All of you. I feel insane as a mother for letting you guys go on this dangerous journey, but I know it's right for some reason. You three are the guys for the job. Knock 'em dead!"

"Likewise. Go do some adventuring."

"I'll be fine." D sounds so brave.

"We've got each other's backs," Z asserts.

"All we need is each other. That's true power!" I finish it off.

"And you…" My dad says to Vizor, who's cross-armed and leaning beside the corner of the room.

"You heard me at the detention center, right?"

"That was very brave, talking about your personal life like that. But do I trust you with my kids yet? Maybe not entirely, but I know The

Legend of V involves you. So, Vizor, you've got to go too. Find yourself in this next journey."

"It'll be easier now that I have friends with me. They're the nicest people I've ever met. I didn't know that kind of compassion existed in the world."

"You guys said the evil could attack at any moment? Then go! We'll be waiting here for all of you."

"Sounds good. Let's go, everyone." We all walk out the door, re-group, and head for Egypt.

In about an hour, we arrive in Cairo. We dash through the modern city to the west bank of the Nile and reach Luxor. The second we land in the stark and dusty Valley of the Kings, we're met by mounted troops waiting for us.

"Is something wrong here?" I ask them.

I gasp at *his* face. I immediately remember. I narrowly escaped that lame commander the last time I was here.

"Yes. You. Die."

"Woah!" A hail of bullets ensues. Like last time, though, the Dark Spirit makes all of the bullets go through me.

– *Thanks!*

– *Don't even mention it.*

"Azilez? Griff? Z? D? Are you all OK?"

"V, up here!" Azilez waves from the valley's entrance. Everyone's safe there and out of harm's way.

"Whew… thank goodness. Now, to deal with you. I've had enough of you for one lifetime."

"I could say the same thing." He's certainly a lot more straightforward this time around. But it doesn't look like I'll be getting any help from the San Francisco Police Force. I'll be fine. I'm stronger than last time.

"Bring it!"

"I won't lose this time. You won't escape, terrorist."

"Whoa! TERRORIST?"

"Number one in the Middle East. No one will leave you alone now."

"What? It was you, wasn't it? Grr…"

– *V, behind…*

"OOOWWW!" Before the Dark Spirit could finish, something sharp pierces my back. The Dark Spirit can't transform quickly enough. I can't move my legs! Now we're both paralyzed.

"Ha. Checkmate. Take him away."

"Not on my watch!" A flying golf club clobbers the commander on the back of his head.

"Who threw that?"

"You could at least, you know, pretend that kind of hurt."

"…"

"No? OK."

The one club was to no avail, but then, suddenly, the Earth starts to tremble. A giant sequoia tree erupts from out of the ground, and all of the military forces fly high into the sky. D grabs me from out of the air and rips out the giant needle in my back. The Dark Spirit immediately wakes up and revitalizes me.

"D?"

"Don't worry, V! I got you."

"Thanks, buddy. I knew you'd find the courage in you."

He smiles, and we land alongside Azilez, Z, and Griff at the base of the sequoia.

"Very cool!" Azilez is even more enamored by D.

"The entrance is somewhere this way, guys. C'mon! You OK, V?"

"Still a little dazed, but yeah."

"Cool. This way." Griff bolts and the rest of us follow. Down the road, we encounter military guards, who, from the looks of things, were ordered to keep us from reaching King Tut's tomb at all costs. Azilez helps us avoid them by creating a wall with her brush.

OK, can I just take the time to elaborate on how AWESOME Azilez's brush is? It fixes ANYTHING, can be used as a means of trans-portation, and can serve as a defensive maneuver, like that wall I just mentioned. The only down side is if Azilez goes into THAT state… the one where she fires purple stalactites from her brush and she's ruthlessly power-hungry. I'm still a bit confused on what that is, but I'm sure I'll figure it out sooner or later.

"There it is!" Griff sees the light at the end of the tunnel. Although underwhelming from the outside, this relatively small tomb is copiously inscribed with incredible luxury hidden inside. King Tut's tomb, as expected, is the most guarded part of the valley.

"Oh, wait… V?"

"What's up, Griff?"

"THAT commander is here again."

"But wasn't he at the entrance?"

"He was, wasn't he? I'm confused, but this is definitely him."

"How do you know?"

"I just do. I'm not sure. It's weird. I can't really explain it. It's like a sensation I feel for a quick sec, but then it's gone."

"That is weird." What could that be? I don't remember Griff being able to tell who a person was without even talking to him or her. Wait… is this his power? His unique, inner strength? Did he just find it? Oh, this thought is not finished!

But back to the topic at hand. "That same idiot who tried to backstab me an infinite amount of times?"

"Yeah, that one."

"Ugh…"

"How'd he backstab you, V?" Azilez asks.

"I kinda wanna know too," D adds. "No one tries hurting my brother and gets away with it!"

"Thanks, D. I'll tell you all. First, let's hide though. Make sure the guys in there don't see us."

We all hug a wall and disappear into the shadows so no one can spot us if they look into the alleyway from the tomb.

"He was here when Griff, Rodger, and I came here last time and met King Tut. The guy was the definition of human stupidity and redundancy: he tried to bottle me up in a tube, and even got me one time. That knocked me out, but Melok and the Dark Spirit helped me out."

"Melok? Oh, the spy, right?"

"Yeah. The cool spy!" D recalls from my stories.

"Guys. Shhhh." I remind them that the commander isn't supposed to hear us.

"Who's there?"

"Too late. Ha."

"How is that funny, Z?"

"C'mon, V. You know I'm very easily amused by things."

"Very true. I guess blowing cover is one of those things."

"Ah. I guess so."

That's Z for you. He's the simplest yet most complex human being I've ever known. Considering the adventure I just embarked on, that's saying a lot.

"If you guys aren't gonna show yourselves, then I'll just drag you all onto the floor!"

"Wow. I wonder how I would respond to that if I were one of your 'gang' members."

"YOU…! BIG MISTAKE COMING BACK HERE!"

– *V? Thank goodness!*

– *King Tut? Is that you? Where are you?*

– *Run, V. Not only do they have their tubes, but they also have found a way to contain spirits. They unearthed my treasures and found something they can use for such a dreadful deed. I tried to stop them, but because of my exerted efforts, I'm very weak now. I got a taste of my own medicine…*

– *WHAT? So, then, the Dark Spirit… It can be caught?*

– *I'm afraid so.*

– *How are they able to do this, King Tut?* the Dark Spirit thinks.

– *A form of magic. It's been forbidden since my time. Friends, save yourselves. Ugh…*

– *Pharaoh? Pharaaaaooooohh!*

– *Come on! You heard him! Ready, Dark Spirit?*

– *You don't even have to ask.*

We quietly transform into Dark V and climb the wall to make

sure the commander can't see us.

The rest of my team show themselves. D is intimidated by the tyrannical, cross-armed expression of the Alexandrian commander, whose name I STILL don't know. And I don't really care.

"Where's your 'gang' leader, kiddies?" They're all bewildered — except Griff. He knows exactly where I am.

– *How are you doing that, V?*

– *Wait. Griff? How are you talking to me telepathically?*

– *Huh. I am, aren't I?* His pride can't refrain from a good, hearty chuckle.

– *You suddenly got some sort of power. But what is it? And more importantly, how?*

– *I'm just as confused as you are, buddy. I have NO idea.*

– *But, wow! You can tell who people are without even talking to them, AND you can sense spirits. That, in my book, is cool!*

– *But can't you, too, talk to spirits, V?*

– *Yours is different though, Griff. I can't put my finger on it right now, but I just somehow know it is. You, too, sort of feel it, right?*

– *Sort of? It's burning through my veins!*

– *Like fire?*

– *Is that a trick question, Extreme V? Mr. Sun's son?*

– *Hahaha!*

That ignorant, boring commander interrupts my laughter. "You can't scare me now, boy! I can bring you out from the crack you slipped into. Almost like I have a can of wasp poison ready to go." The commander whips out a shiny, unidentified object from his right pocket. It is a radiant red jewel.

– *There it is. My jewel that can contain spirits. Run… NOW!*

"Oh, shiny!" D throws his pickaxe with utmost precision. He manages to knock the jewel out of the commander's hand while giving him a bonk in the head with the shaft of the pickaxe.

"Insignificant little misfit!" the commander immaturely barks at a ten-year-old.

"Whoa, buddy. Let's take that down a notch, like all the way maybe?"

"What are you saying, smart mouth?"

"Basically, shut up, and that King Tut's stone, which you stole, is not in your hand."

"You little…! Wait, WHAT? SINCE WHEN?"

"Since you got a serious anger-management problem." Vizor flicks the stone in his hand.

– *Nice going, Vizor!* Griff thinks. *I knew you'd pull through, again!*

"Oh, so that's where you were, Vizor." I come down from inside the ceiling. I actually knew he was there the whole time. The Dark Spirit helps me out with that sort of thing.

"ARRRGHH! Men! Seize everyone in here!"

"You wish, grandpa!" Azilez insults him. She busts out her brush and whips all of the guards against the wall, except the commander. We're going to make sure he never forgets the lesson we're about to teach him!

"Wh-what are you guys…?" The commander stutters.

"Drop the act, dude! You're such a fake!" Griff sees right through him with his weird, new ability.

"H-how? Whatever! I don't even care! DIE! ALL OF YOU!"

Our eyes feast upon the commander as he disintegrates into nothingness, along with his comrades. All of them combine into the most hideous-looking monster the human mind can fathom. Picture a squirrel, mixed with a rhinoceros, a hydra, and a snake. Yeah… that was definitely the worst eye feast ever.

Chapter 7

The Squirrel-Rhino-Hydra-Snake Thing

"What is that?" I yell out.

"I DON'T EVEN CARE WHAT I AM! AS LONG AS ALL OF YOU ARE NOT HERE TO SEE IT!"

Let's do this! I've wanted to shut this guy's mouth since the moment I met him. He's so arrogant — molding the world around him as he sees fit, just because he has the "authority" to do so. The worst part is, people actually have to listen to him. This is one of the most common dilemmas in everyday human interaction.

"What are you even accomplishing with this?" Azilez asks him. She doesn't know better. This guy's head is just about as thick as hardened clay. And it'll never, EVER soften.

"LIKE I SAID, ALL I CARE ABOUT IS YOU GUYS DISAPPEARING OFF THE FACE OF THE EARTH."

– *Off the face of the Earth…?*

– *What are you thinking, V?*

– *Well, Dark Spirit, maybe we actually COULD disappear off the face of the Earth.*

– *What are you saying?*

– *I'm saying surprise attack. This guy's mind is so messed up right now that we could probably pull it off. Right in front of him.*

– *That's a good idea, V!* Griff intrudes.

– Uhh… Griff?

– Yeah?

– I know you have the ability to interject thoughts now, but remember that sometimes people's thoughts are used as templates for their next action. Invading something like that has its risks. I'd know because I've been able to do it for a few weeks now. Most of the time, limiting the use of that is the best way to go.

– Oh, I've never looked at it that way. I guess I got too carried away.

– No worries. Ready, Dark Spirit? Let's get my friends under the ground.

– Yes!

– 3… 2… 1… NOW!

In a split second, we all fall into the ground, except the squirrel-rhino-… You know what? I'm just going to refer to it as the jerk monster.

"WHAT? WHERE'D THEY ALL GO?"

– This is what you wanted, isn't it? I mess with his thoughts to make him seem like he, or it (I don't even know), is crazy.

– Pay attention, Griff. THIS is fun.

He chuckles.

"WHAT IS THIS? WHERE ARE YOU GUYS?"

"I'll say it again. This is what you wanted, right? We're off the face of the Earth…"

"NOT FUNNY."

"I thought it was."

"WHO SAID THAT?"

– I guess that sneak attack is coming sooner than I thought…

I signal that it's time and we all feast on the jerk monster in our own, special ways.

"ARGH! STOP IT! CEASE! HALT! AAAAAAHHHHHH!"

"FOR THE LAST TIME…" I reiterate, "THIS IS WHAT YOU ASKED FOR!" With one last axe kick to the head, the monster falls apart. The commander and his entire crew come back, unconscious.

"OK! How did that just happen?" Azilez realizes that she had just fought a fused mutant.

"Anyone? I kinda want to know too!" D looks around.

"That couldn't be…" Vizor thinks out loud.

"What is it?" Z walks toward him.

"That technique looks very similar to the trick I can pull off. It might be EXACTLY the same, actually."

"Whoa! How?" I ask.

"Sometimes Omoh sapiens invade this planet. When they do, some people might get a hold of that Omoh sapien. And when that happens, well… the rest you can kind of imagine."

"Oh, God… I definitely could."

"I think we all could at this point, V. We've all been through something that helps us fathom something like that," Griff adds.

"Agreed." Azilez nods, placing her brush in her jacket pocket.

"Everyone!" King Tut pops out of undead nowhere and scares the living daylights out of all of us. D even opens the golden sarcophagus and tries to hide in there, having no idea what he's trying to hide in.

"No! D! WAIT!"

Too late. He crawls inside, and we all hear the most blood-curling scream a ten-year-old could muster (because, you know, there is a MUMMY IN THERE). He runs out so fast, he nearly teleports behind me.

"My apologies. I just feel too good right now. I got the red jewel back. And all my energy has been restored. Quick! Don't hesitate! The Solar Prophecies' master temple is this way." The pharaoh creates a nice hole in the ground for all of us to jump into. "Come on! It's like a slide!"

"Oh, slide!" D eagerly goes in first. I shrug and follow him. Z, Azilez, Griff, and Vizor follow me.

Chapter 8
A World and its Puppeteer

"Weeeee!" I hear D's echo from the front of the hole. King Tut wasn't kidding when he said this is a slide. It reminds me of an amusement park. Wait a second… I hate amusement parks! Bad analogy.

All of us make it to the core of the prophecies' master temple. This room is gigantic. It's an empty, white-marble, grandiose hall, and in the very back lies the master tablet.

"Great! We found it! So… what now?" Griff asks.

"HOW ABOUT YOU LET US OUT SO WE CAN HELP YOU?" A thundering scream erupts from Griff's backpack.

"Ow! Owwww! My ears!"

"You're a ROCK, Speedy. You don't have any!"

"Then how can we hear anything?"

"That might be the smartest question you've asked all day." The Chaos Prophecy half-compliments the Speed Prophecy.

"Just come out, guys." Griff sighs and unzips the backpack. All five of them pop out. Their colors are so vibrant, it's as though there were a rainbow hiding in Griff's backpack.

"Wow! The master tablet is a bit low on power!" the Prophecy of Solar points out.

"How can you guys tell?" Z asks.

"Well, the master tablet isn't ever this dormant. It's usually packing way more heat."

"Is that true, guys… err… prophecies?" Azilez quickly corrects herself.

"Well, miss," the Wisdom Prophecy starts, "yes. In fact, this tablet is far more powerful than any of us could ever be. It may even know some aspects of The Legend of V that even we don't know.

"Seriously? Wow!" Vizor sounds quite fascinated by that confession. I guess he has never seen anything like it. In a world like his, how can he see anything cool?

"So… how do we power something as powerful as the master tablet?" Griff asks.

"The five of us are the prime ingredients. But we need more. How about the Dark Spirit and everyone here, including King Tut? Would that be enough, Wisdom?" the Speed Prophecy asks.

"That might be enough. But are you all willing to give a part of your strength to power it?"

"Why would we not?" Azilez abruptly bursts.

"It can't hurt, right?" Z adds.

"I wanna help!" D continues to be the most adorable thing on, and under, the planet.

– *Do You think it's all good, Dark Spirit?*

– *Well, what do you think? I'm willing to do anything you do.*

– *It DID help me relocate all the prophecies, so it does have SOME type of connection with them.*

– *Then we're good to go.*

"Griff?"

"Don't even ask, V. I'm way ahead of you. Of course!"

"You mind reader, you." I pat his back.

We walk up to the master tablet. The Dark Spirit flies out of my body and rests on top of it.

"I'm ready."

"So are we!" All five Solar Prophecies line up on top of the tablet.

The rest of us look at each other and nod our heads. Azilez places her hand and brush on the tablet, Griff and I place our hands, Z places his golf club and hand, Vizor places his blade and hand, and D places his pickaxe and hand.

When D finally joins us, the tablet begins to charge.

"It's working!" Azilez smiles.

"Looks that way," Z adds.

Then the tablet starts to take a little TOO much power, and some of us start to feel faint.

"Uh, how much longer? I don't feel so good…" D holds his stomach.

"Just a tad longer! Hold on, guys!" the Power Prophecy encourages us.

"AHH! It hurts!" I can hardly take it anymore.

"There! Finished!" As soon as the Chaos Prophecy says that, we all collapse. We are still conscious, but have a hard time standing up. Some of us hold our thighs so as not to fall forward.

"Ahh! Good as new! I needed that power boost!"

"You talk, too? Not really a shocker at this point."

"Aww! You're no fun, chosen one!"

"I mean, I've hung around your five prodigies for a few weeks now. What did you expect?"

"How about a 'Hi! Nice to meet you?'"

"Hi! Nice to meet you! I'd shake your hand, if you had one."

"Really? That's getting kinda old now, V."

"See what I mean, master tablet?"

"Hahaha! Always there when you don't want it! That's Speedy, without a doubt. Hohohoho!" For a tablet, it has quite the hearty laugh. I like it! Rocks with personality. This takes "pet rock" and multiplies it by a ton.

"Well, I appreciate that you all came here to see me. How can I help?"

"A gateway. To Hell," Vizor says bluntly.

"Wow! You waste no time! But… WHAT? WHY WOULD YOU EVER WANT THAT?"

"NO, NO, NO! We don't wanna die! We just want to visit Treah, Vizor's home world!" D says.

"Ahh, I see. Could you all actually hold on for a second? I need to brush up on my information regarding The Legend of V. I've been on low power for a while now."

"Sure, go ahead. We've been trying to get here for hours now. What's a few more minutes?"

"Thank you… er… your name?"

"Z."

"Ah! A relative of the chosen one. Well, thank you." The master tablet projects a loading bar, to let us know how fast the information is processing. The loading bar quickly reaches 100%, but then is replaced by three red exclamation marks. "Th-this is awful!"

"What's wrong?" Vizor asks.

"No… NO! The Devil is not supposed to do something like that! What's It thinking?"

"What is It doing? Where is It?" Griff comes closer to the tablet.

"The Shadow Prophecies… It… It's trying to find them!"

"MY PROPHECIES?" Vizor slams his palms on the base of the tablet. "WHY?"

"I'm not sure. But if those prophecies are yours, then go! You must!" "Great! Lead the way!" I remind it what we're here for.

"I personally can't. But I can lead you to Someone who can."

"Who?"

"God, the Father of the Universe. After all, He created the universe. Quick!" The master tablet opens up a gateway to Heaven. "Through here, everyone!"

"NO WAY! The one and only God?"

Suddenly a bullet is fired and hits D's pickaxe. It goes flying to the floor. "HAHAHAHA!" The now-conscious commander then fires a net at D and captures him.

"You again?" I eye him.

"THAT. KID. IS. MINE."

"NO. WAY. IN. HELL." I try to rush him, but then I realize I can't move. In fact, no one could move. We all seem paralyzed, except Vizor. He runs up to the commander, blades in hand, and attempts to get D back.

"That child has done nothing wrong! Give him back!"

"Why would I? He will be the bait to lure you all to me. You have no choice now!" His paralysis gas wears off, so Azilez, Griff, and Z can move again.

"Quickly!" the master tablet says to them. "This portal to Heaven can't stay open very long."

"What do we do? V, Vizor?" Z is legitimately concerned.

"GO! We'll catch up," Vizor responds.

"Fine! But you better do it fast!"

"Don't worry. WE WILL!" The Dark Spirit and I fuse. Dark V comes out of the sidewall and knocks the commander to the ground. Unless you directly target the Dark Spirit, Dark V is impervious to a lot of things. Paralysis is one of them.

"Good! C'mon, guys!" Z leads the way for Griff and Azilez.

"You can do it, guys! I'll be waiting." Griff follows Z.

"YOU BETTER SAVE D!" Azilez stresses to Vizor and me. I mean, she's right. Just look at his adorable face. Who would have the heart to hurt him? She runs through the portal, trying hard not to look back.

"GRRR! ENOUGH!" The commander throws a cube next to D, who is still in his net. A giant cage forms. I hear electricity starting to charge up within it.

No, he's not planning to… HE'S GOING TO KILL D! HE'S TRYING TO ELECTROCUTE HIM!

"Sayonara, PIPSQUEAK! WATCH HIM BURN, YOU TWO!"

"NOOO!" Without a moment to think, I rush through the cage, give D the Dark Spirit, and throw him out of the cage.

Good. He's safe. Wait… "AAAAAAAARRRRRGGGGGGHHHHHHH! BUUURRRRNNNNNNNNNNNNIIINNNNNGGGG!"

"V!" Vizor watches in horror as my skin catches fire, like a piece of steak that sizzles when the barbecue hood closes on top of it. If I didn't have the power of the prophecies shielding me, I would've been toast — burnt, dry, nasty toast.

"Buh bye!" The commander's voice sounds as pleasant as nails scratching a blackboard. He whips out another cube, but uses it on himself. It doesn't electrocute him. It's a teleportation cube. He disappears, and, immediately afterwards, so do I.

Vizor stumbles a few steps back, takes D, and runs off. Then he remembers. – *Maybe… just maybe. Can she help me?*

Chapter 9

A Desolate, Ominous Prison

Ugh, my head. Where am I? And how long have I been here?

The last thing I remember is that insane amount of electricity charring me, and that commander getting away with me. Everything else is a blur.

I grumble.

"Sir! He's starting to wake up."

"Excellent! Keep him there."

I try to grasp something near me, but nothing is close enough. I fall over. I open my eyes, but can't see anything. It's pitch-black.

"Ow…" I grasp my leg as I get up. I'm badly injured. I have pus-filled scabs all over my body. Some of the big ones even have blood oozing out of them. I guess I'm still as subject to injury as everyone else. I'm not used to feeling like this. The Dark Spirit usually helps me when I'm hurt. But… It's gone now.

Oh, right! I remember now! I gave It to D. I know Z, Griff, and Azilez are in Heaven with God right now (gee, I make it sound like they're dead. That's weird.). But where did Vizor and D go? I hope D isn't too rattled. If I know those two, they're probably trying to find and save me. Do it soon, guys… I really need the Dark Spirit right now.

"Well, someone's a fighter!" an eerie, familiar voice bellows. "Even with that much concentrated electricity to your body. You somehow stomached ten megavolts of electricity."

"Ten megavolts?" I try and sound surprised, but come off as pathetic instead.

"You have to have SOMETHING inside you that's protecting you. And we WILL find it, whether you want us to or not."

"N… nrrgh!"

"What's wrong? Aren't you going to try and bust out of the tube now?"

Tubes again? Really?

The lights come on, and my hideous, tattered skin is revealed. All of the scientists in the room gasp and whisper things I can't really hear too well.

"What… what are you going to do to me?"

"Whatever I please. And no one's going to tell me otherwise! NO ONE!"

"Why are you doing this to me?"

"Our experiment might turn up some really significant results in terms of anatomy. And a fortunate side effect is that you will die. Plain and simple."

"Wha…? What did I ever…?"

"I DON'T CARE WHY. I. WANT. YOU. DEAD. WITH THESE EX-PERIMENTS, I FINALLY MIGHT BE KNOWN FOR SOMETHING IM-PORTANT. BUT THAT'S JUST AN ADDED BONUS."

"You sick, twisted monster!" I finally, somewhat, stand up.

"Excuse me? A little louder so I can hear that squeak of yours."

"I SAID," I muster the very little strength I have left, "YOU SICK, TWISTED MONSTER! Don't you realize killing me will accomplish abso-lutely nothing? Whatever you can't comprehend, you drag down to your level." I fall over a bit. "Don't you get it? Even if I am dead, you'll always have to live with a trapped conscience because you and I both know that you want to kill me FOR… FOR PURE REVENGE! What does that accomplish? Nothing! Absolutely…!"

A gas fills my tube. I gasp for air.

"Hmph. Good. He finally shut up." The commander barks orders as he walks away. "Let the boy suffer his wounds for two days while he's conscious. After that, we'll dissect him. And find that freak power deep inside him."

With that, everyone leaves the room. I'm all alone now. Since no one can see me, I start to cry. I'm in excruciating pain. I think back on the time I was nearly beaten to death by that bully. Physically I feel like that right now, only ten times worse. I'm still bleeding profusely enough to feel extremely weak, but not enough to succumb to death. Eventually I cry myself to sleep, hoping that Vizor and D will be back for me within two days.

I hear banging noises on my tube. "Hey… up!"

I think I'm dreaming, so I just ignore them.

Then hot water pours from the tube ceiling onto my back sores. The sensation of 10,000 needles entering my body wakes me up, compelling me to get on my feet. When I do, my hair absorbs most of the water. The commander then turns the water off.

"Good. You're up. About time!" He sounds annoyed. Then again, it's hard for this guy not to be annoyed by anything. "How did you survive the ten megavolts of electricity?"

"What do you mean?" I answer as I try to maintain balance.

"What's this alien power you possess? You're not human; I know that. So I'm going to give you a chance to respond. In exchange, I'll give you one more day to live."

"DON'T YOU GET IT BY NOW? This power inside me is something you can't just extract! It's something unique, something extraordinary, something AWESOME! You're just trying to characterize me as an alien because this is probably the first time you've ever seen anything like this."

"Hmph."

"AM I RIGHT?"

"…"

"Whatever! Keep silent! You can't even comprehend something like this. You're a product of society. Whatever society can't comprehend, it ostracizes, calls it dangerous, and tries to hunt it down and eliminate it with all the weapons at its disposal. CAN'T YOU SEE THAT THIS IS SOMETHING SOCIETY COULDN'T EVEN TOUCH? IT TAKES WAY, WAY

MORE THAN JUST WEAPONS TO TAKE DOWN REAL POWER! TRY IT! I DARE YOU! SOMEONE LIKE YOU COULD NEVER TRULY DESTROY ME!"

The commander walks around the room thinking. He stops at the exit and says, "That's an interesting theory, kid. Can't wait to try it out in a few hours. Enjoy your last 300 minutes of living." A timer above the door appears, showing "299:99:25." The countdown begins.

I have to try to break out. There has to be a way. I won't let the commander kill me that easily! Come on…!

"No, no, no. Wouldn't want you to move too much. I think I'll numb your body a little bit before I CUT IT OPEN!"

An insane amount of paralysis gas fills the tube. I try not to breathe it in. I focus on transforming into Extreme V.

C'mon! DO IT! I HAVE TO TRY! MY LIFE IS ON THE LINE! *Cough*… *cough*… *cough*.

AIR! I NEED IT! I take one huge breath. It's no use. My entire body is now paralyzed, again. I can't focus on my strength like this… I can barely focus on breathing. *Cough*… *cough*… ugh… I knock out for what I think will be the last time.

Is this really it?

Am I… dead?

Chapter 10

V's Hour of Judgment

I wake back up to my grim situation. I look up at the clock: "004:57:16." Less than five minutes left to live. The worst part is, I can't even put up a fight. I feel hopelessly weak. My wounds are even worse than before.

What am I supposed to say now? Goodbye? I see flashes of Z, D, Griff, Azilez, my entire family and friends. Have I told them how much they mean to me? How my life has been so much richer with them in it? No one can hear me from in here. I'm trapped, confined by a menace called society. Its snare took me in, and now it plots to wipe me off the face of the Earth — this time, for good. I can't use the Dark Spirit to fall through the Earth.

"KEKEKEKE!" The commander sounds exceedingly happy, especially since he's about to commit murder. "I bet you never want that clock to run out."

"…"

"What's up? No words of wisdom this time? Or has my paralysis gas at last permanently shut that big mouth of yours?"

"Why… why are you still angry?"

"HUH?"

"Listen to yourself. You… *cough*… aren't even happy… even though you're… about to… physically… de…destr…" I'm cut off by my lack of energy. My heart is barely beating. Even if the commander doesn't kill me soon, my wounds will. I really do have three more minutes left to live, whether it's by the commander's will or not…

That's when a miracle enters the room: a siren.

"WHAT NOW?" The commander is as irked as ever.

"Sir! There's someone knocking out all of our researchers!" a guard answers the commander's question.

"I SWEAR, IF IT'S THAT LITTLE PUNK OR THAT BLUE-HAIRED FREAK, I'LL…!"

Wait! That means the Dark Spirit might be…

– *DARK SPIRIT! *Cough* Hurry! I'm… I'm… about to… die…*

In a matter of seconds, the heavy, metal door that blocks off the entrance blasts open and sends five guards flying with it. I can't even make out what made the door fly, but then the commander suddenly flies toward the tube. He slams against it so hard that it shatters on impact. The commander has a few thousand pieces of tiny glass in his body.

"AAAARRGGGHHH!" he screams in pain. I take a look at everything around me to see if I can spot just who is trying to save me.

"Vizor? D?" I say in the loudest voice I can muster. I take one more look at the timer: "000:00:00." My fingers and toes go numb. A frozen feeling spreads through my arms and legs. This must be it. I relish my last breaths as I anticipate the numbness about to spread to my torso next. The last bit of blood is seeping out of my body… but then… "OW!" Something bites me. Strangely though, there's no piercing pain. In fact, I start to regain my strength! The sores on my body start to disappear, and are replaced by new, fresh skin. The blood on my body starts to evaporate, and new blood rushes through me. Just what exactly is biting me?

I turn around and see a patch of silver hair. I can't see anything else, but I can tell that there is now a person biting my right leg. Wait… a person biting into my leg, and it's somehow making me stronger? No way! Could this being be what I think it is?

"Uh… thanks?" I mean, what else do I say? I'm really confused. That's when she looks up. Wow, she has red eyes too! And a clean face that is white as silk. Her white sweater looks ultra-soft and fluffy. I can barely see the tips of her fingers. Her sweater is way too long for her.

Her mouth gently retreats from my leg and she stands up, offering me a hand. In lieu of words, she gives me a smile. She's wearing jet-black sweats. It's a very plain outfit, but now I see what I really want to see: her fangs. There are two of them, and she quickly hides them inside her mouth. It's very safe to assume now. She's a…

"Vampire, huh?" I smile back at her.

"This isn't the place for a chitchat. Take my hand. The two you're concerned about are waiting for you."

"You know where they are? Have you done anything to them?"

"One way to find out, right?" She places her hand closer to mine. I like her tone. It is playful and soothing. I think I can trust her. After all, she went through all this trouble just to bite me.

"NO. WAY." The commander rises from the glass shards that he lay in. He looks like a demon: blood dripping down his head, with a gun pointed at me. The vampire doesn't hesitate. In a split second, she pimp-slaps the commander's gun out of his hand.

"Come on! Let's go!"

"Where exactly?" I grab her hand and we transform into a purple mist and fly away. "WOOOAAAHHH!"

"Don't worry. You're safe now."

"Who are you?"

"Like I said, not right now. Let's just get back to your friends."

"Where are you taking me?"

"Ugh… you and all these questions. I will answer them when we get back. Trust me, it'll be easier, and your mind won't be in COMPLETE shock."

"I guess you're right. So much happened in the last few minutes. Thanks for the save back there, really. I would for sure be dead by now if you didn't… help me in your own special way."

"Trying to put it delicately, I see." She looks right through me. "Don't worry. Anything for a friend of Vizor's."

"You know him?"

"Just chill with the questions for a little bit, 'k? You think you're strong right now. But trust me, being on the verge of death doesn't exactly heal in minutes."

"Sounds logical. You probably know more about that than I do."

"Just take a nap, buddy. We'll be at our stop in about an hour."

"Yes, ma'am." I finally get some shuteye, and one that's not brought upon by blood loss or knockout gas — for a change.

Chapter 11
Bloodline Connections

Zzz… zzz… zz… zzz…

"We're here."

"Zzz… huh? Where exactly is 'here?'" I gaze upon the castle in the moonlight. It's very tall and looks like a cathedral. In fact, it even has the same, colorful glass panes that a church would. The moonlight is so bright that it bounces off the windows and burns my eyes. I can barely tell if the light is coming from the moon or the sun.

"My home. Transylvania."

Transylvania? Could that mean that…? Nah. There's no way, right? "So can we stop being mist and actually become physical again?"

"Not yet. First we have to go to where D and Vizor are."

"Why exactly?"

"You'll see." She sneaks under the castle gates and makes sure to travel along the cracks in the ground, trying to stay hidden. The weird part is that as I'm following her, I see nothing that resembles life in the castle. I'm tempted to ask, but she's telling me that she'll explain eventually. Plus, I have a feeling there's more to this place than meets the eye. I mean, I just met a vampire; I'm pretty sure it gets only weirder from here. "Here it is. Hurry."

"Uh… OK." I'm still pretty confused.

"I'll explain. Trust me." She understands me. I follow her into what looks like a trap door. As I enter, I see that it's VERY deep. I press on, about 300 feet, until I reach the ground. There, I see a mist waiting for me. The vampire turns us back to normal and lands on her two feet while I land on my face.

"Was that intentional?" I say with my face still on the brick floor.

"It's a mystery…" She says sarcastically.

"That's just like you, Hazy." A figure appears out of a shadow in the room. It's Vizor!

"Can I talk as I please in here… uh… Hazy? I'm bad with names. It takes me a while to remember some."

"Yup. No harm done."

"VIZOR!" I reach out to hug him.

Hazy jumps a little bit. "This is normal, Vizor?"

"Oh, it gets better."

"Can someone please explain what's going on? How do you two know each other? It doesn't sound like you just met."

"That's because they didn't!" I hear the most innocent voice ears can comprehend. D!

"Buddy! I missed you!"

"V! OH, I'M SO HAPPY YOU'RE ALL RIGHT! I've wanted to give This back to you for a while now."

– *V! You're alive!*

– *And well. Thanks to Hazy.*

– *Incredible. I've never seen anyone survive that many volts of electricity.*

– *What can I say? The bond we have is enough strength to live through anything.*

– *I'm truly happy you believe that, V.*

– *Welcome back, Dark Spirit.*

– *Happy to be back!*

It transfers from D's arm into my body. I miss this feeling… NOW everything's back to normal.

"Whoa! What was that?" Hazy notices the Dark Spirit.

"What was what?" As if I don't know.

"That mist that crawled up your arm!"

"Oh, this?"

– *Ready, Dark Spirit?*

– But of course.

I walk toward Hazy, and, after one step, fall through the Earth.

"Wh-WHHHAAATT? Where'd he go? Vizor, did you know he could do that?"

"Maybe."

"Explain it, then!"

I reappear as Dark V. "Not until you explain what your deal is, Hazy."

"I guess that's fair. OK, what do you want to know?"

"Well, first, why'd you come and save me?"

"Ah, that was my idea. I had to try and find you, and let's just say that Hazy is good at that sort of thing." Vizor smiles at Hazy.

"Yeah, she took out all of the guards and I didn't even notice her."

"Nice. Nice!" Vizor gives her a high five.

"So… hmm…" I try to think of what to ask her next. "Oh, yeah! D just kinda touched upon this, but how do you and Vizor know each other?"

"We've been friends for centuries now," she says. "Our parents used to get along really nicely."

"Best friends, huh? I've known mine for what seems like centuries too."

Vizor laughs hysterically. Hazy follows suit.

"Oh, V, that 'centuries' part wasn't hyperbole. Literally, we've known each other for centuries."

"Wait. How old are you guys?"

Hazy replies: "I'm about… hmm… 350 years old. Vizor here is about 450."

"NOOOO WAAAYYY!" D and I scream. "Are you two immortal?"

"Pretty much. Vampires are descendants of Omoh sapiens, after all. They take after their creators."

"See, V," Vizor starts, "the vampires' fangs originated from the blades in the Omoh sapiens' hair. Over time, the blades gradually shrunk and moved into the mouths of our people. These vampires evolved and were much, much friendlier than Omoh sapiens. They were pretty much banned from Treah for that. Since we were 'inherently evil', we dumped the vampires here."

"That's confusing." D is trying to process all of this. "If that were true, shouldn't you two hate each other?"

"That's where our parents come in," Hazy takes over. "See, our parents are leaders of both our peoples. Think of it as public relations. The two meet often to make sure one group isn't plotting to outright destroy the other."

"Wow. What a beautiful friendship."

"No need for the sarcasm. We know full well that it's quite sad; pathetic even." Vizor sees right through me.

"We started seeing each other more often. That's when we realized that… well… we liked each other, even if it was kind of forbidden by our people to even see each other."

"So is this why you had to sneak into your castle?"

"Bingo. My dad doesn't take well to outsiders anymore. He used to, but he changed one day… suddenly."

"Changed? Like how?"

"I'm not sure… He just wasn't himself one day and he's been that way ever since. I'm glad Vizor's back though! I haven't seen him for a long time!"

"Is your dad who I think it is?" I stand up and walk up to Hazy.

"I think so." She giggles. "Care to guess?"

"You're a descendant of Count Dracula, aren't you?"

"Ding, ding. Good job."

Chapter 12

Transylvania Terrors

"So what exactly do we do now?" I ask. "Vizor, should we head back to Egypt? To try and get to Heaven, where the other three are?"

"Slow down, V. After all, you did just almost die."

"I guess. Hazy mentioned that too."

"Did you grab my pickaxe, V?"

Oh, right! D's pickaxe got shot out of his hand! I knew there was something off about D when I got here. It's a shame too. He loves his pickaxe.

"Uhh… I think it's still in King Tut's tomb, right where you dropped it."

"Actually I still have a question for you, V," Hazy chimes in. "How'd you fall through the ground just now? And how did your hair just cover your right eye?"

"Ah, that. Meet the Dark Spirit." It flies out of me and I revert back to my normal form.

"I've heard of This somewhere. I can't quite remember. Hmm… Oh, yeah! Daddy said something about You!"

"Do you remember what it was exactly? It might help us."

"No. Not really. Nice to finally meet You though."

"The pleasure is mine, Hazy." The Dark Spirit retreats inside me. This time, we don't merge to become Dark V.

"Did you want to know anything else, Hazy?" I ask.

"Well, since you're being oh-so generous with your offer right now… how about how you two met?"

"Who? The Dark Spirit and me? Or Vizor and me?"

"Both. Why not?"

I explain by recounting the day Vizor took my family from me, how the Unbound Evil possessed him, and how it affected my life. In particular, I emphasize the differences between possessed Vizor and normal Vizor. It's enough to somehow drive Hazy to tears.

– *V, don't you notice anything different about her?*

– *Hmm… wait, something's missing.*

– *Exactly. What is it?*

– *Please don't tell me it's the Unbound Evil…*

– *No, I would've felt that. But this change is much more subtle. I didn't really notice it until now.*

– *Should I ask her?*

– *I guess so. If she doesn't mind.*

"Hazy, what's wrong? Why are you crying?"

"Because… the way you described Vizor… reminded me of daddy."

"What about him?" Vizor kneels down next to her.

"His attitude about things. He's so much more hostile now…"

"If you don't mind me asking, Hazy," I get straight to the point, "what was that dark barrier around your eyes?"

"Wait… IT's GoNe?" Her psychological state is suddenly changed: she looks like she's going to vomit any second now. It's as though she's feeling five different emotions at once.

"What was it?"

"An emotional lock."

"How does that even work?"

"Dark powers can be UsEd to hide more than your physical bEinG. V, it seems like you don't KnOw why your people so greatly fears DaRknEsS. It fears it will LoSe itself inside of it beCaUsE no hUmaN could ever grasp what it tRuLy is. DarKnEss is tO Omoh SapiEnS and VaMpiRes as LiGhTNess is to HuMAns."

"If that were true, Hazy, I'd be a vampire, an Omoh sapien, and a human. But I'm not. The only things that darkness and lightness can be are the things we make of them, human or not."

"Whoa… what?" Vizor's face is flooded with shock by what Hazy said. "How, and more importantly, why, would you put something like that on yourself?"

"Don't you get it, Vizor? No one, no one could help me at the time…"

"I could've…"

"NO, YOU COULDN'T, VIZOR." She takes a deep breath and gets a grip on her emotions, at least enough to express herself. "You were gone. Your world was gone. I tried to look for you, but there was nothing there…"

"WHY WOULD YOU DO THIS TO YOURSELF?"

"Because I couldn't help daddy. Don't you get it, Vizor? He was acting, and still is acting, like you did when you took V's family from him."

Vizor's reaction implies that he finally realizes what she means. "So… what has he done?"

"He never lets me leave the castle anymore. What's worse, he has scared the rest of my family away. I'm the only one that's left here. But I can't leave. I am to be raised by him… forever."

"Who told you that?"

"He said if he ever found me leaving the castle, he'd kill me and the people I was seeing. I had to put an emotional barrier around myself so he'd never suspect anything I did."

"WHAT?" THEN WE'RE IN TROUBLE! WE'VE GOT TO…"

"Too little. Too late." A powerful force sends us back onto the castle floors.

"You honestly think you were outsmarting me, daughter? I always had an eye on you."

"D-daddy…" Hazy puts her head down, trying not to remind herself why she ran away from herself for who knows how long. The weird part is, Dracula is nowhere to be seen.

"What have you done to her?" I step forward. "Don't you realize she's like this because of you?"

"Drac, why have you become so violent?" Vizor comes up from behind me.

"Ah, the son of the Omoh sapien king and the chosen one of The Legend of V…"

"How do you know who I am? And the legend?"

"I used to consult with Vizor's father all the time. How can I not know about the legend he despises so much?"

"How do you even know that he hates The Legend of V?" Vizor asks. "I'm not even sure he does anymore."

"You were never sure of anything, Vizor. Maybe except for thinking vampires and Omoh sapiens could be friends… but look where that got you."

"Grr…!"

"Not the time to lose your head, Vizor."

"And you… my prize. I'm so glad I get to see you, finally."

– *I sense IT, V.*

– *It was so obviously here from the start. The fact that Dracula and Vizor behaved similarly is a testament to that.*

– *Its actions are not mere coincidences. It has gathered all of us here today to drain us of our strengths. Let's be cautious!*

– *As always.*

"You are one sick puppy, you know that, Unbound Evil?"

"What…?" Hazy finally looks up.

D angrily walks forward, without his pickaxe. "You are going down!"

"I wonder if you can say that after I'm done with all of you!"

"Try all You want. You'll never win!"

"Bring it on." Vizor whips his blades out from his hair.

"WITH PLEASURE."

Chapter 13

The Unseen Enemy

"**U**hh... Vizor?"

"Yeah, V?"

"How do you think your blades will be of any use right now, when you can't see Dracula?"

Vizor's expression changes from that of being ready to fight to the death on the battlefield to one of just having gotten 2+2 wrong. "You know, you'd think I would've thought of that..."

"Guys! Duck! He's behind you!" D tackles us to the ground.

"Argh! I remember you! That nuisance with a tree!" The count finally reveals himself. His black cape with the crimson interior; his slick, black hair; the fancy suit; and those two fangs that are as valuable as ivory.

I walk up to the legendary vampire. "As opposed to the nuisance without the tree?"

"I don't need to remember a tree to remember you, V. You're pretty much burned inside my mind. I won't let you escape."

"Is that the cheesiest line you have?"

"Wait, V, what's going on...?"

Do I even want to respond to Hazy? "Can I explain it later? Your dad is out for my blood. ALL OF IT."

"... I guess."

I can't even imagine how she's feeling. How long has she had that mental lock on herself? Even worse, she's immortal. She could've had that thing on for decades!

"I won't waste any time with you anymore. I've already done it enough."

"Your judgment hour is here, Unbound Evil! You've toyed with me for long enough! I remember EVERYTHING now!"

"But did you even know everything to begin with, Vizor?"

"What are you talking about?"

"Do you honestly think you have the whole picture in your head? You've barely scratched the surface."

"Care to fill us in?" D clenches his fists in anger.

"I've made that cliché mistake once. I won't again."

– At least It finally acknowledges that…

– What real difference does it make?

– I guess You're right, Dark Spirit. If anything, it's worse for us. It has finally adjusted to Its mistakes.

"Die. All of you, including you, Hazy."

"D… D… dad… dy… WWHHYY?" Tears erupt as if spewing from a volcano.

"You sleaze! What are You trying to pull?"

"Nothing different from last time. Or do I have to remind you?"

"ARRGGHH!" Vizor charges with blades whirling. "I can't tolerate someTHING like You!" Before he launches his attack, though, he takes out his grappling hook and starts bouncing off the walls like some insane dodgeball.

"VIZOR, STOP!" I try to make him come to his senses. "Look at this! It has barely attacked us, and we're already frustrated. Don't let it divert your attention! Remember, Dracula isn't evil; it's what's inside him that's evil!"

"Nrrgh!" Vizor retreats with a bitter taste in his mouth.

"That's right, sit tight. Obey your master, you filthy mutt."

"At least I…"

"DADDY!" Hazy charges into Dracula with all her strength, sending him into a wall with a force that can be mistaken for thunder. "STOP! WHAT ARE YOU DOING? YOU'RE NOT BEING YOU! WHAT'S WRONG

WITH YOU?"

"Senile, little fool. So naïve. So young to DIE."

The count flies through the roof and descends onto the ground with such force that it makes the San Francisco earthquake feel like an aftershock. We go flying into the air.

Except when we start to fall back down, we don't. Something catches us: a tree. No way…

"D! How did you…?"

"I'm not going to wait for you to get pummeled again! I've got your back." Extreme D flies out. The colors of the sun really suit him. After saving our behinds, D forges a pickaxe out of thin air. "Join me, V, why don't you? You too, Vizor!"

"Quite the eager one. I LIKE IT!"

"That's my little bro right there!" I point to him. He gives me a taste of my own medicine and gives me a "V" sign. "Hey, that's copyright-ed!"

"Really? I never saw a patent on it."

"Hahaha! Let's go!" Vizor and I ignite into our extreme forms. Vizor's is a little different from D's and mine. His dark-blue hair catches fire, his red eyes turn into a deep crimson, and the force he exerts feels darker. The three of us jump onto the ground, ready for the possessed Dracula!

"Good! GOOD! This'll be fun!" It doesn't waste any time. The brain-dead figure attempts to hit us with the same shockwave that robbed us of our strength late in our last adventure. This time, though, we expect it. With one swing of his pickaxe, D completely deflects the evil's attack and sends it right back.

"TOO SLOW!" He drives me into the ground with a kick so hard that the ricochet effect actually sends me flying. I immediately recover.

"Ha! …Huh?" He disappears.

– *Where did he go, Dark Spirit?*

– *Whoa!* Without warning me, the Dark Spirit makes me invisible for a second, making the possessed monster fly right past me. – *I think Pure Extreme V is in order!*

– You said it. Let's get the other two in on this.

– Definitely!

"Guys! This isn't enough!"

"What isn't, V?" D asks.

"The extreme forms!"

"Oh, I get it! C'mon, Vizor!" D flies up to where I am, and Vizor follows. The Dark Spirit taps into our displayed strength, but the vampire attempts to strike at us in the process. I see him coming and dodge immediately.

"Ha! Sucker!"

"STILL TOO SLOW."

That's when something I never saw coming happens: the Unbound Evil, in Its spirit form, flies into me. Wait… how? Wasn't It just a part of Dracula a second ago? Wait… no… did It just ditch the Prince of Darkness to get a piece of me?

"HAHAHAHA! YOU'RE MINE NOW, V!"

"Grrr! AAAAHHH!" It happens so quickly that I can't react in time.

"Yes, YYYEESSS! BEND TO MY WILL, V!"

"Get out of him!"

"AAAAAAAARRRRRRGGGGHHHHH!"

"V…?"

"………"

"Is he…?"

"KEKEKEKEKE! KNEEL BEFORE THE CHOSEN ONE! MORTAL OR IMMORTAL, ALL WILL BEND AT MY WILL."

My sun-like aura becomes a bit more crimson, and light starts to emit from my hands like steam. Unbelievable… Evil V has arrived.

Chapter 14

The Evil Lightness and the Heroic Darkness

"ALL OF YOU ARE NOW PRONOUNCED DEAD!" It's no use. I have no control over my thoughts. This is what evil does to people; it takes their minds, puts it on strings, and bends it to its will.

"V…?" D looks sad, scared, and confused.

"D! NO! Don't touch him!" Vizor throws him out of the way.

I backhand Vizor, sending him flying since he heroically took D's place. "HA! YOU STRUGGLE TO SURVIVE! AND FOR WHAT?"

"You don't faze me, Unbound Evil. I WANT MY FRIEND BACK."

"HE'S RIGHT IN FRONT OF YOU. ALL YOU HAVE TO DO IS ACCEPT THE GIFT HE'S ABOUT TO GIVE YOU." I dash right in front of him. He tries to counterattack, but I disappear, and then reappear behind him. My "gift" to him is an uppercut to his lower back. "TOO SLOW."

"Not if… AAHH!"

I give him no reaction time. I grab him off the ground, by his shirt collar, and then assertively drive him back onto the ground. Please… stop me. "D! Run!" Arrgh! No! COME BACK!

"GHAHAHAHAHA! IT LOOKS LIKE EXTREME V WINS AGAIN!" I mock.

"Silence, fiend." A cool, calm, and collected voice bellows throughout the castle.

"WHO WAS THAT?"

"Let me remind you." There's a flash of darkness that lasts a split second. Then I'm on the ground, but it doesn't take me long to recover. After all, my body is in its extreme state. It's the Prince of Darkness himself, Dracula. "Did you honestly think you could just dispose of me by tossing me aside like that?"

"GRR! NO MATTER! IT'S ONE VERSUS ONE AND A LITTLE STAIN THAT DOESN'T WANT TO GO AWAY." Don't listen to me! D, fight it! It's no use though… he has never seen me like this. As a result, he's shaken to his bones.

"I… don't…"

"Don't even mention it, D. You shouldn't have to."

"NOW WHAT?" Another voice irks me.

"Now what? Now I take out the THING THAT RUINED MY LIFE FOR THE LAST FEW DECADES!"

Hazy flies out of the tree that D spawned, looking as sharp as ever (get it? Vampire? Sharp? … I hear the "boo"s already). Her mental state is now in her control, and she even wields the Dark Spirit! C'mon guys, destroy me! Wait! WAIT! No! That came out wrong. You know what I mean! Drive this evil out of me!

"Hazy! Baby!"

"Daddy!" The two try to hug each other, but I won't have any of it. I blaze past them, but they both merely stick their feet out, causing me to trip.

– *Ha! Pathetic!*

– *I WOULDN'T BE TALKING, V. I COULD JUST… WAIT… WHY HAVEN'T I THOUGHT OF THIS BEFORE?*

– *Wait, uh-oh! You wouldn't!*

– *OH, YES! THIS WILL TAKE ONE VERY BIG OBSTACLE OUT OF MY WAY! SAY YOUR PRAYERS, V.*

– *NGH…! GUYS, HELP!*

– *AND TO MAKE SURE THOSE TWO VAMPIRES DON'T FOLLOW ME…*

The Unbound Evil, which is controlling me, flies out of the castle and into the sky.

"The Unbound Evil is getting away! Hazy! C'mon!"

"OK! Wait!"

It makes a giant hole, and flies… onto Earth?

– *Wait. We were underground?*

– *DUH! HOW DO THINK THESE MONSTERS LIVE IN ISOLATION? THEY LIVE WHERE NO HUMAN COULD EVER FIND THEM.*

– *Wow, You finally tell me something.*

– *I'm REALLY going to enjoy killing you.*

Transylvania becomes filled with light — which, for a normal place, would be a good thing, except that…

"AAAAAHHHH!" Hazy and Dracula's skins start to burn. After all, the sun is their mortal enemy. The two immediately seek refuge.

"Vizor, hurry!" Hazy extends her arm out. She wants to give Vizor the Dark Spirit. Vizor nods, accepts It, and flies off to catch me, Evil V.

Pure Extreme Vizor (a mixture of Vizor, the prophecies' power, and the Dark Spirit) is on Evil V's trail. By that time, though, Evil V has already reached the sun. The Unbound Evil releases Its grip on me and sends me plummeting toward the sun.

"OH, THE SWEET, SWEET IRONY!" It yells out. "THE VERY THING THAT DRIVES YOUR POWER WILL NOW KILL YOU!"

As I get too close to the sun, my skin feels crispy, like a well-done rotisserie chicken. Fortunately, Vizor swoops in from behind and catches me before my entire body combusts.

"AAAARRRGGHHHH! I'VE BEEN INTERRUPTED TOO MANY TIMES TODAY!"

"V, are you OK?" Vizor realizes that I'm out cold. The Unbound Evil has drained all my power. "Here, I'll give This back to you." He transfers the Dark Spirit over to me. Within a few seconds, my body is back to normal, and I become PURE EXTREME V!

"Wooo hooo! Thanks, Vizor!" We exchange high fives.

"YOU FOOLS! FORGOT ABOUT ME ALREADY?"

Oh, yeah, the evil drained my powers, and now It's even more powerful than It was before — Pure Extreme Evil.

"It doesn't matter. It's two against One now."

"HAHA! GOOD. VERY GOOD. DON'T HOLD BACK, YOU TWO."

Chapter 15

The Real Enemy at Hand

"I'm not letting you two fly away from this fight. I'll just enjoy draining more power from both of you."

– This is bad, V. It doesn't seem to care about anything except the power that you two possess.

– It's almost like a virus. There seem to be so many of It and It lives off others' strength.

Vizor places his hands inside his hair so they catch fire. Then he takes out his hair blades. The fire spreads from his hands onto the blades! "Eat blue-flare tornado, Villain!" Vizor spins around and the blue fire spreads into a mighty twister. With one whack of the blade, Vizor hurls the tornado at the Unbound Evil.

"With pleasure!" The evil literally opens Its mouth to swallow the tornado's energy.

I see an opportunity to strike. Without a word, I grab the Unbound Evil's tail end, flip It over, and deliver an axe kick that sends It rocketing down. "Vizor! The Unbound Evil will eat all projectile attacks you throw at It. Try not to be too careless around It. The Thing is out for our power."

"Understood. I'll use melee attacks, then." Vizor absorbs the tornado he unleashed.

"Ooof!" I stomach one of the evil's body slams. It tries to grab me, but Vizor won't have that. He gets to the Unbound Evil with his ignited blades first.

"AHHH! What? Not bad at all, Vizor. I wasn't expecting something that powerful!"

The flame on the evil's body seeps in. It makes It stronger.

"What? So my fire is useless?"

The Unbound Evil dive-kicks Vizor in the face. Around that time, I recover from the body slam. "Vizor! Hold up!"

"Not today!" The Unbound Evil confronts me.

What am I going to do? All I can do is shake It off. It's absorbing everything that isn't a physical attack. If only there were a way Vizor and I could combine our strengths in one huge hit to knock It out. The Unbound Evil is focusing on one of us at a time, so maybe I can wait for an opening. Also, Vizor's fire has to go away. It's useless in this type of combat.

"Give me your power, V! I'll spare you the misery that's to come!"

"Why would I ever agree to that?" Oh, good. This'll distract It.

"Why would you NOT agree to that?"

"Really? That's the best You have?"

"EXCUSE ME?"

Yes! Got Its weakness!

"C'mon. I mean, all You're doing is waiting for us to attack You so You can become even stronger than before. So why should I even fight You?"

"Do you want your galaxy taken over?"

"And just who's gonna take it over? You? By Yourself?"

"YOU LITTLE PUNK!" There It goes… like a fuse about to go BOOM! "AAAARRGHH!" It conjures up all Its stored energy. It is stronger than ever. It grows giant horns and wings, and two blades erupt out of Its arms. They resemble Vizor's a bit.

"YOU WANT IT? NOW YOU'VE GOT IT!"

"That's enough."

"WHAT? WHO SAID THAT?" The Unbound Evil sounds a little frightened. Why?

"Come back to Me, now."

"Who's there?" I ask.

Out of nowhere and with his bare fists, Vizor clocks the Unbound Evil on the side of Its head. "Did I finally get a good hit?" Vizor sounds frustrated. Then again, why wouldn't he? Until now, his attacks have been further fueling the Unbound Evil.

"Come, My child."

"AAAAAAAAARRRRGGGGGHHHHHH!" Much like at the end of our last adventure, the Unbound Evil burns to nothingness. It vanishes.

– *What was that?*

– *Yeah, what WAS that?*

– *I don't know. I'm dumbfounded!*

– *It just killed the Unbound Evil though, whatever It was.*

– *But more just keep coming. What exactly is going on? I'm not even sure anymore. V, stay alert.*

– *Roger that, Dark Spirit.*

"Vizor?"

"Yeah?"

"Let's go back to Transylvania now! The others might need us."

"Right. Let's go!"

We jet back underneath the Earth to Transylvania. There, the light is still focused on the castle, so I assume that not much has happened since then. I hope I didn't just jinx that…

"D! Hazy! Dracula! Are you guys here?" I want to make sure they can hear me.

Vizor sporadically flips over the roof's debris to see if there is anyone under it. As he gets closer to a certain area, he hears: "Vizor? Is that you?"

"Huh? Who's there?"

"Calm, calm, my boy. It's me, Drac! I can't handle light, remember?"

"Huh? Oh… uh… sort of."

"What do you mean?"

"It's a long, convoluted story that I can't even explain adequately. I've had a few rough decades…"

"You don't say! So have I. That THING took control of me. It wanted to control this place."

"Why?"

"It could've been for any number of reasons. I don't know."

"Well, maybe because…" Please don't, Vizor. Only you and I would get that.

"V!" I hear a high-pitched voice coming from the top floor. "Come check this out!"

"D! What did you find?"

"Just… come on! I can't even explain it!"

"Is Hazy OK?"

"Hazy's up here with me! I wanted to make sure that she would stay out of the light, so I brought her up here where it's pitch-black."

"Then why isn't Dracula with you?"

"I offered, but he refused."

"Refused?" Vizor is confused. "Why Dracula?"

"Do you know the properties of that Thing, Vizor?"

"Well… which one? It has a lot of–"

Dracula cuts him off. "My memories are returning."

Vizor knows exactly what he means. The events of what happened during his possession suddenly crash down on him like a tidal wave. It's almost too much for him to handle.

"What did you do?"

"I… I was vicious. A cold-blooded predator, out to find something."

"Find something? What was it?"

"It was the portal… to Hell."

Chapter 16
Omoh Relations

WHAT? A gateway to Hell is in this castle? And the Unbound Evil tried to find it? Wait, It can't go into Hell? Its home? It can't just teleport back there? I would think It would have no problem pulling off something like that. I feel like I'm missing something big.

"Wait. Which room, D?"

"There's a door here with a sign that reads: 'Do not enter. This means you, Hazy.'"

"So this is what that Thing was hiding from me…" Hazy murmurs.

"Huh?" D asks.

"I always felt something powerful from this room, but I knew I would be killed if I looked inside. Daddy was really scary…"

"Don't worry. You should be safe now." D tries to reach up and pat Hazy's shoulder.

"Thanks, D." Hazy picks him up and hugs him. D starts to lose himself inside her soft sweater.

"What's going on, Drac? A portal to HELL?" Vizor wants an explanation. "That's not something you just find lying around."

"No, it's not." Dracula stands momentarily, but then buries himself in debris once more because of the sunlight.

"Is there any way to shield you from the sun?" Vizor asks.

"Not as far as I know. It's what makes us who we are."

– *Is that really true, Dark Spirit?*

– *Their dark powers are strong. I doubt they could just mask them.*

– Or can they?

– You have an idea?

– Well, the Solar Prophecies do contain the power of the sun. What if I shared it with them?

– But that would… Wait… Would it burn them?

– It shouldn't. And if it starts to, I'll pull it all back.

– So kind of you, V. Unless you burn them… That's just rude.

"Hey, Dracula?"

"Just call me Drac, my boy. Dracula is too formal. It gets me itchy."

– Says the guy wearing a suit…

"OK, Drac. There might be a way to cure you of your solar curse."

"Well now. I've never even heard of any human who's willing to help out a vampire."

"Trust him, Drac. V has helped me pass through my tribulations."

"Ah, a friend of Vizor is a friend of mine. OK, then, what is this idea you have?"

"See the sun?"

"I would if it didn't burn my eyes."

– Smooth, V, smooth.

"Uh… well, do you know what the Solar Prophecies are?"

"I think so. Vizor's dad did mention them at one point."

"Well, combined, they have the power of the sun. Care to have a taste?"

"Wait, whoa, whoa, whoa. WHAT? You're pulling my leg here, right?"

"Nope. Have some, Drac." Vizor helps me out. "These tablets actually make you feel like you are the sun."

"Well…" Dracula tries to make a sane decision. "Enough crazy things have happened today. I guess this is kind of normal in comparison. Why not? Let me have it!" I reach into the fallen roof parts to grab Drac's hands. I release my extreme powers and let him feel what it's like to have the sun gently rub his skin. "What… what is this?"

"This, my friend, is what the sun feels like."

"It's like… it's like a heartbeat; it feels pure, strong, and gentle all at once. I feel… I feel…" Drac slowly smiles, and even gets a bit teary. He rockets from under the scrap, and faces the sun with his majestic cape flying in the wind.

"I've never seen a vampire so happy to see the sun in the sky." Vizor looks at the count.

"I'm just happy I can look into the sky again, sunlight or moonlight. I'm glad I'm myself again. I'd rather burn to a crisp than serve that wretched evil!"

"Oh, come on, daddy!" Hazy jumps down from clearly above 100 feet. Landing unscathed, she makes sure to stay in the very corner of the room where there's no light. "Let's not go there, OK?"

"Fair, my darling. That's perfectly fair."

"Uhh… daddy?"

"Yes?"

"How are you not burning?"

"Would you like to know this beautiful power that has been bestowed upon me? Do you want to know what the sun really feels like?"

"Uhh…"

"Darling, I know you have doubts, but look at me! It's inside my body, and I haven't burned down. Come on. We won't be creatures of the shadows anymore!"

"I suppose…" She strokes her left arm with her right.

"Come, my child… Actually, never mind. Stay there." The count walks over to his daughter. Vizor and I stay behind and smile at Hazy to let her know that she'll be fine. She smiles back. D walks down the stairs, jumps onto his giant tree, and slides down from the trunk onto the floor. He walks over to Vizor and me.

The count takes Hazy's hands, and the process starts anew. Hazy's eyes glitter as dazzlingly as when a light hits a diamond. Her arms fall to her sides, and her eyes widen. She slowly takes a step into the sunlight, feeling warm and fuzzy on the inside (and outside with her sweater). She gazes at the sun, with a brand-new smile on her face.

"I… I'm not sure what to say, daddy. This… this feeling…"

"It's not me you should be thanking, darling, but rather the handsome curly-haired one next to you.

I smile, but then…"Oh! Thank you, Vizor! So, so much!" Hazy hugs him so hard that he gasps for air.

The count, D, and I all receive the blankest expression you could possibly imagine.

"Uh… honey?"

"Yes, daddy?"

"That's the wrong curly-haired boy."

"Oh, well…" She turns around and faces me. "Thanks a bunch, V!"

"Hey… uh… no problem!"

"So come on! You've got some explaining to do, daddy!"

"About?"

"The portal, and how we have it. I don't even know how it got here, and it's in my house."

"Ah, yes. Well, come along, everybody."

We follow the count to the top floor, where the room with the gate to Hell resides.

As we get closer to the door, the Dark Spirit and I feel the powerful aura that the portal is emitting.

– *Whoa! It's like when we sensed that the Devil was in Vizor's castle. Remember? When It took it over?*

– *I couldn't forget.*

"Here it is!" The count slowly opens the door. I'm not sure why. It's either because the portal is unstable and/or reactive, or he's just trying to be dramatic. Inside, we see an empty room with an energy field that could easily have been mistaken for a black hole. Wait…

"Count, is that actually a black hole?"

"Ah, I see how you'd think that, but no. It's a portal."

"But it resembles one in so many ways."

"Yup. The wonders that exist in the places least seen are truly remarkable. This is probably one of the best I've ever come across."

"Right…" Hazy walks up to her dad. "Now how did it get here?"

"I'll get to it, sweetie. But, well…" The count looks up to the ceiling that's no longer there. "Where do you want me to start?"

"Anywhere's fine, daddy. I just want to know everything you know."

"Alrighty then… I'll start with how I first saw this seemingly impossible force. I was meeting with Vizor's father…"

"Count, stop there." Vizor interrupts and sounds eager to know. "What was my father's name?"

"You mean to tell me that you never knew?"

"I knew only my brother's name, X. He never told me."

"That seems odd. But, nonetheless, I shall tell you. His name is Syzor the Second."

"What happened to the first one?"

"How should I know? He never really liked me, remember? He told me only what was necessary."

"Ngh…" Vizor doesn't sound too happy.

"Well, anyways, I had a meeting with Syzor on Treah. He seemed rather odd that day."

"How so?"

"Well, he just offered me this portal like it was nothing. He never seemed so generous."

"What was the meeting about?" I ask.

"You know, the general 'we're not going to kill each other' thing."

"Oh, right. Continue."

"So, at first, I thought it was supposed to be a peace offering, but…"

"But…?"

"Hazy, remember that day?"

"Which? Wait…" Hazy's eyes widen.

"Yes. The day I was possessed, and the day everyone left the castle for good. When my memories eventually returned, I saw that the Unbound Evil came from this portal."

"So then… he used this to try and wipe you out?"

"That's the gist, yes. However, after he knew I was possessed, he tried to take it back from me. That's when Treah was erased from this universe."

"So his plan backfired. He knows it's still here then?"

"Yes, and the worst part is that I don't even know where inside Hell this portal will take you. I've never been through it."

"Why not?"

"I guess I was just keeping people from ever going inside it."

"So that's it then? That's how this hole got here?"

"Yeah, I know it's not much, darling, but it's all I really know. All I can do is warn all of you."

"What about?"

"There's a big picture here. We have only a few pieces of this convoluted puzzle. Syzor is after something, the Unbound Evil is after something, and it seems like the Devil is after something. All of them play major roles in this scheme."

"How horrible! They're messing everything up!" Hazy points out. "All of this, and for what? Personal gain? I won't stand for it! I'm gonna stop them! All of them!"

"Now, darling, I don't think you should..."

"But daddy, this is something I feel like I need to do! I've been oppressed by that Thing for long enough."

Those words really speak to Drac. He realizes why she's doing it, and starts to look inside himself as well. It doesn't take him long to chime in with regard to this adventure.

"All right, you win, Hazy. But there's no way you're going alone with just V, D, and Vizor."

"What do you mean? Do they have more friends?"

"You're looking at him." Drac winks at us.

"No way! You want to come too?"

"Why not? I feel like thwarting these menaces as much as you do. Let's do it together!"

"You know what? I wouldn't have it any other way." The two of them hug. The sun disappears from the hole in the Earth. Nighttime is upon us.

"That's odd. I kind of miss the sun now..." Dracula crosses his arms.

"Want to see if it's still out there? In the real world, daddy?"

"Great idea! Where do we go, fellows?"

Vizor, D, and I huddle together to figure that out.

"Why exactly are we doing this?" Vizor whispers. "We're going to Egypt, right?"

"Yup. OK then. Let's break."

"This isn't football, V."

Is it, though? Because this is a game where we don't know the opposition's strategy or tactics. We can't even really grasp what our enemy is yet. But we do know that they are prepared to trample us on every down. I guess there's only one way to meet the enemy: on the field.

"To Egypt! And to Heaven! We've got to find the others!"

"Who might 'the others' be, D?"

"Z, Griff, Azilez, and the Solar Prophecies. After all, they complete our team."

C h a p t e r 1 7

Heaven: the Source of All "Good"

Wow, I never expected to be back here alive and well. After all, I did almost die here. But let's look past that. I'm back now, and that's all that matters.

"Where is this Valley of the Kings?" Hazy asks me while we hover above Cairo.

"South. Along the Nile, come on!"

We get closer and closer by the minute. The valley is still under guard. In fact, it looks like it's been fortified. That jerk commander REAL-LY doesn't want us in there.

"Do I have to go through all this stuff, again?" Hazy sighs.

– I don't know. Do we?

– We… I'd imagine. They must have something planned for us by now. After all, that's the commander's life mission: to make sure we don't live.

– Good point. So here's what I think. We barge in, through the front, in our extreme states.

– Careful, V. Who knows what they have inside there? The Unbound Evil could even be helping them.

– Let's get a little closer to see if You can sense It.

– Good idea.

"This way, guys, c'mon." After crossing the staircase near the tomb of Merneptah, I signal everyone to stay put. The Dark Spirit and I hide inside the ground and stop just outside King Tut's tomb.

– Anything?

– No, not really. It doesn't seem to be here.

– *Just what exactly is going on? The Unbound Evil seemed hell-bent on killing us, but then some mysterious voice caused It to EXPLODE.*

– *It seems strange, but there had to be a reason for that blast.*

– *We really don't know what our opposition is plotting. You were right: we have to be extremely cautious from here on.*

– *Glad you agree.*

– *Well…how about that red stone? The one that interferes with spirit energy…or something of that nature?*

– *Listen to this! It's hilarious!*

"C'MON! THIS THING WON'T OPEN!"

"You'll never get it open!" King Tut mocks him.

"WHO THE HELL IS SAYING THAT?"

"Sir! What else should we try?"

"Did you try the crowbar?"

"Yes, sir! It snapped in half, sir."

"AAAARRGGHHH! I GIVE UP! BLOW THE PLACE UP, MEN! THAT PESKY BRAT WON'T EVER COME BACK IN HERE, AND I'LL SEE TO IT!"

– **Gasp*! We've got to hurry!*

– *We don't have much of a choice. The prophecies' temple is essential to The Legend of V!*

– *Let's go back to the others. We've got to get the commander and his men out of there.*

– *Hohohoho! That won't be necessary, my boy.*

– *Huh? Wait, the master tablet!*

– *Indeed! Now that my power is back, I can repel these stingy people from this place!*

– *Really? How?*

– *Just get back about ten miles, and you'll see.*

– *You're not going to kill them, are you?*

– *Heavens, no! I couldn't. Even people as terrible as this.*

– *OK! Let's go, Dark Spirit.*

– *As you wish.*

We resurface.

"What's the plan, V?" Drac crosses his arms.

"To retreat. Temporarily. For a few minutes."

"Huh? Why? I want my pickaxe back!" D pouts.

"Don't worry, I have a feeling it's still there. The commander wouldn't think much of an ordinary pickaxe. Oh, and about retreating: the master tablet told me to do it."

"Wait… master tablet?"

"You'll see, Hazy." Vizor places his hand on her shoulder. She smiles to let him know she trusts him.

"All right then. Off we go."

We all make sure we fly far enough, to the point where we think it's ten miles away. We fly a little farther to make sure.

"OK, so… now what?" Vizor asks.

"We wait."

"For what?"

Suddenly, a loud thump rocks the Earth.

"Was that it?"

"I'm not sure, Drac. It never really told me what to wait for…"

That's when we spot rain, but it isn't made of water; it's made of people! "AAAAAHHHHH! HELP ME!" Vizor, D, and I all recognize the commander's voice. The cries of agony behind him are those of his crew.

"That kind of impact would kill them all, right?" Vizor sounds half-disgusted, half-excited.

"Uhh…" I have no idea. The master tablet didn't give me much information. As I close my eyes to make sure I don't see the enormous amount of bloodshed that's about to take place, more crazy events transpire: the commander and his crew all stop just feet before impact on the ground. They're all stuck in midair. Pretending we all know exactly what's happening, the five of us run right in front of the commander. Vizor, D, and I start to kick him like he's a piñata. Hazy and Drac exchange confused looks, but after a few seconds shrug and join us.

"GRR! IF I COULD MOVE RIGHT NOW…!"

"Oh, you'd probably have us all eviscerated and our corpses burned, but too bad you CAN'T MOVE." I make sure to emphasize the last part to pour even more salt on his mental wound.

After a couple of minutes of kicking him until he's sore, the commander and his entire squad fall face first on the sandy, rock-textured ground.

"I will have my revenge!" The commander points his finger up in an attempt to be threatening, but it just comes off as lame. In fact, D thinks it's so lame that he kicks his arm down. "Ow…"

"How did I do, guys?" Hazy whips her hair out of her eyes.

"Ten out of ten."

"I'll give you a seven. Just because you came in late."

"You suck, Vizor." She chuckles.

"You're welcome."

"We go now, then?" Drac rubs his foot. It's sore from kicking the commander too much.

"You want to fly?"

"Please!"

He cloaks himself in darkness and transforms into a bat.

"Wait… WOAH!" I pet the creature to make sure it's real. "How'd you do that?"

"One of the many powers of a vampire. We can manipulate darkness to shape our bodies in any way we want! Even in the shape of an object, like…" Drac shapeshifts into a wooden stick.

"Huh." I lift my foot, and before I even start to bring it down…

"Don't you dare step on me."

"Yeah, c'mon, V. That's my daddy."

"I guess I was just curious about what would happen if he broke in half."

"Well, picture snapping a human in half. So don't snap a vampire stick."

"No worries. Especially with the image you just painted in my brain."

"Well, can we go now?" D is jumping up and down in a steady rhythm.

"Sure, buddy. Let's go."

Vizor, D, and I run to the Valley of the Kings, but Hazy and Drac don't follow.

"Why are they not running with us?"

"Probably because they're transforming into..." Of course, the two bats fly directly above us.

"This is fun! I can't remember the last time I flew with you, daddy!"

"You too, huh, Hazy?"

"Well, why not? It's easy on the legs to fly."

"Do everyone's legs hurt?"

"Well, it doesn't matter that much. We're here already." The entrance to the pharaoh's tomb is open, and, best of all, there's no Alexandrian cop in sight.

"Whew! Finally!" I stretch my arms. "I wonder if the master tablet's still here."

– *It's not like I can grow legs and walk away, V.*

– *Oh, yeah, I forgot you could do that. And trust me, with what I've seen in the past few weeks, a rock growing legs and walking off wouldn't surprise me.*

– *Very true. Well, c'mon! I'm waitin' for ya!*

– *Be right there!*

We head inside the pharaoh's tomb, and the hole that leads to the master temple is still there. We each head into it, and as everyone goes inside, I stop to see if King Tut is OK.

"You there, King Tut?"

"... zzz... zzz... zzz..."

"He's asleep."

"I wonder why."

"Probably keeping the jewel safe is mentally frustrating work, especially if you're hiding it from the commander." I jump inside, and meet everyone in the room with the master tablet and the Heaven portal.

"Ah! You all made it! And you brought vampires! Exotic!"

"The thing TALKS?" Hazy rushes and grabs the tablet on both ends. "Is there a switch that turns it on and off? This can't be real..."

"As real as a vampire, my dear! Hohoho!"

"It's actually alive!" Hazy uses her power to shape her body like the master tablet.

"Very creative! The dark power suits you!"

"Thanks! And the hefty voice suits YOU."

"Hohohoho! ...Oh! D!"

"PICKAXE?" The boy REALLY wants his pickaxe.

"Uhh… yes. It's over yonder."

D dives onto the pickaxe and hugs it as though it were made of fine silk.

"So is this the portal?" Hazy says as she returns to her vampire state.

"Yes! Enter, my friends."

"No time to lose, guys. C'mon!" I run into it. Vizor, Hazy, Drac, and D all follow.

The portal acts like a wormhole and sends us through many vibrant colors. The amount of colors here is enough to put a rainbow to shame. I can't even identify some of them. The visual overload is enough to give some people an epileptic seizure. So for most of the trip, I close my eyes.

Before I know it, we're dumped in… Cairo? Wait, were we tricked?

"Did that thing seriously just boot us outside?" Vizor crosses his arms in frustration. His question is very easily answered though. It did transport us to Heaven. How can we tell? There are angels and demons duking it out in what looks like the Valley of the Kings. In the midst of the crossfire, we spot them: Z, Griff, and Azilez are all in their extreme forms, and all five Solar Prophecies are behind them.

"Guys!" I yell out to get their attention. Sadly though, it doesn't work. They're too busy dodging demon fire and helping the angels ward off the unwanted visitors. "I don't get it. How are there demons here?"

"Who cares why? All that matters is that they ARE here. And it doesn't look like showing them the door will make them leave." Hazy's hand starts to emit a purple energy.

"All right! Let's go!" Vizor grabs his blades from his hair, and, without thinking, charges into the field. We all follow behind him, toward Azilez, Griff, Z, and the prophecies.

"Get back!" Azilez's rainbows cover Griff and Z as they attack the raging enemy. Griff uses his bare fists, and Z uses an infinite supply of golf balls and his driver to smack the menace from a distance. A good strategy, but how long could they last?

A lot is going on in that one little area. Azilez is trying to deflect and intercept every fireball the demons throw their way, but eventually one breaks through. Luckily though…

"Watch out!" Vizor breaks into his extreme form and uses his blade like a bat to return the fireball back to the mouth it was spawned from.

"VIZOR?" Azilez turns around and sees who saved her back. "Does that mean…?"

"Looking for us?" D and I jump into the party in our extreme forms.

"Took you guys long enough! Where have you been?" Z notices us.

"We were starting to worry!" Griff adds.

That's when the two vampires descend from up above, ready to assist.

"WHO ARE THESE TWO?" Azilez tries to be heard over the roaring fire.

"We'll explain later! All that matters now is helping you guys!"

"Appreciate it. Welcome back, V!"

"Glad to be back, Griff. Now let's get to work!"

Madness ensues. We all split in different directions, taking out the hoards of enemies that come our way. D uses his pickaxe like a hammer to meteor the foes into the Earth (or into Heaven…? Never mind. That's confusing); Z and Azilez use the same teamwork they've been using, only it's more effective because the amount of demons they're fighting now is much less than before; Griff and I combine our melee tactics like axe kicks, roundhouses, and hammer fists to dish out some pain; Vizor uses his blue-flame tornadoes to wipe out whole groups of demons at once; Hazy and Drac shape their bodies into massive T. rexes and smash through any threat they find; and the prophecies warn us of oncoming attacks.

This goes on for quite a long time. In fact, the amount of demons we've fought now seems infinite. We have to find out where they're coming from. Otherwise we'll get tired and lose! I try to get some info out of Griff. "What exactly is going on here, buddy? Is this all you guys have been doing here?"

"No! We found God, but talked with Him for only a few minutes." He dodges a quick fireball. "That's when some angels revealed themselves as demons."

"What does that mean?"

"They were disguised. They opened a gateway from Hell!"

"Well, why don't we close it?"

"Gee, that's easier said than done! Let me just flick the 'off' switch on the portal!"

"Oh, so that's the problem. You guys never knew how?"

"Exactly! And those things are keeping God busy. There are thousands of them just inside the tomb and the master palace."

"Well, there's got to be something that's opening it. Let's go inside that portal that was opened."

"Trust me, V, we've tried, but there are just too many in there, even for our extreme forms. The force is too much!"

That's when I remember the portal back in Transylvania. "Wait. There's a way we can get into Hell."

"How?"

"Transylvania."

"This is not the time for a vampire reference, V."

"No. Transylvania actually exists. That's where those other two are from." I point at Hazy and Drac.

"Those two are vampires?"

"I'll explain on the way. We've just got to get back to Earth!"

"Let's consult God then!"

"C'mon!"

"EVERYONE!" Griff flies to a central spot where all of us can hear him. "FOLLOW US!" We fly into the tomb, trying to lose the demons through its maze-like corridors. Sadly, though, not everyone knows where the location of the master temple is. We end up losing Hazy and Drac in the process.

– *Dark Spirit, can You go find them and meet us back here?*

– *Sure! Especially if it means you won't be electrocuted again.*

– *Hurry!*

I try not to reminisce about that near-death experience. The Dark Spirit leaves my body and uses Its dark power to fish out the other two in the monster-infested pathways. I jump into the hole that leads to the temple. I meet the others in the room. There's a ball of light. It speaks.

"Why would you choose to enter this room? It's dangerous."

"We're here to help!" Griff replies. We all position ourselves near the portal and use all of our strength to delay the demons' arrival. "Can You make a portal that leads to Earth?"

"With a snap!"

In a split second, it's there in front of us.

– *C'mon, Dark Spirit!*

– *V! I'm almost back. I've found them. Just go into the portal.*

God then holds the wall so we can pass through. "Go. Hurry!"

We all, one by one, enter the white field. As I'm about to walk in, the Dark Spirit, Hazy, and Drac rocket into the portal before me. I fall over for a split second, but get back up in time. I make it through, the gateway vanishes, and as God lets go of the wall, demons bounce off it like the most ridiculous game of pinball you've ever seen.

Chapter 18
Crossroad Junction

The portal all of us jump through dumps us on a lush, green hill in a forest-like mountain range. We lie down on the grass and take in the refreshing, cool air around us. The grass feels like cotton, and the wind acts like a blanket that's neither too warm nor too cool. I roll over, but just before I get too comfortable…

"V!" Azilez wakes everyone up. "WHERE HAVE YOU BEEN? WHO ARE THOSE TWO? AND…!"

"Calm, calm, child. I'll explain."

"YOU BETTER! YOU JUST LEFT US HANGING!"

"He probably has a good reason, Azilez…"

"That, and Vizor and he did eventually return. With me, no less. Just get that intense fire out of your head, sit down on the fluffy grass, and… zzz…" D knocks out.

"Just explain. I'm an anxious gal. You know this!"

"Right, of course. So here's how it went down…" I go into detail about the horror they managed to avoid seeing. I tell everyone about the electric cube, how I saved D in the nick of time, how the commander snatched me, what ALMOST happened to me, and how Hazy saved my life.

"Uhh… seriously? That dude finally caught you?" Azilez has a hard time believing that. (You could also sense the disgust in her voice when she brought up "that dude").

"And he nearly KILLED YOU?" Z really doesn't believe that, especially in view of my extreme power.

"I was really weak. Ten megavolts of electricity would do that to any person."

"Actually, that'd immediately kill 'any person'."

"Point is, I was weak, and the Dark Spirit wasn't there when I needed It."

"'Cause you gave It to D to save him?"

"Exactly. I didn't have time to think, really. In a situation where your little bro is about to die a gruesome death, you'd do anything to save him, right?"

"Right." Z can agree with that.

"So… that leads to these two." Azilez glares at the new faces, Hazy and Drac. "Who are they? And why does it look like they're cosplaying vampires?"

"That's not a very nice thing to say to a vampire," Hazy replies in a smart-guy tone.

"Right, like I'm gonna believe…"

"Hold up, Azilez," Griff uses his new ability to see whether she's genuine. "She's actually telling the truth."

"How can you tell?"

"I just… can. I don't know how."

"Seems like the star-boy has a good head on his shoulders." Hazy refers to Griff's shirt.

"Well, that, and if what V is saying is true, then he wouldn't be here if this girl didn't have the ability to heal him."

"I guess that's also true…"

Drac sees that Azilez still isn't satisfied and jumps in. "Little girl, what do we have to do to get you to believe that we're vampires?"

"Well…" Azilez then immediately sees a contradiction within the scene. "Wait, how are you guys not burning? You're in broad daylight!"

"Let me show you how we aren't." Drac walks up to Azilez and offers his hand. Azilez looks at his pale hand with long, sharp fingernails. Rather hesitantly, she takes it and begins to feel the reason. The surprising warmness of Drac's hand makes her realize that he has felt the prophecies' strength.

"The prophecies..." Azilez drops her hand.

"Huh?" The two scratch their heads.

"Oh, that would be us!" The Wisdom Prophecy jumps out from behind a bush.

"Wow! Talking rocks!"

– *That's probably the sanest reaction I've ever seen when someone is meeting the prophecies for the first time.*

– *Well... bear in mind that her dad did meet with Syzor on a regular basis.*

– *Good point.*

"A vampire? That's a first for me."

"Nice to meet you." Hazy makes sure NOT to offer a handshake to the Prophecy of Wisdom. "Hazy's my name."

"How lovely. My name is Wisdom."

"Wait... Really?"

"AND I'M SPPPEEEDDDDD!" Of course, the green rock starts flying everywhere to steal the limelight.

"Ah, so I finally get to actually see you all. But where are the other three?"

"The other three?"

"All here. Ready to serve!" They say in scarily close unison, almost like troops standing at attention. But then they all loosen up. Hazy finds them quite fascinating, and Drac lets out sighs of relief at being able to finally meet the Solar Prophecies that he had discussed with Syzor.

"So you guys DON'T want to help Syzor, right?"

"Goodness, no!" the Power Prophecy answers Drac. "Why would we? We don't even know HOW he'd use us."

"That's good to hear..."

"By the way, where's D?"

"Shh. He's over here, sleeping." Azilez gushes about how adorable he is when he's curled up in a fetal position.

"Hey, Drac?" I turn to him.

"Yes?"

"Where exactly are we?"

"Above Transylvania, my boy. Why do you ask?"

"No, I mean, the land we're standing on now. What land is Transylvania buried under?"

"Oh, this place? This is where the vampires were before the 'incident' occurred."

"Incident? Do tell."

"Gather around the imaginary campfire, boys and girls. Hazy and I will fill you in."

"Oh, boy, story time!" D wakes up and makes Azilez's heart jump a little.

"This place is actually where the castle used to reside. It was never underground. Hazy and I moved it there."

"Why?" Now Vizor, too, is interested. (He never knew this story? And Hazy and he have been friends for centuries? I wonder what they talk about then…).

"I'm getting there. The humans ravaged this place after I slipped up."

"Slipped…?"

"I'll get to it. Don't worry." Having expected that reaction, Drac intercepts it. "So the castle had always been rumored to hold vampires, but no human could ever verify a sighting. That changed one day. I was walking down after taking a shower, and slipped!"

"OK, OK. Stop right there." I see two things wrong with that. "One: how is it that NO HUMAN heard the running water?"

"The castle was much bigger than it is now. So big, in fact, that most humans got lost inside it."

"OK… but two: why didn't you just shape yourself into a bat and hang on a shadowy ceiling?"

"All I can say is, I made a mistake."

"Wow… *seriously?* So what happened next?"

"Well, I was seen. And the humans threatened to burn the place down."

"How'd you react?"

"Well, since I knew that was the most likely reaction from any human sighting a vampire, I had to be prepared…"

"DID YOU KILL HIM… OR HER? Do you remember?"

"No! Of course not! That would be a last resort!"

"So what did you do?"

"I went up to the top of the castle to talk with all of the humans roaming around the area. I told them that we had no intention of hurting them."

"What'd they do when they heard that?"

"Did they believe you, Drac?"

"Patience, children. That's when it happened: the evil corrupted me."

"Wow, really?"

"That's when I scared everyone away from the castle for good. I always meant to bring them back, but I don't think I can at this point."

"That sucks. Sorry, buddy." Griff pats him on the back.

"So, after that, Hazy and I forced the castle underground, never to be seen by any human again. Until you guys."

"I didn't want to help daddy." Hazy adds. "This was his first death threat to me. I had no idea what was going on, or what to think. After that, a part of the castle was blocked off from me, and I was forbidden to ever roam that area. That's when the dark mental lock was created inside my head."

"So then this place would be where the original Transylvania was?"

"Yes. Romania," Hazy answers. "This is where the vampires used to reside."

"There were more than just you two?"

"Oh, of course. They were a whole race at one point. They all died off now, though. I don't like to talk about it too much…"

"Never mind then. Don't force yourself. You've already done too much for me."

"So now that we all know each other…" Speedy starts, "how's about we go to Hell?"

"After a short nap." I fall back down onto the hill and close my eyes.

"I'm OK with that," Griff notes.

"Me three. I'm beat…" Azilez just falls over.

D returns to his fetal position without a word, cradling his pickaxe in his arms; Z does the same things as D, except with a golf club; Hazy and Drac make sure to find an area that has sunlight; and Vizor leans against the side of a tree as he sits down. The prophecies? Griff makes sure to stuff them inside his backpack. He then throws it onto the ground so nothing would make him uncomfortable as he sleeps.

Rest well, guys. We're going to need it…

Chapter 19

Hell: the Place with Answers (and FIRE)

— How long have we been napping?

– … Zzz… zzz… zzz…

– Dark Spirit?

– … Zzz… hu… huh?

– I think we should wake up now.

– We shouldn't waste any more time, you're right.

"Get up, guys! C'mon! Hell awaits us!" *That couldn't have sounded worse…*

"Really, V? I was in the middle of a dream!" Azilez begrudgingly gets up and shakes her head.

"Five… more… minutes." Hazy rolls over.

– Gee, it looks like Monday morning. And this is the group that's about to dive HEAD FIRST into Hell?

"Seriously, guys. We can't waste any more time!"

"Are you sure, V?"

"I'm sorry, D. We have to."

"Aw… really?"

– I sound like a parent…

– That's a bad thing?

– In this case, yes.

D isn't as reluctant as Azilez, and happily gets up. It's almost as if his complaining was for nothing. "Then let's go, V! What are we waiting for?" I hold out my hand and D suddenly realizes that he wasn't the only one on the ground. "Oh, right… get EVERYONE up!"

Everyone looks pretty groggy as they wake up. They — especially Hazy and Drac — take their time standing.

"All right… where to, guys?" Z gets up and faces Vizor and me.

"The hole should still be there, right?"

"What hole?"

"The one that the Unbound Evil made while trying to fling me into the sun."

"That happened?"

"Did I not tell you about it?"

"Y'know, you probably did. I was just in a mood where I zoned out. Sometimes I sleep with my eyes open… like a fish."

Note to self: Z's a fish.

"I'll go check if it's there." Vizor grabs the grappling hook inside his hair, throws one end onto a tree, and flies up. With the view he gets, he's able to spot the hole that leads to Transylvania (the newer one). "Found it! Over here, guys!" Vizor lands on top of a tree and waves at us.

"No fair! I want to tree-climb!"

"You can literally do that anywhere. You can spawn them, remember?" Hazy reminds D of what he's capable of.

"Oh, yeahhh…"

"Let's get moving!" We run toward Vizor, but after a few seconds…

"HEY! YOU GUYS FORGET SOMETHING?"

"What was…? OH! The prophecies!" Griff runs back to retrieve his backpack. That is when things start to get bad.

Something that resembles a claw flies past us, takes the prophecies, and flies into the Transylvania hole.

"What was that?"

"You tell me!"

– *Was that the Devil's hand?*

– *How is that Your first guess?*

– Think about it: the portal is very close to us. If it drops us somewhere near the Devil, it wouldn't be an inconvenience to snatch it!

– You're right. We've got to hurry! C'mon! Pure extreme form, all the way!

– At your service!

I burst into action. Griff, Azilez, Vizor, Z, and D all follow, but just as we're about to let loose…

"WHAT HAPPENED TO YOU GUYS? VIZOR, YOUR HAIR'S ON FIRE!" Hazy's mouth hits the floor.

"Wait, honey, this feels like what we felt back then, remember?"

"Huh? Oh, it does! But it's a little different. It feels… darker, more complete."

"This is what the prophecies combined with the Dark Spirit feels like."

"You can combine them?" Hazy's eyes glisten with excitement.

"Yup. This is the power of chaos energy: an energy that is comprised of two forces. It's really something special."

"I feel it!" Hazy holds out her hands and looks at them like she just discovered something groundbreaking. She bursts into a pure extreme state. Her hair turns pure black, except for one strand of silver; her eyes form a gentle, pinkish color, and the aura around her feels like dark, heavy heat.

"I can get along with this!" Dracula spins and hides himself inside his cape. When he reveals himself, his hair's color is the opposite of Hazy's: all silver, except for one strand of black. His eyes' color shifts from dark gray to a sparkly silver. Here is the coolest part though: when he opens his cape, it looks like I'm staring into space! It looks like a void with white specks inside.

"Wow, you two, you've gotten the hang of this thing pretty quickly."

"What can I say, Vizor? I guess I learn quickly."

"Come, children, we have no more time to waste! The Solar Prophecies are in danger!"

"Right!" Griff gets a head start on all of us. We all catch up to him, fly into the hole, find the castle, zoom inside, get to the portal, and enter the highway to Hell. (Cue: awesome AC/DC song!)

We find the other side of the portal, though we land in a spot that none of us really expected: a single, isolated prison cell. It looks like one you'd find on Earth.

"What is this?" D hammers one of the cell bars with his pickaxe.

"It's exactly what it looks like: a jail cell. Nothing too special about it…"

"I'd beg to differ, Hazy." Vizor is knelt down in one corner of the room. He picks up a tiny piece of scrap metal from the ground. But he can't hold on to it for long. It shocks him. The pain makes him drop it.

"You OK, Vizor?" Griff asks.

"Yeah, I'm fine. But…" Frantically, he looks for more of those strange pieces. He finds three more, one in each corner of the cell. "Just as I thought. This is advanced Omoh sapien technology."

"What's it do?" Z asks.

"It can trap anything, no matter what it's made of, within its snare. However, it takes a lot of power to charge one. I can't imagine what four of them would be needed for. Wait…" Vizor places the puzzle pieces together. Or at least he tries. "Didn't the Unbound Evil come through here?"

"Well, yeah," Drac confirms. "I'm sure it was that Thing."

"If what you're saying is true, Drac, then the Unbound Evil, or at least a part of It, was trapped inside here."

"How do you know that? Couldn't It have just come in from the outside?"

"No, V, you don't understand. This tech was used to trap the most powerful beings on Treah. And let me tell you, in a world run by greed and self-lust, power was abundant. We needed a good defense system just to keep our so-called 'society' intact. Also, you can figure out what type of being was kept here just by checking the little devices. It's why I picked one up."

"Let's look at one WITHOUT picking it up."

"Just what I was about to do. Come here."

We examine one of them together. He shows me how they detect and measure the type of energy being trapped. There are two meters on each side of the tech, one with a blue number, and one with a red number. The red number detects regular-matter content, and the blue number detects dark-matter content. Right now, the red number reads "0.01%", and the blue number reads "99.9%".

"So… what does that mean?"

"It's as I expected. Only two beings are strong enough to possess this kind of configuration without collapsing in on Themselves: the Unbound Evil and the Devil."

"Then it probably was the Unbound Evil…" Azilez chimes in. "Unless It found a way to trap the Devil!"

"That's highly unlikely, considering the Devil created the Unbound Evil AND the Omoh sapiens."

"Right. So where to from here?"

"To the Devil, I guess. Right up to It. After all, It's got my world in Its hands."

– *Not the helpful kind of hands, that's for sure.*

– *I think we all got that, V…*

"C'mon!" D picks at all the cell bars with one massive swing and bends them open. "No time to waste then!" We all fly out, into open Hell.

This place looks more like I envisioned it. Everything is on fire. But as we fly around, Hazy and Drac recognize their surroundings. They know exactly where we are.

"Guys, it looks like we're still in Romania! Above the ground!"

"WHAT? HOW? Why do Earth, Heaven, and Hell all share the same places?"

"Actually, V… since you brought that up," Vizor decides to add more, "Treah has similar destinations."

– *Gee. One mystery to another. I can't even keep track of all of them.*

– *Yes, but I think I can help you with My insight here, V.*

– *Fill me in. I'm curious.*

– *I think of it this way. Heaven is watched over by God, Hell is watched over by the Devil, and both Earth and Treah are watched over by Their cre-*

ations.

    – That kind of makes sense actually.

    – Doesn't it? It's pretty simple too.

    "Hold on a second, guys." Griff stops flying and stares at a burning bush. We all stop next to him, to make sure we don't get lost in this place (even though we don't really know where we're going to begin with…). "This bush isn't becoming ash. Sure, it's on fire, but it's perfectly fine."

    Z takes a closer look. "This is all really confusing."

    "Let's try not to get sidetracked." Hazy grabs everyone's attention. "We've got to get the prophecies and Treah back from the Devil!"

    "We know. But where IS the Devil?"

    "You mean US?" More demons. Of course. It IS Hell after all.

    All eight of us turn around, in our pure extreme forms, ready to fight if we need to?

    – Griff!

    – Yeah, V?

    – I think the Devil's close by.

    – What makes you say that?

    – Because a group of about a thousand demons happens to just be prancing around.

    – Well… maybe. It IS Hell.

    Cute. He uses my own line against me.

    – But we just got here. Isn't it kind of coincidental that this group HAPPENED to run into us?

    – I suppose. But I don't sense any huge, concentrated power…

    – Neither do I, V.

    – I just don't want to fight more unnecessary battles. I want to get back what we came here to find, hopefully get some answers out of the Devil, and go back home.

    – Quite the list, V.

    – Thanks, Griff. I chuckle. But how do we stop the demons? Oh, I got it! I need to consult Azilez for this one.

    – Why not meeeeeee?

– Well, I need a rainbow for this one.

– Oh, OK. Whatcha got planned?

– I want to use a rainbow as a shield to fly over the demons.

– If you can do it fast enough, sure. That'd work.

– Let's find out!

"Oh, no! Demons! Retreat!" I fly in the opposite direction.

"Huh? V! GET BACK HERE!" As expected, Azilez is the first one after me. "WHAT ARE YOU DOING?"

Everyone follows behind to try and see what my game plan is.

"We don't need to fight them. Plus, I knew you'd be the first one after me. I need you for my plan."

"Aww! You know me too well."

"I thought as much. Now here's what I was thinking…" I tell Azilez about the rainbow shield.

"That's just crazy enough to work. Let's do it!" She whips out her brush. "You're coming with me!" She grabs my arm and heads above the demons.

"Just what's going through his mind?" Z gets a facial expression like he's pondering the way the universe works. "Eh. He's got this." The other six redirect their flight pattern.

Azilez's brush bleeds a rainbow that flies across the burning sky-line. The demons prepare for a countermeasure, but after staring at the multi-colored miracle, all stop in their tracks.

"Whoa, what is that?"

"I don't know. It's gorgeous!"

Something else happens when the bright rainbow contrasts the musky, hellish background. Dark energy starts to dispel from each and every one of their minds. Eventually, all of them become HUMAN! They all cheer and rejoice.

"Wow! How'd that happen?"

"They… they had them too." Hazy lands next to us. "The dark locks. They're exactly like the ones I had."

"But you never changed as a result of it. Just look at all of them. They're human!"

"This lock was much stronger. It didn't just simply block emotions; it blocked who they once were."

"I wonder how…"

"Ask them. They might remember now."

One of the "demons" walks up to Azilez. "I haven't felt anything like that in a long time! Thanks!"

"My pleasure!" – *HOW THE HELL DID THAT JUST HAPPEN?*

"We're in your debt! What do you need?"

"Where's the Devil?"

"It? Oh, It's just under here."

"You mean Transylvania? It's there?"

"No, the whole underground realm is Its. That's indisputable."

"We finally got It right where we want It!" Griff fist-pumps.

"DO YOU NOW?"

Uh-oh. Brace yourselves, everyone!

Chapter 20

The True Devil

An unseen force pulls every human on the surface of Hell even far-ther down. It's not like the ground opened for anyone, no. Everyone just started going through the ground. So for people who aren't a part of our group, it's painful. Really painful. That phase is short-lived though; for most of the time, we fall while we're INSIDE the underground realm.

This place is HUGE. At first, it almost seems unnecessary. But then I figure it out… I think.

"Is that?"

"YES."

Oh, God… the Devil is GIGANTIC! No, that's an understate-ment. How do I describe something like this…? Hmm… demongous?

"WELCOME, THE LEGEND OF V, TO MY TRUE, ULTIMATE DO-MAIN!"

"WHOA! That Thing's huge!" D finally realizes what he's looking at. "What's that It's holding?"

"OH? YOU MEAN… THIS?"

To give you some prospective, It holds out an Earth-sized plan-et in the palm of Its hand. However, the planet is a little different than Earth. It has "V"-shaped blades, like Vizor's, as rings.

Vizor immediately comments: "THIEF! GIVE ME BACK MY PLANET!"

"ARE YOU KIDDING? I NEED TO FIND THE SHADOW PROPH-ECIES FIRST."

"Why's that?"

"I DON'T NEED TO JUSTIFY ANYTHING. THIS IS MY HOME, AND YOU PLAY BY MY RULES."

OK, yes. I'm convinced this is the Devil. Its heart is as cold as dry ice. Touch it once, and you burn. All It cares about is how much It gains — the epitome of evil.

"… TOLD… WHERE… ARE!"

"What was that?" Z looks around like someone just yelled "fore" and he can't spot the ball.

"ONE SECOND, PLEASE." The Devil proceeds to lean Its head closer to the planet. "SAY THAT AGAIN, SYZOR."

"I told you! I DON'T KNOW WHERE THEY ARE!"

"OH, WELL… I GUESS YOU WANT TO STAY HERE EVEN LON-GER…"

"IMBECILE!"

"SILENCE! YOU'RE IN NO POSITION TO SAY THAT!"

"DO YOU WANT MY PROPHECIES OR NOT?"

"Ugh! Can someone tell these two to shut up?" Hazy holds her head in pain.

"THE VAMPIRE'S GOT A SHARP TONGUE NOW. IS THAT IT? FIGURES… A MISTAKE FROM OMOH SAPIENS MEANS DISASTER. THEY'RE BOTH DYING RACES. OH, WAIT, ONE OF THOSE RACES IS DEAD. MY BAD."

"Cute attempt to reminisce, Satan."

"DON'T EVER CALL ME THAT AGAIN. I AM THE REAL DEAL AFTER ALL."

"Real deal?" I'm confused.

"YOU REALLY HAVEN'T CAUGHT ON YET, V? THAT VERSION OF ME YOU SAW ON YOUR LAST QUEST WASN'T ALL OF ME. WHERE DO YOU THINK THE UNBOUND EVIL INHERITED THAT ABILITY?"

"Oh…"

"Is that my dad?" Vizor asks.

"WHERE? I DON'T SEE ANYTHING BECAUSE HE'S USELESS IN EVERY WAY!"

"IS THAT MY SON?"

Vizor quivers, "Y-yes!"

"Bring him up here! I have something to ask him!"

"I wonder if he misses me." Vizor can't wait to find out, so he flies up happily, yet braces himself at the same time. Hazy follows him as an assistant.

"Dad?"

"Where are they?" Syzor calmly asks him.

"What are you…?"

"THE SHADOW PROPHECIES! WHERE ARE THEY?" He wastes zero time getting angry with his son.

"I don't know! I've been possessed for the past few decades!"

"SURE. LIKE I'LL BELIEVE THAT! C'MON! BACK TO THE BIN FOR YOU!"

"No."

"EXCUSE ME?"

"He said no, Syzor." Hazy appears from behind. "Respect it."

"YOU'VE BEFRIENDED THE VAMPIRE?"

"This isn't anything new, dad. You never gave me the opportunity to have any friends to begin with."

"YOU ARE AS DEAD TO ME AS YOU WERE WHEN I LOST YOU! SO YOU KNOW WHAT? GET LOST! SEE IF I CARE! I'M STUCK HERE ANYWAY!"

"Fine!"

As Vizor turns around and leaves, Syzor realizes something important and stops him. "Wait! Vizor! How did you get here?"

"What do you mean?"

"There are only two ways in here. Death or… *gasp*… you have it, don't you?"

"Have what…?"

"GET OUT OF MY WAY!"

"AND JUST WHERE DO YOU THINK YOU'RE GOING, HMM?" The Devil encloses the planet in a giant barrier. Everyone inside gets trapped, including the two that just went up there.

"HA. I CAN SIT HERE ALL DAY. NO… MAKE THAT FOR ALL

ETERNITY. IT'S PRACTICALLY MY JOB."

"Huh?" Drac ponders.

"DO YOU GUYS NOT KNOW ANYTHING AT ALL? IF GOD OR I LEAVE OUR CHAIRS IN OUR KINGDOMS, OUR HALF OF THE UNIVERSE TIPS OUT OF BALANCE."

– *Wait… really? It has never mentioned THAT! Well, my chance is now at hand then!* Syzor clicks a button on his hair blades, and the planet's rings turn into giant jet engines. It's going out of Hell. "SAYONARA, CRIPPLED!"

"WAIT… AAAAHHHH! I WASN'T SUPPOSED TO SAY THAT! CURSE YOUR STUPIDITY! CURSE MY STUPIDITY! JUST CURSE STUPIDITY ALTOGETHER! CAN YOU ALL BE DOLLS FOR ME AND GO GET THAT PLANET BACK?"

"Uhh… no."

"WRONG ANSWER."

Wrong answer? What is that supposed to mean? Either way, before I find out, I remember that the Devil probably has the Solar Prophecies. "Wait!"

"WHAT?"

"Give me my prophecies, and I'll get back 'Your' planet." It DOES have them… right?

"OHH, ENTICING… HMMM… NO." It didn't really think about it too much. I guess I should've expected that…

"NOW HOW ABOUT YOU GO GET THAT PLANET BACK BEFORE SYZOR TERRORIZES YOUR WORLD?"

"Whoa, slow down." Griff steps in. "Say that again?"

"YEAH. TERRORIZE YOUR WORLD. WHAT ABOUT IT? IT'S WHAT THEY'RE INCLINED TO DO. THOSE SELFISH PETS ALWAYS WANT MORE…"

"How do You know that?"

"HELLO? HELL TO V'S BRAIN! I CREATED THEM! THEY TAKE AFTER THEIR MASTER!"

– *Wow… I'm really out of it today.*

– *Not the best time either.*

– I'll recover, don't worry. "We have questions first though."

"I FEEL A SLIGHT AMOUNT OF REMORSE FOR YOUR STUPID-ITY. WHAT DID YOU WANT TO KNOW?"

"Well…" I try to think of something to ask It. Let's see… what did we recently do that warrants further explaining? That's right… "Why was the Unbound Evil trapped inside a cell when we first got here?"

"OH? THAT? IT WAS MISBEHAVING ITSELF, SO I HAD TO PUN-ISH IT."

"How so? How did It misbehave?" Azilez asks.

"IT WASN'T OBEYING MY ORDERS. LIKE A DOG AND ITS MASTER… EXCEPT I'M THE ABSOLUTE MASTER. I CREATED IT. IF IT DOESN'T FOLLOW WHAT I SAY, THEN I JAIL IT."

"Won't It just hate You more then?" Z asks.

"YES. THAT'S THE POINT. MORE HATE MEANS MORE POWER. THAT'S ALL I CARE ABOUT. AT THE END OF THE DAY, ALL OF ITS POWER BECOMES MINE."

"Wait… what?" Drac stops It there. "You DRAIN Its power? For what purpose?"

"LIKE I SAID. IT. DOESN'T. MATTER."

"I don't think You realize how much it DOES matter." The Dark Spirit echoes within me.

"OH. IT'S YOU. DARK SPIRIT."

"'Tis indeed. Do You even know what the Unbound Evil is doing right now?"

"WELL, YEAH. IT'S INSIDE ITS CELL, FUELING ME WITH POW-ER LIKE A GOOD ENERGY STATION SHOULD."

"I don't think You know… but…"

"WHAT? ARE YOU SAYING I'M INCOMPETENT?"

"Well, considering You can't move Your butt from that chair, kin-da-sorta?" It doesn't appreciate my comment. It's like It owns certain emotions. I don't like it.

"WOW, YOU GUYS AND THE INSULTS. I THINK I'VE HAD ENOUGH FOR ONE CENTURY. COME BACK WHEN THE HUMANS ARE DEAD, DRAC. NOW GET THAT PLANET." *– OH, GOODIE, I HAVE*

ENOUGH STRENGTH TO SHOOT THEM UP NOW. ABOUT TIME. It flings us into the air, toward the surface.

"Aaaaaahhh! My prophecies!"

"GET THE PLANET BACK, AND I'LL THINK ABOUT IT… MAYBE. WE'LL CONTINUE THIS LITTE Q&A LATER."

I think I'm starting to see it all clearly now… This legend of mine is one sick, twisted revenge story. The Unbound Evil, the Devil, Syzor… all of them are out for something. Yet all of them are completely oblivious to some important facts: 1) No matter how much power they gain, they'll always lust for more. In the Devil's case, It wants the Unbound Evil. In the Unbound Evil's case, It wants the entire universe. In Syzor's case, it wants Earth. 2) All of them are out for each other. 3) They're all going to fail, one way OR ANOTHER.

All of this evil is not OK! And my best pals and I are going to be the ones to dispel it!

Chapter 21

A Split Team

That boy… The Legend of V has finally arrived. Time for my secret weapon. It's high time the Great War made a comeback. Syzor runs back to his castle in the midst of the thick fog.

There's something else I've noticed about Treah: there's literally nothing on its surface, except Syzor's stronghold in the distance. All there is to tread on are dry, porous fields of rock.

Vizor and Hazy are hot on Syzor's trail, but since Syzor is much more familiar with the planet than Vizor, he loses them with ease.

"Dad! Stop!"

"WHY ARE YOU FOLLOWING ME? GET LOST!"

"Do you not miss me at all?"

"Son, I never cared that you were gone, nor will I ever. NOW, LEAVE." Just to show how much he doesn't care, Syzor enters the ground, and Vizor and Hazy lose sight of him.

"Hazy!"

"You don't have to ask. I'm on it." Her body takes on a gaseous state, and she enters the hole which Syzor escaped through.

Finally, the rest of us land on the planet, but we can't see Vizor or Hazy anywhere.

"Darling!" Drac calls out to Hazy.

"Vizor!" Griff shouts in the opposite direction. "Where are you at?"

The foggy state of the planet acts like a giant dome. As a result, our voices echo and reach Vizor. "GRIFF! IS THAT YOU?"

"You bet!" Griff heads in the direction of our voices. As I follow him, I realize that the planet is still moving at great speed, heading toward... wherever it's going. That's the question on my mind right now: where is Treah going? The most likely answer is Earth, but I can't say for certain. Being a relative to the Devil, Syzor must have some tricks up his sleeve.

Right then, we see Vizor running in front of us.

"Vizor!" D yells.

"GET BACK, GUYS! I need to deal with my dad!"

"Are you kidding? Have you not learned anything from hanging out with us the past few days?" I try to remind Vizor what we came here for. "We're a team."

Vizor looks back with a single tear shedding from his left eye. "And this is where I take one for the team. I'm stopping my dad's conquest... ALONE!"

"No wa–"

"I'm not debating this. I said I was in your debt, right?"

"Vizor, c'mon! No way I'm watching you die!"

"V, IF YOU GO UP THERE, YOU'LL DIE FIRST!"

We all stop in our tracks. "What do you mean?"

"Don't you get it? My dad wants you here. He's been waiting for his chance to obtain your power and use it to destroy the humans!"

"We've been through this, the power inside me is–"

"WHAT? UNTOUCHABLE?"

"Huh...?" I'm confused. He read my mind. That's exactly what I was going to say.

"The Omoh sapiens have lost to you guys during the Great War once. What makes you think that they're not prepared this time?"

"I'm confused..."

"V, I know more about my dad than you do. I know what he's capable of, the technology he uses to obtain power, and his form of rule. GO BACK!"

"But..."

"NOW! This is how I'm going to repay you guys."

I stand in awe, looking at Vizor's bravery as he flies farther and farther away.

Azilez walks up to me. "Any plans?"

"I don't even know. I'm so confused."

"You know what? I have a plan!" Azilez says as she turns around. "D? This rock looks very breakable. I bet we could go underground and follow Vizor!"

"That's not a bad idea." Z chimes in.

"I guess there's nothing left to do 'cause Vizor's family seems like they want to kill me. Sure, I guess espionage is the way to go."

"All right, brace for impact!" SWING! As Azilez had predicted, D cuts through the ground like brittle toast. However, as we slowly descend, we see a giant, industrial city. I have no idea what city we're in since I'm not very familiar with Romania…

"What IS this?" Azilez busily twists her head in every direction.

"It's a city, Azilez. A city," Z offers an oversimplified description of the situation.

"I think we get that, Z. I think she meant: 'Why is it UNDER-GROUND?'"

"I mean, does it matter? This is actually better, right? We have a better cover to stalk Vizor."

"Wow, you're so matter-of-fact."

"I try my best."

"You try too much sometimes…"

– Is he always like this?

– Oh, yeah. And I love it. I loved it when I was a little kid, and it's the same now. It's a relationship better witnessed than explained.

– I like it already.

"One problem though, Z."

"Yeah?"

"WHERE'S VIZOR?"

"… Oh, yeah."

*– *Sigh*… Here I was thinking that he was on to something.*

– Just not our day, huh?

— I guess not, but that's no excuse to stop now.

Suddenly, Dracula eyes something that he can immediately recognize, even if she isn't solid. "Hazy!"

"What? WHERE?" Azilez turns around one last time and finally keeps her head steady.

"You guys don't see her?"

"Well, I see SYZOR."

Hazy's chasing him, and it looks like Syzor means business. He's headed somewhere in a hurry.

"PESKY VAMPIRE! GRRAAAHHH!"

Syzor throws his hair blades, and they create a vortex of blue fire. Hazy dodges it easily since she's in her spirit form. "Try again, please."

It seems like Hazy already knows how to make Syzor mad: taunt him.

"GGGGGGRRRRR!" – *SHOOT! I'll let her have it later! I need to stay focused!*

"Guys," I whisper to everyone. "Stay hidden. And shut up. We don't want them seeing us."

"Got it," Azilez actually whispers for once.

— Don't you just love how she's the only one that responds to a command involving voice control?

Syzor's hair blades return to his hair, and he continues toward the palace.

Hazy spots us. However, instead of saying anything, she keeps on Syzor's tail, ignoring us.

"I wonder what's going through her mind…" I think out loud.

What am I supposed to make of this? It seems both of them don't want us here. How much do I really not know? Is it really better to just turn around and leave? After all we've gone through to get here? Now that I think about that… no! It isn't time! We're just getting started here!

"Are you still doubting yourself, V?" Azilez walks at my side, again.

"I'm… just not sure. Vizor looked so sure of what he was doing AND saying *for once…*"

"Think of it this way: what do you think is going to happen to him in there? And Hazy? Two against… God knows how many?"

"That's the thing though. He's got his friend for the journey ahead, just like I had Griff and Rodger the first time."

"But then look what happened to all of you. From what you told me, you guys ended up in hospital beds, right?"

"Yeah."

"And what did they do when it was time to settle things?"

"They… they…" I close my eyes, deep in thought. What exactly did they say? Hmm…

"Are you kidding? There's no way I'm going to miss this!"

"Wouldn't miss it for anything else, V!"

They never hesitated… not for an instant. I think I'm starting to see why. They knew that if we were together, no obstacle could stop us, even when… even when… they didn't know what was ahead. Vizor needs us now more than ever!

"So, V, what are we going to do?"

"We're going to help them, even if it means the death of me! Griff and Rodger did the same for me… It's time I do the same for Vizor. And help him create his own legend!"

"That sounds like the V I know!"

"I needed that. Thanks, Azilez."

"Absolutely no problem, V. Now then… the palace awaits!"

"Right! Guys! We're going to barge right into that castle, and help Vizor get what's his!"

Next stop: the Shadow Prophecies! And Syzor's plan!

Chapter 22

Treah's Master Tech

The six of us continue forward, making sure to remain as quiet as possible. The Dark Spirit and I fuse once more to become Dark V, so I can slither through the ground to make sure there is no danger ahead. If there is any, I have enough time to stop, turn back, and warn Azilez, Z, D, Drac, and Griff.

– Anything here?

– Nope. It looks safe.

– Good. Let's…

– Wait a second! Look! V! Up above!

– Huh?

I lift my head and spot Syzor, who is about to power his way back onto the surface of the planet. Hazy is still behind him.

– This is good… Maybe I can lure in ALL of them, not just the chosen one. What am I saying? Maybe? OF COURSE I CAN! With this idea in mind, Syzor rockets through the stalactites and enters his grand castle.

– Uh-oh! He's getting too far ahead! I can't lose sight of him! There's no telling what he'll do with any amount of time! Hazy uses her spirit to her advantage. She silently slips through the cracks of the rocks, and forces her way into the castle.

"Guys! They're gone!"

"THANK GOD! THIS VOICE WILL BE HEARD!" That might've been a mistake actually. Azilez's powerful voice causes a disturbance we hadn't thought possible. The entire city seems to be groaning. It gets louder by the second. Then I realize, the groans are due not merely to the fact that the residents are upset; the residents are actually chasing us!

"This looks hairy…" Griff darts in one direction, without really looking in front of him first. He bumps into three Omoh sapiens, and the impact knocks all four of them on their butts. The three Omoh sapiens recover WAY quicker from the fall than Griff. When he looks up, he witnesses their uninviting faces: cross-armed, and looking down on him — literally AND metaphorically.

"You don't look like you're from here."

"So?"

"DIE!" The female Omoh sapien immediately goes for her hair blades and gives them a nice, thorough swing. Griff backflips in time to counterattack. He parries the blow with his legs as he comes up.

"Whoa, calm down, sister."

"Actually, this is me being calm. You don't want to see me mad, Griff!"

Wait… She knows him? Does Griff know her?

Griff gives her an odd stare. "Who are you? You look a lot like…" Griff turns around and looks at Azilez for a second, then looks back at the girl. He repeats this process over and over until he finally makes the connection. "You're her opposite, aren't you?"

"How perceptive! My name is Eliza." Well, they have the same, booming voice, which I was hoping wasn't the case….

"How do you know us?" Azilez takes her brush out. The others behind her brace themselves as well.

"Syzor. He contacted us. Told us to make sure you guys stay down here for a little while. So come and play! COME, BROTHERS AND SIS-TERS! LET US RAIN MAYHEM ON THE CHOSEN ONE!"

"So you know about The Legend of V as well, then?"

"Duh! Why wouldn't we?"

The second figure comes into view now. Not only is there an Azilez double here, there's one for Griff too?

"Don't tell your name is Ffirg…" Griff slouches a bit.

"What? No! It's Pippin."

"Not gonna lie, but I kinda wish it was Ffirg now."

"OK, Eliza?"

"Yeah? Kill him, right?"

"Oh, for sure. I was just going to ask for permission."

"C'mon! For murder?"

"Right… sorry…"

"Ugh! C'mon! Live up to your name!"

"You are so dead! Ready everyone? CHAAAAARRRGGEE!"

"HAAAAAAA!"

– *Not today! Pure Extreme V time!* As I'm about to lift off, the Dark Spirit tries to stop me. But it's too late. Little did I know this would be a huge mistake.

– *V, wait! NO!*

– *IGNITE!* I blast into the air, with my radiant colors and all.

– *We got him… That was too easy.*

Suddenly, giant red alarms start blaring. A huge box forms around me, and it closes in. I try and burst my way out of it, but it's made of such a weird material, like a mold of plastic and rubber. I can't cut it open!

"Guys! HELP!"

"V!" Azilez runs over.

"HEH! Go ahead and try to help him, my mirror image! No one breaks out of this box. NO ONE!"

Azilez launches rainbows in my direction. As they strike the box, they explode, but the box isn't harmed… AT ALL.

"Who's laughing now, V? HAHAHA!"

Pippin joins Eliza. "YEAH! AAAAHHAHA!"

"Hold on, my boy!" Drac flies up and starts biting the mold with his sharp fangs. Still, nothing happens.

"You honestly thought a VAMPIRE could do anything against our tech?" Eliza laughs maniacally.

Thinking I'm about to be crushed to death, I brace myself. However, the mold simply passes through me. It encases me in, but I can still breathe since my head is sticking out and none of my bones are crushed. I feel fine.

The box falls from the sky, and Pippin catches it. "Good! Now back to the castle!"

"Right! See ya, losers!" As Eliza runs off, she looks back, winks, and sticks her tongue out, specifically at Azilez.

"GET ME OUT OF THIS BOX! AZILEZ! GRIFF! Z! D! DRAC!"

"GRRRR…!" Azilez nearly breaks her brush from clenching it.

Drac places his hand on her shoulder, and she calms down a bit. A little bit. "I'll take care of all this. I've never had to transform into this, but…" He flies up, so everyone can see him. Drac changes into his spirit form then comes out as a dragon. He lets out a mighty roar, and uses his flamethrower to make the other Omoh sapiens flee. "Get on! All of you!"

"Cool!" D trots on, not questioning how that just happened.

Azilez shrugs and gets on, Z follows her, and, finally, Griff runs over.

"COME! Next stop: Eliza and the Pippin."

"Ha. I like the 'the' in front of his name." Z says.

"Came up with it on the fly." Drac flaps his wings and looms above Eliza and Pippin.

"Did it just get darker than usual? WHAT IS THAT?"

"Your pippin-flippin' doom! That's what!" Drac spews fire like a pyro who just got a lifetime supply of flames for Christmas.

Pippin, meanwhile, takes the back of his hair blades and conks my forehead with it, knocking me out. I guess I kinda walked into that one, didn't I?

"Can't I just kill him now, Eliza?"

"No! Master Syzor's orders! Bring V to him ALIVE. You know the master's will is absolute."

"Grr…" Alive? Why would Syzor want me alive? Isn't his end-game to kill me? I'll find out soon enough. I have to be very cautious here. I hardly know anything about him. Not only that, the Devil sent me here to get the planet back. What do I do if I can't get it? Do I just casually fly back and tell It, "Oops. My bad. Forgot the planet. Maybe next time?" I doubt It'd let me leave alive.

"Give the boy back to me, and nobody gets hurt." Drac's dragon form, with his massive size and wings, blocks Eliza and Pippin's way.

"You think we care?" Eliza subconsciously blurts. "Let me remind you who you're dealing with!" She squeezes herself. I've seen this before.

"Drac, hurry! SHOOT THEM!"

Drac coughs out a fireball. It explodes on impact with the two aliens. "Did I get them?"

"Wait, where is V?" Azilez sounds worried. "DID YOU SHOOT HIM?"

"WHAT? No! I wouldn't!"

– *V, are you there?* Griff taps into his unexplainable power.

– *Griff! Up here!*

Eliza and Pippin get out alive somehow. Not only that, Eliza uses her hair blades like boomerangs to carry me to the surface. They have evaded pursuit…

"Nerds!" Eliza pops her head out of the ground and makes an "L" sign with her fingers.

Azilez loses it. "THAT'S IT! YOU'RE GOING DOWN, SISTER!" She explodes into her extreme form so quickly that the blaze trail nearly burns the other three. Drac wouldn't burn because of his scaly skin. Azilez doesn't even bother slipping through a crack embedded in the ceiling; she blasts a hole into it instead. "WELL, DON'T JUST STAND THERE! C'MON!"

"Excuse us for wanting to get those extra cinders off our bodies first," Z replies.

"JUST GET UP HERE! WHATEVER YOU'RE DOING CAN WAIT! V CAN'T!"

"At this point, Z, just let her do her thing." Griff holds on to his shoulder.

"I guess you know better, buddy."

"Drac!"

"Yeah?"

"Go back to your original form. We don't want to make the hole in the wall any bigger, do we?"

"Right you are, my boy." He uses his wings to cover himself, revert into his spirit form, and then back to his normal state. "I'm ready!

We're off!"

"To V!"

"And God-knows-what-else," Z adds. All four are now aimed to get me back from the Omoh sapiens' clutches.

Azilez doesn't even bother to open the front door; she pummels it down to let everyone inside the castle know that she's coming for them. "ELIZA! GIVE MY FRIEND BACK!"

"HAHAHAHAHA! Such anger… it suits you, Azilez!" She jumps down from the second floor of the building, with a paintbrush in hand.

"UGH! You have a brush too?"

"Hello? I'm you!"

"YOU WISH!" Azilez creates two giant fists with her infinite supply of rainbows, and attaches them to her own hands. "TASTE THE RAINBOW!"

"Yes! YES! Come at me with all your strength!"

– *Wait…* Griff tries to make sense of the situation. With his hypersensitive awareness, he scouts the area. "AZILEZ! Stop it!"

"Huh?" She turns around, confused.

Eliza seizes the chance. She uses her brush to spawn purple crystals, much like the ones Azilez used to try and kill Griff and me. It skins the side of her face. "OWW!" One of her rainbow fists flies off. Since her weight is not centered now, she has a hard time getting up. "I'm not leaving without him!"

"THEN NEVER LEAVE!" Eliza fires a volley of crystals in their direction.

"FORE!" A golf ball darts onto Eliza's chest. She falls over on impact and gasps for air. "Hey, I warned you. Had enough already? That's no fun." Z is enjoying this way too much.

"NOT BY A LONG SHOT, SMART ONE!"

"Why, thank you."

"Perhaps you deserve it now… MY FULL STRENGTH!" Eliza tosses her brush into the air, and it becomes a crown-shaped crystal. It automatically attaches onto her hair blades. Then her hands and arms become crystals themselves; even her left eye gleams violet. "KEKEKEKEKE!

Behold! My race's strength!" With one fist-pump, her left arm grows a crystal shield.

"Guys! Avoid her!"

"Why, Griff?" D asks.

"Because! There are energy stabilizers scattered across this castle! Whenever foreign strength is displayed, it copies and stores it!"

"What can they do with it?" Azilez tilts her head up from the floor.

"I don't know. That's the scariest part."

"Smart boy. Stay down. LET ME KILL YOU!"

– *Grr… we can't use our extreme forms here! But we've got to get V back! Who knows what fresh Hell awaits him?*

Meanwhile… in fresh Hell.

"Give us the prophecies' strength!"

"No."

"PLEEEEAAASSE!"

"No."

"I'll let you get out of the cube if you do."

"No."

"I'll even let you be king of the Omoh sapiens."

"Ew. No."

"SILENCE, FOOL! YOUR JOB IS DONE. NOW GET OUT!"

"Yes, my lord!" Pippin scrambles, trips, and does whatever he can to get out of Syzor's sight.

"Ah… the chosen one."

"Why does it matter?"

"Why does it matter? HAHAHAHA! You jest, surely!"

"Uhh… no. What do I have that the others I came here with don't?"

"Well… I'm not sure what YOU have, but I know what I have!" He clicks a button. From a ceiling hatch, two more cubes fall down and crash onto the floor. Inside them, Hazy and Vizor.

"V? Why did you follow us?" Hazy nearly yells.

"V! I TOLD YOU! STAY OUT OF–"

"Why don't you guys see it yet?"

"Huh?"

"We went on this journey together, and you just try and go on your own during the most important part of it?"

"V, this was never about abandoning you. But now that you're in this situation, I'm surprised YOU don't see it."

"See what?"

"Right in front of you."

"OK. It's your dad. So?"

"That's just it. HIM! I WAS TRYING TO KEEP YOU AWAY FROM HIM! HE WANTED YOU FROM THE VERY BEGINNING!"

"I'll just get out of it like I always do."

"This isn't your stereotypical antagonist-gets-his-butt-kicked-by-the-protagonist bit, V. I hope you realize that!" Syzor walks, with his arms behind his back, around my cube. "Do you realize how many things you don't know here?"

"I've noticed. That never stopped me!"

"And I was hoping it wouldn't."

"What?"

"You and your pathetic moral compass; it's the very reason civilizations crumble. They stick to their one 'truth', and look where it gets them. NOWHERE! That's why this empire has thrived since the very beginning of time. We never cared for these pathetic misconceptions. And as long as I'm here, we never will!" – *As soon as Vizor tells me where those stupid Shadow Prophecies are! If he's not going to willingly give them to me, then I'll MAKE HIM.*

– UGH! I'm so dumb! How could I have fallen for that…? Because I actually care about feelings. I'll prove they're worth something… somehow. I'll make Vizor, Hazy, and Syzor see that you can triumph through with them!

– I couldn't agree more, V. But this one IS special in different ways.

– How?

– The king of Omoh sapiens? Think about it: how many tools would a king of a WHOLE RACE have? His people can hide nothing from him!

– Is that why Vizor didn't want me to deal with him? He should know better than that!

– C'mon. Cut him some slack. He was trying to protect you. He knew Syzor's endgame involved you, so he tried to not get you involved.

– Still, though… why?

– Why what?

– Why does Syzor want me?

– I don't know.

Great. Just when I thought I'm getting somewhere, I crash.

"So then, now that I have you right where I want you, I'll make you bear witness to the greatest Omoh sapien tech ever!"

"Greatest tech…?" Vizor tries to think of something worthy of that title.

"It's not that spirit-trapping energy, is it?" Hazy calms down a bit, but there's still a touch of concern in her voice.

"Heavens, no! Why would I limit V's strength?"

Now I'm really confused. What does this guy want from me?

"But first… I must summon HIM."

"Him?"

"That's right. Him. Ever wondered about your ancestors, Vizor?"

"My ancestors? Which ones?"

"Have you heard of Syzor?"

"You mean yourself? Of course. You're my 'dad'."

"What? No. Not me. I'm Syzor the Second!"

– Uh-oh… I know what he's talking about.

– You do, Dark Spirit?

– Yes. He speaks of the original Syzor.

– What's so special about him? He's just the previous king, right?

– V, he's so much more. He was the original Omoh sapien: the very beginning of this race that began millennia ago. It all started with him.

– He's the first-ever Omoh sapien?

– That's not even the worst part. Remember the Great War?

– Yeah? My stomach starts to churn. I feel like I've just eaten way too much chocolate.

– Ever wondered which people opposed your ancestors in that battle?

– …

– It was the Omoh sapiens. And Syzor the First was their commanding general.

– WWWWWWHHHHHHHHAAAAAAAATTTTTT? HE'S PLANNING ON REVIVING THE GREAT WAR? THEN IT'S TRUE! HE IS GOING TO EARTH!

At that exact moment, by complete coincidence, Treah enters the Kuiper Belt. It's on its way to Earth.

"Syzor the First, huh?"

"About time someone caught on! But I felt so smart. You should've stayed quiet. UGH! Regardless. Stay here! I'll go fetch him." Syzor the Second walks off, with his pure black cape gliding in the wind. He shuts the door behind him.

"Syzor the First? What's going on? How did you know…?"

"Calm down, Vizor! Remember, I'm inside him. I know about the Great War," the Dark Spirit reassures him.

"WHAT DOES THAT HAVE TO DO WITH ANYTHING?"

"The original Syzor was the first-ever Omoh sapien!"

Vizor starts to understand, and even calms down a bit. "So then he made everyone else with the Devil. My dad IS planning on another war."

Vizor looks up. As I peer into his eyes, I see a sense of certainty I hadn't seen there before. "Listen, V. We clearly have different opinions on you being here. Right now, though, it doesn't matter. You're here. That's the only thing that matters."

"Not just him!" I would recognize that cheery, happy-go-lucky voice anywhere. As the door flies open, my hunch is confirmed: it's Azilez, and the rest of the gang is behind her.

"V!"

"You're safe, buddy!" Griff appears from behind her. "What have they done to you?"

"Surprisingly, nothing… yet."

"Yes! Then we made it!" D starts twirling his pickaxe.

"C'mon, stud, let's get you out of here." Z grabs the box.

"No!" Hazy orders.

"Huh?" All four of them stop.

"This planet is headed toward Earth right now! If we leave, we'd be allowing the eruption of an interplanetary war! If we act now, we'll save millions of people!"

"I'm in!" Z raises his hand. – *Not like I was going anywhere else…*

"Me too." Griff crosses his arms.

"Me three." Drac smirks along the side of his face.

"You don't even have to ask me!" Azilez turns around to face Griff, Z, Drac, and D.

"So… what now?"

"To Syzor! That jerk's gonna pay!" Azilez cracks her knuckles.

"Excuse you?" A giant, floating square flies in front of the castle. On it are Syzor the Second and a giant block of black ice.

"What's in there?"

"The doom of all humans! BEHOLD, THE GREATEST ACHIEVE-MENT OF OMOH SAPIENS!" Vizor's dad repeatedly punches the black cube next to him. Several blows later, it breaks, revealing someone from inside. He's clad in a glorious, dark-blue robe with an excessive amount of fur on the inside, and his hair blades have two layers instead of the one every other Omoh sapien has.

"Who has summoned me?"

Looks like it's a showdown: Homo versus Omoh.

"What was that? DAD?"

"What you just witnessed? Simple! I resumed Syzor the First's life!"

"'Resumed his life?'"

"Yes. It's the greatest achievement of our kind: the ability to freeze one's life solid, and to resume it at will! THE POWER TO CONTROL LIFE AND DEATH!"

Chapter 23
The Evil Crossbow

— Uh, did you know about this, Dark Spirit?

— No! I've never heard of being able to stop and resume life at will! I thought only God and the Devil could do that!

— They can do that?

— They can do anything. It's THEIR universe after all. They have no limits.

— Except the Devil has to sit on a chair forever…

— Yeah, that's kind of weird actually. During the Great War, It never had to.

— Really? Did It just permanently break Its giant spine while in battle?

— Even if It did, It could heal Itself. Remember what I just said? They can do ANYTHING.

"WHO HAS SUMMONED ME?" Syzor the First's voice echoes through the outside wind.

"I did!"

"Who are you?"

"Your master!"

"Ha! HAHAHAHAHA!"

"WHAT'S SO FUNNY ABOUT THAT?"

"You do not seem to understand that the only one I listen to is the Devil! It, and It alone, is my master! WHERE IS IT?"

"I have contained It."

"Impossible!"

"WHY ARE YOU GUYS YELLING?" Azilez gets hypocritical.

"SILENCE, FOOL!" The two overlords say in freakishly close unison.

"So you say you've tamed the Devil?"

"YES!"

"Prove it. With what did you slay It with?"

"Why… THIS!" Syzor the Second jumps down from the platform and onto the planet's surface. He runs to the castle's front door and jumps to reach the top of the door. There, he clicks a button, which rattles the castle.

"What's happening?" Griff falls on his butt, again.

"OUT! Children, out!" Drac jumps, using his cape as a hand glider to safely descend. Z and D use their pickaxe and golf club as snowboards and ride down the castle walls, Griff grabs my cube and runs ahead of Z and D, and Azilez uses a long rainbow board to fly Hazy, Vizor, and herself down.

"Please keep your hands, arms, and legs inside the rainbow at all times." Azilez pretends to be a flight attendant.

"WE'RE IN BOXES!" Vizor becomes Captain Obvious.

"Thank you for your cooperation!" She begins her 1,000-foot journey from the top of the castle to the bottom. The most intense part of the trip isn't the actual traveling. It's looking back at where they started from that gives them chills. "Wha… what… IS THAT?" Azilez jumps off her board and turns around to look at the castle.

"BWAHAHAHAHA! THE EVIL CROSSBOW! DOES THIS ANSWER YOUR QUESTION, SYZOR?" The castle bends and twists its geometry and takes the shape of… well… a crossbow.

Two figures pop out from the end of the crossbow's control mechanisms: Eliza and Pippin. "Ready at your command, sir!"

– Hold on! Evil crossbow? Th… that's…! AAHH! I REMEMBER! Vizor thinks to himself. "V!"

"What is it?"

"That thing that struck me really, really hard! It was this thing!"

"Really?"

"Seeing it again, I'm certain!"

We try our best to hear each other over the violent wind.

"NOW! ELIZA! PIPPIN!"

"Yes, sir!"

"ARE THE OTHERS READY?"

In a matter of seconds, a few thousand Omoh sapiens pop their heads out from inside the cannon. "YES, YOUR ABSOLUTE HIGHNESS!"

"Hold on! I don't know what's going on here, Syzor, but whatever it is, don't think you can just do it unchallenged!"

"That's right! No way you're touching our friends!"

"You monsters will never touch my darling!" Dracula blocks Hazy's line of sight with his cape.

"How ironic! Calling US monsters when that's exactly WHAT YOU ARE, DRACULA!"

"What can I say? I take after my creators!"

"I'm going to enjoy shutting you up! THIS IS WHERE THE VAMPIRES DIE, AND WHERE THE HUMANS LOSE THEIR LAST SLIMMER OF HOPE FOR SURVIVAL!"

"NOT GONNA HAPPEN!" Azilez fires rainbow bombs at the crossbow.

"CHARGE, SLAVES!" Syzor the Second's order reaches everyone as fast as light. Jumping out from the mist around us, the Omoh sapiens take the bombs and toss them skyward.

"GRIFF! HELP ME OUT!"

"Got it! Z! D! C'mon!"

"Whatcha need, Griff?"

"A big tree!"

"You got it! Z, give me cover!"

"All right! Range practice!" Z materializes 50 buckets filled with multicolored golf balls. "I'm bound to get a hole-in-one with one of these!" He fires away. The strike of Z's golf club is so swift, clean, and precise that if you weren't looking at him, you could mistake it for gunfire. The Omoh sapiens drop to the ground as if they were red-and-white targets for Z.

"GRR…!"

"How do you like that?"

"ENOUGH! ALL OF YOU!" Everything, even the mist which a second ago was racing across the rocky ground, stops in place.

"Who was THAT?" Syzor the Second demands to know. "ANSWER ME!"

"Oh, gladly, 'your highness!'" The original Syzor emerges from underneath the planet, but brings something with him that he didn't have before: a giant tablet. In fact, it kind of resembles a prophecy!

"What is that?" I try to move my head, but nothing happens. All I can do is talk.

"This trinket?"

"Huh… odd calling me a trinket, fool!"

"S…sorry!" Syzor the First actually bows his head for the first time.

"ANSWER THE QUESTION!" Azilez feistily tries to wave her brush, but to no avail.

"My, my. So many victims to choose from… Which do you think is most appropriate, Syzor?"

"Well, if you're asking me…"

"I'M NOT REFERRING TO YOU, PHONY! I'M REFERRING TO THE ORIGINAL THAT'S NEXT TO ME."

"NRRRGGHH!"

"Hmm… oh! How about that one!" He points to me. It hasn't taken him long to decide, almost as if he has wanted to pick me from the very start.

"What's happening? Who hit the pause button on this planet?" Z's eyes move a little.

"Hahaha! I appreciate this one's sense of humor! Too bad I'm going to have to eradicate it!"

"Huh?"

"Whoa, wait, wait! What was that just now?" Z finally gets a little serious for a change.

"ERADICATE his sense of humor? That's cruel!" Azilez grinds her teeth.

"That's not all, you peasants. After this, V is going to work for me!"

"Like Hell I will!"

"Be obedient, puppy!"

"I'm not some mutt! What are you? How can you talk?"

"What do you mean? I've been talking this whole time!"

"Nice try, Syzor!" Griff chimes in. "But I can sense it too! That rock's been talking!"

"Another talking rock?" Hazy's attention is finally captivated.

"Impressive, you two. I'm surprised you managed to figure it out!"

"They have the same voice. It was easy for you two, wasn't it?" Griff would point at them, but… you know… the whole 'planet-pause-button' thing?

"WHO ARE YOU? ANSWER ALREADY!" I lose it.

"I am the Prophecy of HELL!"

Chapter 24
Soul-shattering Destruction

"**H**ELL HAS A PROPHECY?" Griff and I are shocked.

"Not just Hell! I'm pretty sure you've met my brother. The one that resides deep under Egypt on Planet Earth."

"The master tablet?" D pieces that one together nicely. "Does it rule Heaven?"

"You're quite smart for your young age. Yes, that's exactly right!"

"Know what else? Since Treah is modeled after Hell, I control this planet's will as well!"

"So that's why we're all limp!"

"Well… for now."

"What are you going to do to us? I'm ready for you!" Hazy tries to whip the hair out of her face, but isn't able to.

"I doubt it…"

"What's that supposed to mean?"

"You think your little 'moral' fiasco means anything to me? Please. I WRITE AND CHANGE THOSE RULES AS I SEE FIT!" The Hell Prophecy sounds like the Devil.

"No one and NOTHING can change that!"

"Ohohohoho! The chosen one has a sharp tongue. I LIKE THAT. It'll make crushing his soul all the sweeter! Bring him up here."

As though I were almost around a rope, the Hell Prophecy's force pulls me toward it. C'mon… resist… fight it!

"I LOVE IT! I LOVE WATCHING YOU STRUGGLE! LIKE A WORM!

TOO BAD YOU CAN'T SLIP YOURSELF AWAY FROM THIS ONE!"

"AAAAHHH!" With one final pull, I'm in range of the original Syzor's palm. He grabs my shirt's collar.

"Now, should we bring everyone else up here so they can watch?"

"Just what I was thinking! GRRRAAHH!" The Hell Prophecy shines bloody red, and everyone in sight levitates toward space. While out in the great beyond, Treah is passing Mars. It's almost at Earth, and we can't even move!

"GGGGRRRR! THAT'S IT!" Azilez near-explodes into her pure extreme form. She can control her brush without even touching it. She fires a rainbow at Syzor the First, and knocks the back of his head. On impact, he drops the Prophecy of Hell.

"Oh, a fighter! Looks like that fraction of power wasn't enough!" The Hell Prophecy, now with a multicolored vortex around it, seems to be bending space to create a barrier around Z, D, Griff, Azilez, Drac, Vizor, and Hazy. It addresses the Omoh sapiens: "Make sure you remember this one's judgment hour! A reminder of what happens to all of you who step out of line! IS THAT CLEAR?"

"LOUD, CLEAR, AND THEN SOME!" They all hold their hands to their foreheads as if they're saluting a military general.

"Good! Now you seven!" The prophecy floats next to the distorted box it has just created. "Take a last good look at your friend. As of now… HE'S DEAD."

"LIAR!"

"Don't believe me, eh? WATCH THEN, and see with your own eyes!" The top of the Hell Prophecy opens up, and a red button pops out. "You do the honors, Syzor."

"WHAT'S GOING ON?" Syzor the Second body-slams the original and sends him flying.

"I'm answering your question, 'Syzor.' You're a disgrace to the name and all Omoh sapiens. You don't even know where the original Evil Crossbow is."

"Huh? It wasn't the castle?"

"FOOL! The crossbow has always been a part of this planet. Care to guess which part?"

What part of the planet is the crossbow in? Gee, it could be anywhere, unless… Is it THAT big?

"No way. Is it that?"

"That's right! IT'S THE PLANET'S RING!"

"NO! V!" Azilez tries to tear down the barrier she's in, but even her pure extreme form isn't powerful enough to break it down. "GUYS! HELP ME!"

"Right!"

– *V, let me! I can free them!*

– *Hurry! Then find out how to get us out of these cubes!*

– *On it!*

The Dark Spirit flies out of me. However, It doesn't slip under unnoticed. The Hell Prophecy catches it.

"Oh, no no no no no no, NO! We will certainly not be having that! In fact, you're going to help power the crossbow! Come here!"

"NO! NEVER!"

The Dark Spirit is made of the same substance as the Unbound Evil since It absorbed Its power, so the prophecy has a hard time getting a hold of It. Fortunately, it also means that Syzor the First can't press the button on top of the prophecy to activate the crossbow.

What power can break free of this mold? Is there something I'm missing? I'm still so naïve in the grand scheme of the Devil, the Unbound Evil, this new Hell Prophecy, Syzor the First, and Syzor the Second. Regardless, THIS IS MY LAST SHOT!

The fire within me burns… It burns like no other… It can burn only inside me… because… the power within me… IS UNBREAKABLE! GO, PURE EXTREME V! "YOUR GAME ENDS HERE, YOU TWO!" Still inside the box, I ram into the prophecy.

"Ooof…!" The Hell Prophecy takes my hit without a scratch. "Nice! NICE! I like a good fight!" The rock then summons a vortex that shoots flaming stalactites. They look like the exact ones from the Devil's throne.

"Dark Spirit! Behind you!"

"Huh?" In the nick of time, It avoids the crystals and heads for the cage. "Now how do I get this thing open? Ah, here! AAAHHH!"

"Not today! Or any other day, for that matter!" Syzor the First takes one of the stalactites and traps the Dark Spirit inside it. Then he tosses it into space like it's trash.

"Now, V. Are you ready?" The Hell Prophecy asks.

"For…?"

"HAHAHAHA! Now you're just playing dumb. SYZOR!"

"Yes?"

"The button."

Syzor presses the button, and Treah's ring detaches from the planet. It splits into two parts. It reminds me of how Vizor's blades split apart when he used them to attack. The two sharp ends of the ring grab a hold of my prison box, and a giant javelin starts to form on the other end of the ring. Earth is now within the planet's sight. Are we really too late? Is there nothing I can do now?

"Any last words, V?"

"NRGH!" I try to scramble out of the box, but it only seems to be squeezing tighter. I CAN'T BREAK FREE! NOT EVEN IN MY PURE EXTREME FORM!

Out comes the javelin. It pierces through my right shoulder and stays there. It hurts terribly, but only for a second. I don't even have time to scream in pain. The box encasing me finally releases its grip, but only for me to start rocketing toward Earth, unconscious and…

Chapter 25

Is That It?

"**V!**"

"Whyyyyyy?"

"!"

"Did that just happen?"

"My boy!"

"HELL PROPHECY!"

"What do you want, Vizor?"

"WHAT DID YOU...?"

"It's exactly what it seems like. I killed the fool. Power with friend-ship? Inner strength? And to top it off, unbreakable? Funny... almost enough to make me laugh. But it doesn't even deserve my chuckle."

"YOU MONSTER!"

"What? Are you going to try and kill me? Go ahead. Try. I even took the barrier down for you."

"GRRR..."

– V! Answer! C'mon! You can't be dead!

– ......

– V!

"HAHAHAHAHAHA! Syzor! Well done! Now! FOR EARTH!"

"Yes!"

"NEVER!"

"Is that all you've got? Pathetic! Not even worth destroying. You're all nothing without him!"

"COWARD!"

"Funny… weren't golf clubs supposed to be made of metal instead of PLASTIC?"

"No…"

"Griff!"

"What?"

"Let's go to Earth! You and me! We'll find V and…"

"He's gone…"

"Huh?"

"I SAID HE'S GONE! HE'S DEAD! I COULDN'T SENSE HIM! ANYWHERE!"

"THAT'S IMPOSSIBLE! Even if he died, we should sense his spirit!"

"What…?"

"Come! To my castle, Hell Prophecy!"

"YOUR CASTLE? YOU'VE BEEN DORMANT FOR SO LONG. HOW IS THAT STILL *YOUR* CASTLE? What… wait! WHAT ARE YOU DOING?"

"NO! DON'T! DAAAAAAAAAD!"

"Why the drama, Vizor? You were dead to him anyway. Now, he's officially dead to you! And to everyone! At least you still have grandpa, BWAHAHA!"

....
....
.... nrgh …

   – Finally awake, huh?

   – Wha…? What's going on?

   – Hush now… You won't feel a thing…

   – Wait… what…?

....
.... BWAHAHAHAHAHAHA! IT FEELS GOOD TO BE BACK!

   – Wait… WHAT'S…? OWWW! You… You're the…

– Devil. That's right! Your mind and Mine are now one! Unbreakable spirit? CONSIDER IT BROKEN! FOR ETERNITY!

– No... no...

– Your morals mean nothing to Me, nor anyone else anymore. Your spirit is dead. It will be held prisoner here... forever. Fall into evil's embrace!

Chapter 26

Evil V: the Scariest Evil Form of All

KEKEKEKE! WHO TO KILL FIRST?

– What's that supposed to mean? I finally get the strength to yank my fist, but I hadn't noticed that I've been caught in four different sets of chains. There's one chain on each of my arms and legs.

EXACTLY WHAT YOU ALL THINK! I'M GOING TO KILL MY FRIENDS! WHO EVEN NEEDS THEM?

– What's going on? Why can't I narrate?

– DON'T YOU GET IT YET, FOOL? YOU ARE NARRATING! I told you once, and I'll tell you again: I. AM. YOU.

– GRRR! THAT'S NOT TRUE!

– BUT IT IS! IT'S NOT LIKE YOU CAN DO ANYTHING! THAT JAVELIN IS STILL INSIDE YOUR SHOULDER!

– Then I'll tear it out!

– Ah, ah, ah. I wouldn't do that.

– Why not?

– Do you not know how much blood you'll lose, V? And the Dark Spir-it's gone! There's no way in Hell I'd heal you.

– We're in space, not Hell.

– You can at least pretend like the javelin hurts.

– I can at least pretend You're a threat.

– SILENCE, KNAVE! YOU'RE LUCKY YOU'RE STILL ALIVE!

– THAT'S 'CAUSE MY POWER IS…

– JUST SHUT UP! NO ONE LIKES YOUR MONOLOGUING! BE-SIDES, LET'S SEE IF YOU'LL BE SAYING THAT AFTER YOU KILL ALL OF YOUR FRIENDS!

– So that's what You meant…

– JUST HOW THICK-HEADED ARE YOU? WHAT ELSE COULD I HAVE…? UGH! YOU KNOW WHAT? LET'S JUST BOTH STOP.

– Fair.

THAT COULD'VE GONE MILES BETTER. NOW WHERE WAS I? OH, YEAH! KILLING MY FRIENDS! WHO SHOULD I START WITH? HMM… WHO CARES? I'LL JUST KILL WHOEVER GETS IN MY WAY FIRST! NOW FOR THE EVIL V TRANSFORMATION!

DESTROYING ALL RATIONAL THOUGHTS, MY MIND BE-COMES EMPTY. ALL THAT REMAINS IS THE NEED TO ERADICATE. THE YEARNING IS SO STRONG THAT BURSTS OF WHITE STEAM EMIT FROM MY MOUTH AND HANDS.

– It's like I looked into a magic mirror, my reflection knocked me out, and is tying my arms and feet in shackles… Oh, wait, that actually happened.

AHH… HOW CAN BEING BAD FEEL SO GOOD?

– It doesn't!

I NOW AM STARTING TO GET SO CLOSE TO EARTH THAT MY BODY ACTUALLY CATCHES FIRE FROM THE VELOCITY. BUT LET'S BE HONEST, ARE THE LAWS OF PHYSICS ANY MATCH FOR ME? I MAKE THEM MYSELF!

SORRY… GOT OFF TRACK. MY TRAIL OF FIRE BLAZES ACROSS THE NIGHT SKY. COINCIDENTALLY (AND WHEN I MEAN COINCI-DENTALLY, I MEAN TOTALLY PLANNED), I AIM MY LANDING AT SAN FRANCISCO. IF I'M NOT GOING TO KILL MY FRIENDS, MIGHT AS WELL KILL MY FAMILY FIRST.

– No! Don't! OWWW! Wow, that actually does hurt… I'm starting to feel it now.

"Whoa! What's that thing in the sky?"
"I don't know!"

"It's a meteor!"

"Wait a second!" RODGER, FROM AMONG THE GIANT CROWD OF PEOPLE, WHIPS OUT A PAIR OF BINOCULARS. "It's V!"

THE CROWD ACTUALLY STARTS TO CHEER VIOLENTLY FOR MY RETURN… LITTLE DO THEY KNOW I'VE COME FOR THEIR HEADS!

– *I gotta get out of here!*

– *WHY? YOU'RE INSIDE YOURSELF, AFTER ALL!*

– *You know what, I… oww… OWW…!*

– *LOOK AT YOURSELF! YOU CAN'T EVEN FINISH A CLEAR THOUGHT ANYMORE! YOU'RE WORTHLESS! WITHOUT YOUR FRIENDS, WHAT ARE YOU?*

– *…*

– *HA! HE FINALLY WILLINGLY SHUT UP.*

NOW BACK TO THE CROWD OF PEOPLE. I CRASH-LAND DANGEROUSLY CLOSE TO THEM. IN FACT, ANY CLOSER AND I WOULD'VE KILLED THEM ALL! THAT WOULD'VE BEEN NO FUN, KILLING THEM ALL IN ONE BIG BLOW LIKE THAT! THAT'S SO UN-ORIGINAL! INSTEAD OF BRINGING THEM TO HELL, I'LL JUST BRING HELL TO THEM! TRUE, I'LL HAVE TO USE ALL OF MY ENERGY TO DO IT, BUT IT'LL BE WELL WORTH IT.

"V! You made it home!"

THE FOOL! RODGER DOESN'T KNOW WHAT'S ABOUT TO COME TO HIM!

– *Don't you DARE… OWWW… touch him!*

– *I DON'T THINK YOU HAVE ANY CHOICE IN THE MATTER. REMEMBER, YOU'RE DEAD!*

"Where's everyone else?"

"THEY ARE YET TO COME."

"Wh-who is that? That's not V, that's for sure!"

"NAÏVE LITTLE BRATS! NONE OF YOU KNEW ME!"

"V…?"

– *RODGER! NO! DON'T! Wait… What are you doing, Devil?*

– *I'M GOING TO BORROW THE REMAINING ENERGY OF YOUR*

DEAD SOUL. HOPE YOU DON'T MIND… NOT THAT IT MATTERS.

– AAAAAAAAARRRRGGGGGGHHHHHHHH!

I PLACE MY HAND ON THE JAVELIN AND SUCK THE DEAD LIFE OUT OF THAT POOR EXCUSE FOR ME! LOOK AT HIM! HE'S STARTING TO LOOK LIKE A ZOMBIE. WITH IT, I SUMMON A PSEUDO THRONE FOR MYSELF TO SIT UPON, VOLCANOES TO MAKE THIS PLACE FEEL MORE LIKE HOME, AND CAVE STALACTITES. I CAN'T GET ENOUGH OF THOSE!

– I can…

– DIE ALREADY! WHAT DOES IT TAKE TO KILL YOU? I'LL SUCK THIS BOY DRY! I DON'T CARE HOW MUCH POWER HE HAS! I'LL MAKE SURE HE NEVER FEELS ANYTHING EVER AGAIN! I'LL MAKE HIS VERY EXISTENCE VOID!

– GRRRRRAAAAAHHHHHHHH!

– JEEZ! DIEEEEE!

– …

– DID I FINALLY GET HIM?

– …

– ABOUT TIME.

"TIME TO DIE, ALL OF YOU!"

"Everybody run!" A MAN YELLS OUT FROM THE CROWD OF PEOPLE. SAN FRANCISCO INSTANTLY BECOMES COVERED IN A BLACK CLOUD, AND NOW I SIT ON TOP OF IT! IT'S TIME TO WAIT FOR THE OMOH SAPIENS TO TRY AND TAKE THIS CITY FROM ME!

– …

"COME, ALL OF YOU! YOU CAN'T TOUCH ME!"

"V! What's up with you? Snap out of it!"

I FINALLY TURN AROUND SO RODGER CAN SEE MY FACE. VOID-WHITE EYES WITH A RED DROP IN THE MIDDLE OF EACH, WHITE MIST DROPPING FROM MY MOUTH AND HANDS, AND THE MOST HATE-FILLED FROWN HE'S EVER SEEN. HIS REACTION IS SO DELICIOUS THAT I CAN ALMOST MISTAKE IT FOR GHIRARDELLI.

"Where's V?"

"YOU'RE LOOKING AT HIM." I GRAB HIM BY THE SHIRT COL-

LAR, ALMOST TO THE POINT OF SUFFOCATION.

"No… way… I'm… not. No way… in Hell."

"WELCOME TO HELL. YOU PLAY BY MY RULES. GOT IT?" I SPIN HIM INTO A BUILDING. THAT SHOULD KILL HIM.

– …

– *STILL NO REACTION? EH, HE'S PROBABLY DEAD.*

"Freeze! Hands where I can see them, pal!"

"CERTAINLY." I TELEPORT RIGHT IN FRONT OF HIM.

"FIRE!"

HUNDREDS OF GUNS FIRE AT ME ALL AT ONCE. NOT A SIN-GLE ONE HITS ME. NO, I DON'T MEAN THEY ALL MISS. RATHER, THE BULLETS ALL BOUNCE OFF ME.

"I'LL GIVE YOU A FEW MORE SECONDS TO REALIZE HOW USELESS YOU ALL REALLY ARE."

"V? What happened to you?" Rodger's voice cracks.

"THAT'S FOR ME AND THESE FISSURES TO KNOW." OH, BY THE WAY, I SUMMONED FISSURES TO SWALLOW UP ALL OF THESE POOR SOULS. WHAT CAN I DO? I FEED ON THEM.

MEANWHILE, WITH MY CREW IN OUTER SPACE…

"I'm going to look for V!"

"But he's dead, Azilez. He got shot by a planet-sized…"

"SO? THAT'S NEVER STOPPED HIM! IT'S LIKE YOU CAN ACTU-ALLY SENSE HIM OR SOMETHING!"

– *I can.*

– *WHOA! WHAT? GRIFF? HOW…?*

– *Don't you get it? *Sniff* I want to believe V's alive too. But it's like you said: I could literally sense his presence. Now, I can't. He's gone.*

– *Do what you want, Griff.*

– *What…?*

– *I don't care! V has survived worse! I'm going for him! If you don't want to, FINE! But like any good friend, *sniff*, I'm going to be there for him when he needs me most, even if he's dead!*

AZILEZ STARTS TO FLY TOWARD ME TO SAVE THE LITTLE

SQUIRT THAT WAS ONCE IN MY WAY. I CAN'T WAIT TO KILL HER TOO!

"Azilez! Where are you going?"

"Yeah. Where exactly are you going?" – *But… my power… The Dark Spirit even said that I should be able to sense V, even if he's dead. That's just what's frustrating me! Wait a second!* GRIFF FINALLY REALIZES WHAT WAS FISHY ABOUT THE JAVELIN THAT ENTERED ME: THAT THE ENTITY INSIDE IT AND THE DEVIL ARE THE SAME. "Oh, no! Guys! We have to get to Earth, pronto!"

"Why the hurry, Griff? We've got these two to deal with!"

"And for what, exactly?"

GRR…! HE FINALLY CAUGHT ON!

"I don't follow… my boy." DRAC'S FACE GOES BLANK.

"This is all part of the Devil's plot! The reason I couldn't sense V at all is because It has him trapped somewhere!"

"How can you be sure of that?"

VIZOR… I SHOULD'VE KILLED HIM TOO. I'LL DO IT WHEN I NEXT SEE HIM. IT'LL BE EASY TOO. HE'S INSIDE A BOX.

"The energies inside the javelin and the Devil are exactly the same, now that I think about it." – *Azilez is right. V has survived way worse!*

"Are you sure?"

"It's better than just sitting here fighting these two distractions! C'mon!"

"WE WON'T…!"

"Let them, Syzor." The Hell Prophecy blocks Syzor's path.

"Are you sure?"

"Look at it this way: we have more time to prepare our third leader-in-command!"

"It's not Syzor the Second, is it?"

"How could it be? He's dead. You just killed him."

"Right… Then who is it?"

"It's not anyone you'd know. It's someone who actually disguised himself as a human all this time for our sake: to give Earth a taste of the Omoh sapiens' way of life."

"Who is it?"

"It's…"

I APPROACH MY TREE HOUSE TO KILL EVERYONE INSIDE, BUT… JUST MY LUCK! ALL OF YOU GUYS SHOW UP!

– …

"V! YOU'RE ALLLLLIIIIIIIVVVVEEEE!"

"Azilez! Don't!"

"Huh?"

"HE'S RIGHT, YOU KNOW."

"WH… WHAT?"

"I was right… hello, Devil."

"WHO ARE YOU TALKING TO? I'M V!"

AZILEZ, GRIFF, AND VIZOR ALL GET HORRIFIC FLASHBACKS. BACK FROM THE TIME THEY ACTED THIS WAY. THEY'RE WISHING TO BE ABLE TO COMPREHEND IT AGAIN!

– …

"I AM NOW COMPLETE!"

"V…"

"What exactly do you want?" OH, VIZOR…

"I WANT ALL OF YOU. MAINLY YOUR HEADS, BUT I GUESS I CAN FEED THE CORPSES TO MY PETS… IF THEY CAN MANAGE TO CHOW THEM DOWN."

"YOU DID THIS! YOU DID THIS TO POOR V! I'LL NEVER…"

"YOU'LL NEVER WHAT, GIRLIE?"

"FORGIVE YOUUUUUUUUUUUUUUU!"

YES… YES! GIVE IN TO THE EVIL INSIDE YOU! IT'LL MAKE KILLING YOU ALL THE SWEETER!

"YOU MADE ME DOUBT MY BEST FRIEND! NO WAY YOU'RE WALKING OUT OF HERE ALIVE, DEVIL!"

HA! HE TOO! THEY LOOK MORE WELCOMING THIS WAY!

"I remember now…" VIZOR TALKS TO HIMSELF, QUIETLY. EVEN I CAN'T HEAR HIM. "This feeling that those two had… My dad hit me with his copy of the crossbow, and evil grew inside me… but it wasn't even genuine evil. It was one that was fabricated to look real."

"So what are you going to do about it, Vizor?"

"I'm not sure, Hazy. But I do know one thing: I'm going to save V. Just like he saved me." VIZOR'S EYES TURN BLACK. HE DECIDES TO ENTER HIS EVIL STATE TOO! GREAT! WAIT. WHY IS HE CALM? COME! FIGHT ME! NO! THE EVIL ENERGY IS MELTING THE CUBE PRISON! GRR…!

"WHAT'S WRONG? YOU JUST GOT HERE!"

AZILEZ… AND GRIFF IS WITH YOU TOO. PERFECT! I'LL EN-JOY SENDING YOU TWO TO WHERE I'VE SENT V. OBLIVION!

Chapter 27

The Shadow Prophecies

This is the second time something like this has happened… Why am I so weak? Why can't I fight back? It's like they have the strings tied onto every limb on my body. Wait, the Devil literally does have me tied like that… AGGHHH! Where did I go wrong? I have this javelin inside my shoulder, I want my family dead, the Solar Prophecies are with the Devil, and my friends are tapping into their evil selves just to save me… WHY?

– *Maybe it's high time you did the same for them.* In my conscience (within "my" conscience, where the Devil is controlling me), I see a familiar face: mine. Well… not exactly. What exactly am I looking at? Oh… Evil V.

– *What are you doing here?*

– *I think you mean what am I NOT doing here? I'm you.*

– *NO! You were placed inside of here! Ow…*

– *Oh, was I?*

He walks up to me and grabs the javelin inside my shoulder. Instantaneously, I see an image in front of me. It's the beginning of this adventure: the part when Vizor held our families hostage on top of the burning Ghirardelli building. I felt a pinching in my stomach up there, as though something was trying to set itself free. I remember…

– *What… what was that?*

– *That was me, knocking on the door of your soul.*

– *Huh?*

I notice the javelin isn't inside me anymore. Evil V somehow has torn it out, without causing me any pain at all! What's even more surprising is that the hole that should be in my shoulder is instantly repaired!

— *How did you…?*

— *You really want to know what those fools have over you?*

— *What are you talking about? You're a fake!*

He has just about had enough of being called a fraud, so he grabs me by the shirt collar.

— *LISTEN. The only other person who has an evil state like this one is Vizor.*

— *What does "like this one" mean?*

— *Notice anything different about me compared to the other evil forms?*

— *Well, you're certainly tamer. You haven't even tried to kill me yet. On the contrary, you saved me!*

— *Glad to see your conscience isn't entirely shady. Yes, that's true.*

— *I don't see how a tame evil form gets me anywhere…*

— *Of course you don't. You've never experienced it, after all. Well, at least not yet.*

— *What are you saying?*

— *I'm talking about those two.* Evil V points at the cold-blooded Azilez and Griff.

— *How do you know they'll pull through?*

— *Hmph. Come now, that should be easy. With your beliefs in mind, how can I say they WON'T pull through? V, I think you've forgotten something very important: you've lost the ability to trust and place hope in the unseen.*

— *How do you know?*

— *Look at the predicament you've gotten yourself into: you're a slave to your own body now, aren't you?*

— *Ugh…*

— *All because the opposition outsmarted you this time. Are you going to let them do that to you?*

— *What else can I do?*

— *You're right.*

— *What?*

— *Why am I helping you? I'm evil, remember? I shouldn't be doing this.*

I shouldn't be doing this… I. Shouldn't. Be. Doing. This. Wait a second! WAIT JUST A SECOND!

"So, Hazy." No, wait! I was just about to get to the good part, Vizor! "Will you stand by me one more time?"

"I would. If I could stand."

"Ha! Right. Let me get that." Fine, you win. Vizor's evil energy melts the cube that confines his most trusted companion.

"So… where to?"

"The real crossbow."

"WHAT? Why? That's crazy!"

"I know. But it's the only way to save V right now. It's the only power source available right now, even if it means destroying myself in the process. V nearly gave his life to save mine, and I'll do the same for him! It's evil or bust! You saw how useless V's pure extreme form was, didn't you?"

"As long as it's OK with you, it's fine by me. I just want to make sure it's what you really want."

"Right now? I couldn't be sure-er."

"Heehee. Cute. We'll have to patent that word one day."

"Definitely not today."

"Right. Let's go."

"OH NO, YOU DON'T! AHHH!" Azilez's dark-purple crystals distract the Devil enough for Vizor and Hazy to fly back to Treah, which is pretty much next to Earth at this point. In fact, it's so close that Syzor the First, the only Syzor still alive, and the Hell Prophecy are almost ready to raid and destroy Earth. Whatever those two are doing, they better do it fast!

"Is the ring still there?" Vizor asks Hazy.

"Hmm… I don't know. It's not like I can clearly see it or any-thing."

"No need for the sarcasm."

"Are you kidding? ALL the need for the sarcasm. It's literally right in front of you."

"Um, that's not all that's in front of us.

"What do you…? Oh."

"Now who needs the sarcasm?"

"Hush, child."

"Yes! Indeed! HUSH, VIZOR!"

The Omoh sapien army is now here, with Eliza and Pippin at Syzor's right and left hands. At the helm is the Hell Prophecy.

"So, you guys finally escaped those cubes, eh?"

"Hazy! I almost forgot! The Dark Spirit!"

"Right! On it!" She breaks down into her gas state.

"This didn't work last time, so what makes you think it'll work this time? I can sense you, even if I can't see you."

– *That's true. So why then did Vizor…? Wait a second… No! He's not TRYING to get kidnapped, is he? That crafty little snitch! Quite creative! And we could possibly get back the Dark Spirit too, while stalling the war.* Hazy thinks to herself.

"You're mine!"

"Not even in your most delightful nightmares!" Vizor tries to dive-tackle the Prophecy of Hell, but is stopped by Syzor's blade toss.

"Slaves! Charge! MAKE SURE HE DOESN'T ESCAPE AGAIN!"

"For the Omoh sapiens!" The battle cry that echoes in the starry sky fades away, and, behind its unveiling curtains, an army of aliens, out for their own kind (not that it means much at this point).

– *Wow. This is going swimmingly. I'm killing three birds with one stone. That's one more than two.*

– *Hazy!*

– *Huh? Who's That?*

– *Over here! On the bottom of the ring! Hurry! Before Hell lets loose.*

– *You're telling me… Are You in here?*

She zooms toward the bottom-left sharp edge, where a stray asteroid lies.

– *Yes! Swiftly, now! We must stop this catastrophe from even beginning!*

– Right! Use my body as a vessel for now.

– Thanks! Much appreciated!

The Dark Spirit slithers onto Hazy's nonexistent arm and enters her body through her invisible shoulder.

– So where's everyone else? Is it just you two here?

– V has been hit by the crossbow and is thought to have died. Weirdly enough, though, the shot didn't kill him; it possessed him. He's now brutally evil, wanting to eviscerate everything eviscerate-able.

– Oh… does it look like I can fix it?

– You're asking the wrong gal.

– It's OK, I'll figure it out. I just wanted to be prepared for the worst, is all.

After playing an extensive game of "gun the runner", Vizor finally gets caught by his home planet's army, and is stuffed in another impossible-to-escape box prison (even though he just got out of it and clearly knows how to). Does he really want to save me that badly…? I'm very touched. Honestly.

"Nrgh…!" Vizor struggles to get out of there. Why though? He probably wants to stall more. That would make more sense. But then again… why is one person… er… alien stopping an entire army's advancement? Haven't the Hell Prophecy and Syzor recognized that by now? If not, Vizor has both of them eating out of the palms of his hands.

"Now… to get rid of you! Just like your late pal, V!"

Vizor and Hazy exchange glances one last time, as Vizor is taken to his "judgment" place.

"He's a disgrace to all of us!"

"Let his corpse fly in space for all eternity!"

"Why is he even here?"

"Those blades don't belong in his hair!"

All sorts of nasty comments bombard Vizor all at once, but he is unfazed, and maintains the same confident smile smeared on his face.

Vizor is finally brought to his two old comrades, Eliza and Pippin.

"I can't believe you, Vizor." Eliza puts her right hand on her hip.

"You could've been so much more."

"What's with you? Teaming up with humans AND vampires? The very definitions of enemies! Do you realize the level of treason you've committed?"

"Well, I wasn't the one who chose to go to Earth, now was I?"

"Do you think that matters? Your objective would've been clear to any one of us! Yet it wasn't to you. Why is that?"

Vizor remains silent, but this time, his smile runs off and tosses a frown onto his face. It spells: "You two have NO idea."

"It doesn't matter! Like you said, Eliza!"

"Yes, Pippin, I agree. For once."

"What's that supposed to mean?"

"Exactly what it sounds like, genius."

"SILENCE! EVERYONE!" Syzor's scream is heard across the entire army. "Now, for the death of our corrupt little one who can't even find some prophecies and destroy his counterpart! KILL ONE PERSON! THAT'S ALL WE WANTED! COULDN'T EVEN DO IT. How shameful. You are now stripped of the title 'Omoh sapien'."

"Good. I never wanted it."

The crowd of aliens gasps and freezes when their ears register what they just heard.

"Excuse me? I didn't know you had such a big mouth."

"The feeling's mutual, o' great commander." The sarcasm is so sweet that I could've replaced maple syrup with it and not tell the difference.

"I'll enjoy slaying you with my hand, just like I did to your father before you. Hell Prophecy, do you mind if I claim this one?"

"Be my guest. You've been a good boy."

"I'm deeply obliged. Thank you. NOW THEN!"

As soon as Syzor's arms are lifted, the crowd goes wild... more than usual. They seem happier about death than power. Opposites of humans, yet so many parallels can be drawn between them.

"Give him death! Give him death! Give him death! Give him death! Give him death! Give him death! Give him death! ..." The crowd keeps chanting, over and over and over again. Vizor is strapped to the tail end of the crossbow, and it loads another javelin. Now the crowd's cheers change to: "Spear of death! Spear of death! Spear of death! SPEAR OF DEATH! …"

"I know he's doing this for V, but I can't watch!" Hazy, now in her actual vampire form, covers her face with her hand.

The anticipation builds. The crossbow stretches back to fire, and suddenly…! It passes through… Wait. It shut down? IT SHUT DOWN!

"What's this? THAT SHOULDN'T HAVE HAPPENED! IT SHOULD'VE FIRED! WHAT ARE YOU DOING? HUNK OF JUNK!"

Syzor kicks the crossbow. As he does, a giant Windows error message pops up, saying: "evilcrossbow.exe has failed to run. Please check hard drive for any possible corruption." To make it funnier, the Windows error sound plays repeatedly, almost as if it's intended to piss Syzor off. "MAKE IT STOP! MAKE THIS INFERNAL NOISE STOP!"

In the best way possible, his wish is granted. Suddenly, the giant ring itself starts to shake, breaking Vizor free of his prison. Then it trembles so violently that it seems like the very fabric of the space-time continuum around it is shaking. Even all of the Omoh sapiens spin around because of the unimaginable force. In fact, the quake is so powerful that all of Earth feels it.

"VIZOR!" The Hell Prophecy charges at him in a fiery comet blaze, but is repelled by the force of the ring breaking into five separate pieces. Wait… Five pieces? This isn't what I think, is it?

The ring parts decompose further. As they do, a final burst of dark mist blasts through a hundred-mile radius to make sure the entire Omoh sapien army, Syzor, and the Hell Prophecy feel the presence of the shadow… the Shadow Prophecies! Finally, the Windows error message changes into one that says: "Behold, the first true Omoh sapien. All of YOU are the disgraces."

Oh, boy! Serious stuff's about to go down! But…

– *I think I get it now, Evil V, I mean… me.*

– *What is it?*

– *I feel it. I mean, I'm not quite sure what I just felt, but I'm almost certain about what it means. Evil power and evil intent are two different things. Much like a gun can be used to harm the innocent, it can also be used to protect them. Evil power can lead to evil intent, but only if you let it. Only the ones that stay true to themselves can wield evil power for good intent. Evil is all around us. We can't pretend it's not there and then pretend to live in harmony. We have to first recognize evil power, then control it, and only then can we feel total power as a complete being. This is another form of chaos, isn't it?*

– Good job, V. I can now completely enter your spirit, with no fear of corrupting you.

The evil half and I now become one, but at that point it's too late. Through the vision of the Devil, I see Griff and Azilez on the floor. Both are completely still. Azilez's back is broken, and the same can be said for Griff's neck. Noooooooo!

– My work here is done. Sayonara, V… if you can take it.

The Devil exits my body before I say anything. The possessed Evil V immediately subsides. I have no idea what to say, think, or do. The pounding sorrow in my head is too much. I feel faint and fall into a coma… lying beside my two best friends.

Chapter 28

A Step Above Extreme

You're not going to fool me that easily, Devil. Sure, it seems like they're dead, but they really aren't. I can still feel their energies. If they stay like this for too long though, they will die. The same goes for me, but all I have to do is touch them, because with my evil power, I can restore their bones back to their original shape. Just one problem: I'm in a coma!

– How did this happen?

– Idiot! You let that one sight of your friends get to you! You have to wait a while now before you can move!

– Why?

– Our combined strengths have to reach the tips of every limb in this body before we can move.

– Really?

– Yup.

– That's weird.

– Well, it works. I'll tell you that much.

– I feel like I can trust you at this point.

– Good to know you trust yourself.

– Oh, yeah… that's confusing.

– Less talk! More power!

– Right.

– Let's go to your arms first! Since all we have to do is touch Griff and Azilez.

We start to run (yes, inside my unconscious) to my right arm, but I have to get the snarky comment in there first. If you'll excuse me…

– Don't you mean "all I have to do is touch Griff and Azilez?"

– OH, SHUT UP! DO YOU WANT HELP OR NOT?

– Just making fun. Jeez!

– Let's not talk for the rest of the way.

– Sounds good to me.

Running up my arm is quite the trip. I'm not physically running on my bones, no. I'm running on my imagination! I'm in the middle of space, dashing on a starlit path with several types of weather conditions blocking my progression: tornadoes, hurricanes, lightning, blizzards, fire, waterspouts, sandstorms. And the list goes on!

– What's with all this stuff?

– It's what I was interested in when I was a kid: space and weather. It makes sense that they're all here. I'm running inside my mind, after all.

– Right. AND WHERE AM I IN HERE?

We run around a bit longer, and after jumping over the last glacier in our path, Evil V spots something.

– There! Look!

– What exactly is that?

– Your… er… our right-hand generator. It's the thing that translates the brain-nerve code into hand-nerve code. As you can see here, it's been clogged.

It looks like someone has jammed a hot dog into a computer. As I continue to stare at it, the entire room trembles.

– What was that?

– That was our stomach rumbling.

– Good to know that it still works. Even still, that jam looks like it's gonna be hard to fix.

– AND I PLAN TO KEEP IT THAT WAY.

A dark-purple stalactite shoots at my evil half. Without looking, he grabs and crushes it.

– You're. Still. Here.

– YOU THINK I'D EVER LEAVE? NO WAY I'M LETTING YOU TOUCH THOSE TWO. THEY WILL STAY LIKE THAT AND SLOWLY DIE!

– How did You know to come here?

– Really, V?

– What?

– In case you haven't noticed, you're talking to the DEVIL, the MASTER and CREATOR of evil energy. It knows how to use evil energy inside and out.

– THANKS FOR THE DIMWITTED EXPLANATION. MAYBE V FINALLY UNDERSTANDS FOR ONCE. BWAHAHAHAHA!

– I'll show…

– NOPE!

In a flash, more stalactites fire from the Devil's palm. Evil V thought he could use my hot-headedness as a distraction. Boy, did that end well…

– SUFFER IN THESE CHAINS!

– DEFINITELY NOT!

I burst into Pure Extreme V and dive-kick the Devil across the face.

– NOT BAD! NOT BAD AT ALL! TOO BAD IT'S NOT GOOD ENOUGH!

– Nice! Mind if I borrow some of that lovely energy there, partner?

– My power IS yours… I mean, ours.

He smiles and uses his evil energy as a chaos supplement to the prophecies' power. He also becomes Pure Extreme V.

– Now we're ready! We both point to the Devil.

– TRY ME, BOYS.

Back to Vizor, Hazy, the Dark Spirit, the Hell Prophecy, Syzor, and every other Omoh sapien there is.

"CAN SOMEONE PLEASE EXPLAIN WHAT JUST HAPPENED?"

"Why should I? You never did." Vizor gets sarcastically cocky.

"I'LL HAVE YOUR HEAD IF IT'S THE LAST THING I DO!"

"Then it's a shame you're going to stay around for a long time."

"NNNNNRRRRGGGHHHH…!"

With the power of the Shadow Prophecies, Vizor notices something glowing inside the Hell Prophecy. "Ohhh! What's that you got there?"

"WHAT DO YOU MEAN?"

"THOSE!" Vizor's hand transforms into a black thundercloud and he whips it into the Hell Prophecy.

"NOO! NOT THOSE!"

He finds five other tablets inside the Hell Prophecy. Five other…?

"VIZOR? Is that yoooouuuu?"

Vizor rolls his eyes. It's the Speed Prophecy.

"Phew! Finally out of that machine!" the Chaos Prophecy adds. "Hold on! Are those the Shadow Prophecies?"

"Well, I say!" The Wisdom Prophecy gets really excited. "I think they are, brother! It seems that Vizor has finally found them!"

"I can't wait 'till he tells us how he did it!" the Power Prophecy adds.

"Guys! We've got to help Vizor! Hazy and he have a full army to deal with!"

"I agree, Solar! Let's go!" The Chaos Prophecy speeds up.

"YOU… ACTUALLY… WERE ABLE… TO GET INSIDE ME?"

"Not too shabby for a disgrace, now is it?" Hazy crosses her arms and legs in midair.

"YOU SHOULD KNOW! WHATEVER! IT MATTERS NOT! EVERYONE! DESTROY THESE TWO, ALONG WITH ALL TEN OF THOSE PROPHECIES!"

"Not happening!" Vizor goes into his pure extreme form, but he doesn't use the Solar Prophecies' power; he uses his own set this time, and… Wait… It's the same thing? "Hold up! WHAT?"

"KNOCK KNOCK!" Syzor uses the very edge of his hair blades and gives Vizor a miserable flesh wound on his forehead.

"Aaaahh!"

"RUNNNN!"

Vizor, Hazy, and both sets of prophecies blast away toward Treah, further prolonging the army's advancement. All of them hide in a crevice inside the planet. It almost looks like a cave. Since there are so many cracks on the planet, the entire army overlooks them. But they're noticed by the Hell Prophecy. It can sense them, wherever they are (especially since Hazy has the Dark Spirit).

"Oww! OWW!"

"You need help, Vizor?" Hazy reaches out to him.

"No! I got it! Prophecy of Shadow, do your thing!"

"Wha...?"

With one spin around Vizor, the Shadow Prophecy instantly masks the wound and gets rid of it.

"WOW! That's like something I can do!" The Dark Spirit finally comes out of Hazy. "Wait... guys! Look out!"

"Huh?" Vizor turns to see the Hell Prophecy charging at him. Before he is struck, all of the Shadow Prophecies gather around him and make a shield, which the Hell Prophecy promptly runs into.

"NOW YOU'RE ALL TRAPPED!"

"Uh-oh..." The Power Prophecy tries to think of something, desperately.

– *What now? I've got BOTH sets of prophecies at my disposal, yet I can't seem to use both at the same... Wait a second. Solar Prophecy of Wisdom...*

– *Yeah? What is it, Vizor?*

– *Have you guys EVER crossed paths with the Shadow Prophecies?*

– *No. Never... Wait. Why?*

– *Hmm........... THAT'S IT!*

– *What? What is it?*

– *The sets of prophecies are another form of chaos!*

– *That's never been attempted before! It could go horribly wrong!*

– *We don't have much choice. Here goes...*

Vizor braces himself, takes the Shadow Prophecies' energies and the Solar Prophecies' energies, and creates a link using the Chaos Prophecy from both sets.

"Whoa! What's happening? QUIT IT WITH THE SURPRISES, VI-ZOR!"

Suddenly, there's a huge explosion and the Hell Prophecy is launched a few miles upward. Vizor's appearance changes. His hair flares in two different directions. To the left, his hair is red, and the right is his signature blue. In addition, his hair blades and hands alike are lit with black flames, which resemble a shadow. Prepare yourselves. Here comes CHAOS VIZOR.

"Good riddance."

"How did you…?" Hazy can't finish her sentence.

"No time. V and the others could be in danger. With the army distracted, now is the time to go."

"Uh… right." Hazy is a bit confused, but can still tell she's looking at Vizor, so she goes with his idea. All of them head to Earth, seeking to help my friends and me in the coming war… and the war we're already in.

Chapter 29

How NOT to Enter a Hospital

"What happened here?" Drac walks out the front door of the tree house. "V? Griff? Azilez? Are you guys OK?"

No answer.

"Guys?"

No answer.

"THEY'RE NOT MOVING! Z! D! Get over here! Help!"

"Calm down, Drac. What's the…" Z drops his golf club as he stares at the three of us. "D! We've got to get them to the hospital, NOW!"

Just as Z runs down, ambulances and police start to crowd the area.

"And what are you doing exactly?"

"ONLY HELPING MY BROTHER AND HIS FRIENDS NOT DIE! Also, I live here."

"That won't be necessary. We've got it all under control."

"No, you don't! Do you even know what their mental state is like?"

"I would if you'd stop interrupting."

"You're missing one, by the way."

"Missing one what?"

"Another child. Last I checked, he was about to fall from the back of that tree house."

"WHAT? WHY DON'T YOU TELL ME THESE THINGS?"

– *People. Am I right?*

Z waits for him to run off, and D asks, "Are they OK…?"

"They will be. Just summon a tree to carry them, and take them to the hospital. But remember, they're fragile."

"Uh… OK!" Trying to not collapse at the fact that I'm nearly dead again, D slowly unearths a nice, soft tree from the ground. Wow, he does a good job. I feel like I'm on top of a cloud. Back inside my bed… one sheep… two sheep… three sheepppp… Zzz….

"That way! Follow me, you two."

"Right!"

"I'll be behind you, my boy!"

They fly to the hospital.

Back inside my right hand, the Devil isn't really trying to harm us, but rather is blocking our progression. It just wants to keep things the way they are.

– *You two are pathetic! You can't even get past a few shiny, purple crystals.*

– *If You weren't so BIG, maybe we could!*

– *YOU'D THINK I'D GIVE UP MY SIZE FOR ANYTHING?*

– *V! C'mon! Rush It!*

– *BAD IDEA, EVIL V.* The Devil's palm is enough to snatch Pure Extreme Evil V right out of the air. No matter how he struggles, the Devil won't let go. It never does. – *OHOHOHOHO! THIS IS THE BEST PART! THE SUFFERING!*

– *NO! Evil V!*

In a final act of bravery, I leap-dash into the Devil's wrist hard enough to knock Evil V loose… but not fast enough to avoid a final black stalactite into the back of my head.

– *SUCH A WASTE… IF ONLY YOU WEREN'T SO WEAK!*

– *…*

– *WHAT'S WRONG? IS THE EVIL ONE FINALLY STARTING TO HAVE FEELINGS?*

– *You don't get it, do You?*

– *HUH? WAIT. NO, THAT'S IMPOSSIBLE! THAT CAN'T BE…!*

– *Ha. Surprised?* Evil V looks up, and now his right eye is brown… my eye color.

– WHAT IS THIS? YOU TWO CAN'T FUSE!

– Why not? We are the same person, after all.

– SILENCE! GOOD AND EVIL ARE NOT SUPPOSED TO LIVE IN HARMONY! AND THEY WON'T! BECAUSE YOU'RE NOT LEAVING!

– Why should I? Remember, Devil, You're in MY home field. YOU'RE the One who needs to leave.

– YOU THINK THAT ACTUALLY MATTERS TO ME WHEN I CREATED THE UNIVERSE YOU TREAD IN?

– Did You though? Look there.

– WHAT ARE YOU TRYING TO PROVE?

– That space is one that I created during my childhood — all of my likes, all of my dreams, accumulated here. THAT'S NOT SOMETHING YOU CREATED! In fact, that's not something anyone but me can create!

I open my fist and out comes a giant laser beam.

– NO! NOOO! NNNNNAAAAAAAARRRRRRGGGGHHHHHH! Without another word, the Devil vanishes from my body. Speaking of bodies…

– Ouch! Look at that. Let me get that out of there… Good as new! With Evil V's powers, the wound in my head is gone. *– Now, to restore this hand!* The meshed version of the two of us disintegrates into a gust and envelops my body (the one that got shot with the crystal). I open my eyes — my two big, brown eyes. I get up and deal with the clogged nerves. *– That goes there and… done!*

Back in reality, Griff, Azilez, and I are all in adjacent hospital beds. Perfect! I'm in the middle! That means all I have to do is reach out and touch them so they will heal! This'll be quick.

– I'm ready now…

– You always were. It just took you a while to realize it and gather all of your inner strength.

No time to waste. Next stop: the left arm!

Meanwhile, outside my sanity…

"Z, is he going to be OK?"

"I'm not sure, buddy. I'm not sure."

"I can't believe they're not letting us in." Drac comments.

"They're not supposed to. We're technically not even supposed to be out here."

"Why's that?"

"Usually, when they admit a patient to the hospital, they don't want anyone in critical condition to have visitors. But look inside, closely."

Drac squints to see and realizes that the doctors are frantic. They have no idea what to do, since normally a shattered back and a shattered neck would result in instantaneous death. To top it off, they have no idea what has induced my coma. They know I'm IN one, but they can't find a reason for it because physically, they say, I'm in perfect condition.

"Bob, what's going on?"

"I'm not sure, Phil. These patients' behaviors aren't like anything I've seen!"

"What to do! What to do-hoohoohoohoohoo!"

"Pull yourself together, doc!"

"Say that to these two. Some of their most important bones have been completely crushed. How are they alive?"

"The one in the middle is even stranger… His physical state is perfect, yet he's not moving or showing any signs of activity!"

"What do we tell the ones outside who brought them here?"

"Nothing yet. We've barely done anything to help them."

"How do we help them, huh?" Phil grabs Bob's coat. "We can't move these two from their spot. They're fatally weak! And how do you help someone in a coma if you don't know the cause?"

"Grr… let's ask the ones outside. A few questions may help determine the cause."

"What about the other two?"

"Just make sure their vital signs are as stable as possible. Whatever it takes!"

"Yes, doctor!"

Bob approaches Z, D, and Drac. "Can we have a word with you three?"

"About what?" Z asks.

"The curly-haired boy's state. Do you know how this coma could've happened?"

"Afraid not. Why, do you not have any answers?" Drac replies.

"We were all inside our house, protecting our parents…" D twirls his pickaxe around, trying to remember anything that could possibly explain my mental condition. That's a hard one. I myself can barely explain it, and I'm INSIDE my body.

"Hmm… it's probably because of some extreme emotion he's feeling if it's not physical."

"Well, he did go evil."

"Go… what?"

"N-nothing, sir. Just a little-kid hiccup." Z quickly covers up D's comment.

"Ah, I see. Distraught over seeing someone in this condition, eh?"

"Well, he is my brother. "

"Oh, I'm so sorry."

"Well, I think we've told you all we can."

"That's a… unique getup."

"Well, I am…"

Z quickly puts his hand on Drac's mouth. "A cosplay! Of Dracula! Doesn't he look cool? It's his Halloween costume!"

"But it's not even close to…"

"Never too early to practice, right? Oh, look! Phil calls for you!" Z turns Bob around, pushes him into the door, and bolts. "OK, guys, what the hell was that?"

"I should be asking the same of you, Z."

"You can't just say things like 'I'm Dracula' or 'Well, V was in his evil form.' Do you think the doctor would understand something like that?"

"Well…" Drac thinks for a moment. "I guess not."

"Besides, we don't want to get anyone else involved in our business." Just as Z finishes speaking, Vizor, Hazy, the Dark Spirit, and the ten prophecies fly into the hospital by crashing through the roof (not minding that it's a HOSPITAL).

"What the Devil was that?" Phil cowers behind Bob. As the dust clears, Chaos Vizor becomes visible for all to see… And that's a problem, especially in a civilized hospital.

"Vizor?"

"That's hot."

"No need for the pun, Z."

"C'mon. Everyone else, too, would've done it."

"…"

"You're no fun."

"Does it look like I'm here for fun?"

"True. If you're looking for the other three, they're in there."

Hazy looks first, and her stoic attitude breaks. "What HAP-PENED? They're not dead, right?"

"Close. Griff has a broken neck, Azilez has a broken back, and V is in a coma which we can't explain…"

"Hold on…" the Dark Spirit cuts in. "I feel all their spirits. They're still alive, but Griff and Azilez are barely hanging on. V seems to be fine."

"How is that possible?" Hazy looks confused.

"It's right. I feel him too. He's running. Fast. Inside his own con-sciousness."

"That's interesting. But regardless, they might need help. I must go back to them."

"Good idea. Just don't be seen by…"

"Too late." Hazy turns around and spots two little children, fro-zen in awe of the two vampires, two kids with clubs and pickaxes in their hands, the floating purple phoenix, and the tri-colored alien. One is so awestruck that he drops his lollipop.

After that, silence. Absolute silence. Yup. Just… standing. Wow, how riveting.

"Well, this is awkward."

"You didn't have to say it, Z." Vizor turns around and palms his forehead in humiliation.

"Just go, Dark Spirit."

"OK then. Hang on, you two." The Dark Spirit slowly makes Its way to Griff's body.

"Is that real fire?" The little girl points at Vizor's head.

"Don't get closer to it!" He says a little too loud, and the girl starts to bawl mercilessly. And, usually, when there's a crying child in the hallway, there is a worried mother somewhere near. Yup. There she is. Right on schedule. She looks like a mess. Her hair looks like she just rolled out of bed, her lipstick is smeared way past just her lips, and everyone can smell her morning breath.

"Where have you two been?"

"Sorry, mom, we ran into these cool-looking guys!"

"What cool-loo… AAAAAHHHHH! Call the police!"

"Uh-oh."

"Wait, wait! We're not…!"

Nice try, Hazy. She's not going to have any of it… AT ALL.

"SECURITY!" She goes to the nearest fire alarm, smashes it with her purse, and pulls it so hard that she nearly breaks it.

"Should we escape, Vizor?" Hazy asks.

"And leave V, Azilez, and Griff? Are you kidding?"

"Well, how are we gonna deal with the incoming guards?"

"Leave that to me. They won't lay a finger on any of us."

"You're not killing them, are you?"

"What? No. What made you think that?"

"Just making sure."

– *Griff!! GRIFF! Where are you? GRIFFFFFF!*

– *Nrrg…*

– *From there! Near his head!* The Dark Spirit blazes over to where It heard the noise. Bad news: his mind is blocked off, and the Dark Spirit can't understand why. – *What is this? A door?* It tries to sneak underneath, above, through, and even around it. Nothing works. It seems like his head is inaccessible.

– *Are we too late…? GRIFF! Answer me! It's the Dark Spirit!*

– *Huh? Dark Spirit?*

– *Griff! Thank goodness! Open up!*

– *I can't…*

– *What? Why not?*

– *Only one person can undo this lock. Nothing else can get through it. You already know who it is, don't you?*

Griff… why? At the risk of killing yourself? But then again, I'm what he fought against, fought with, and fought for. He wants his battle prize, but, above all, his friend, in one piece.

– *I understand. Are you sure you're fine until he gets here?*

– *I'd break my neck again for V. As long as my bro is here, that's all that matters to me. Bring him here. I know he's alive! I can feel it!*

– *You can "feel" it? Friendship between these two is…*

– *No, no! I can sense his presence! Like you! He's sprinting, right?*

– *How did you…?*

– *I'm not even sure. All I know is that I fought for V and that he's alive! Just bring me V!*

– *Uh… OK! I should go to Azilez to make sure she's OK too.*

The Dark Spirit flies out of Griff and heads to Azilez. Evil V starts to pick up on It.

– *I sense Its presence.*

– *Whose?*

– *Not whose. It's a What.*

– *The Dark Spirit? It's well and here?*

– *HEY! GET IN HERE, DARK SPIRIT?*

– *WHOA…? V? ARE YOU OK?*

– *Just get in here and I'll explain! I'm on a mission to save Griff and Azilez from certain death!*

– *Then let Me help you.*

– *Exactly what I was hoping for.*

– *We'll go to Azilez first. The Dark Spirit finds me and enters my body.*

– *Any particular reason you chose her over Griff?*

– *I checked on Griff. He says he can wait.*

– *Azilez first it is. Just help me get over this massive tornado here, and we'll be at the neuron generator.*

– *I go through this all the time.*

– To heal me, huh? I never realized how difficult it is for You.

– It's no big deal. These are your childhood dreams, after all. I feel like I get to know you a little better every time I pass through here, and the same goes for anyone else's body. Griff, Azilez, Vizor…the list goes on. I've seen many things from My healing times. All of them intrigue Me in little ways that make Me smile, and sometimes make me feel otherwise.

– I never knew. Here it is!

– Oh goodie! Let's get to work!

– Hopefully there's no Devil this time.

– Huh?

– Never mind…

– Oh ok. As It's about to fix the neuron generator, It realizes that I'm going up to try and help It.

– What are you doing? Are you trying to fix this?

– Uh…yeah?

– It takes certain types of energy to fix something like this. I don't think you have the type to…

– I'll say it again: uh…yeah?

– Was that Evil V? What's he doing inside you?

– I've learned something from this whole fiasco, Dark Spirit. I place my hands over the neuron generator. *– Everyone has an evil side, whether they know it or not! It just takes a while for it to manifest itself in one's mind. How people react to it is up to them. Some people try and shut it out, some try to destroy it, but there are a select few who embrace it. However, some people are not strong enough to control it, and it consumes their entire being. What most people don't understand is how evil coexists within us is up to us.*

It doesn't say anything.

– No words?

– Only…congratulations.

– Why that one?

– You truly are going on a journey unique to you. You're finding out about aspects of this world in your own rite. In a way, that's all that life is: using the experiences from your special and unique journey in life to shape it, even change it.

– Seems like You've had quite a few journeys Yourself.

– I've certainly had more than you.

– Haha! Almost there! Concentrate!

– Right!

With our combined evil and dark energies, the healing of the second neuron generator goes smoothly and quicker than last time. Time to reach out to Azilez!

– Can I move now? I try, with all of my strength, to reach out to the unconscious art master to my left. I lift up my pinkie, then my ring finger, then my index, and lastly, my thumb. My left hand works!

"BOB! LOOK! The one in the coma is moving!

"WHAT? HOW? He came out that quickly?" The two look in awe as my hand slowly creeps toward Azilez. I place my hand, gently, right below her neck.

"What's he doing?"

"I-I'm not sure."

"Shall I see if his brain functions are working?"

"Yes!"

"Er…yes, sir!"

Outside of the room, Vizor, Hazy, Drac, Z, and D all have their own problems.

"Freeze! All of you!"

"Oh dear! What is that?"

"It looks like something from the mid 70s lit on fire!"

"Vizor, now what?" Hazy whispers to him, reminding him about his supposed plan.

"I got it."

"Hold on, men! Hold your fire!" The leader of the security guards decides to show up late, but why'd he ask to hold fire?

"WHAT 'HOLD FIRE'? SHOOT THEM!"

"Did you even stop and ask who we are, first? Or did you just assume we're a threat because your children were yelling right next to us?"

"Well, I don't have to! Judging by your appearance…"

Vizor walks closer to the woman.

"Should we still not shoot, sir?"

"Hold your fire."

"Yes, sir…"

Vizor doesn't even say anything to the woman in front of him. He just stands there, staring at her with his two cold eyes.

"AAAAHHHH!" The woman screams, as if something is happening to her. Even though Vizor hasn't even laid a finger on her. "FIRE YOUR GUNS! SHOOT!"

"Don't do it, men! DON'T!"

"WHY? LOOK AT HIM!"

"Yes everyone. Look at me. What am I to you?"

"Uh…"

"I'll answer that." The head guard walks forward. "You're Vizor, an alien from another world that looks like the kid inside of there, V."

"How did you…?"

"You don't recognize me?"

"Uh, to be honest, no."

"Hahaha! I'm playing around, son! You've never seen me, but I've seen you."

– Awkward? Guaranteed.

"It was during that interrogation, remember? I was one of the many officers standing outside the room."

"Oh right, that day was all over the place. What's your name?"

"Erik."

"Nice to meet you, Erik."

"Now, if you don't mind telling me who these two are."

"The vampires? Their names are Hazy and Dracula."

"WHAT?"

"THE Count Dracula?"

"One and only, my little children!"

"And this woman next to you?"

"My daughter."

"No way…"

"The legend is real…?"

"Who could've thought…"

"Yes, well. These are stories for later days. Right now, those three poor souls inside there need help. We're gonna wait right here for them to…V?"

"What is it? DRAC? WHAT IS IT?"

"V's hand moved!"

"He's alive!" Z face plants against the stainless glass window (fun fact: it's perfectly stainable).

"Let me see! D isn't tall enough to look through the window on his own. He goes on the tip of his toes, and with that, can barely see what's going on inside the room. "IT'S TRUE! His hand! It's on Azilez!"

"There's hope after all!" Hazy grins, and her eyes brighten.

"So, Erik. Want to tell your men to stop shivering with their guns in their grasp?"

"Sure thing. Men, cease!"

Everyone gets to know each other outside, while having hope that the three of us will make it through. Hang on, Azilez. I'm coming!

And hopefully there's no Devil this time. I've had enough for one day.

Chapter 30
Majestic Minds

— Now we just go through my fingertips into her neck?

— Pretty much. It's easy.

— Well, let's go then.

— Since technically you're still in a coma, you should be able to step outside of your body with no problem.

— Why would that be an issue in the first place?

— Think about it for a second. Your consciousness is walking out of your body.

— Oh. So there's no soul inside the body then?

— Exactly. And that's a problem.

— Good to know if I run into a problem like this again.

With that, we're off! Up my fingertips and into Azilez's lower neck area. Since what we run into depends on our childhoods' likes and dreams, I should be running into many different assortments of… wooooooooaaaaahhhh!

— THIS PLACE LOOKS EPIC!

— It's as if unicorns flew through here!

Can I even describe what I'm looking at right now? It's the entire visible spectrum and everything in between. There's an assortment of coloring sheets, canvases with some of Azilez's life moments like her 11th birthday, the day she met Griff and me, paintbrushes that act like hovercrafts, and RAINBOWS. Lots of them! A rainbow here, there, over there, THEY'RE EVERYWHERE!

– How do we know where to…?

– Here. This rainbow leads to her brain.

– How do You even know that?

– When you do this for a while, you'll see that most bodies have the same composition. See how the path stays narrow going through there?

Now that I think about it…that does make sense. The bodies keep their compositions, even in this bizarre world.

– Oh yeah!

– It's the same for everyone. Maybe you just didn't see it in yourself because the storms blinded you.

– Maybe. I'm not sure. That doesn't matter right now, though. To her head!

– I'll lead the way!

– Sure.

We jump on the rainbow that leads to the narrow straight and run along its many colors. I try to pay attention to some of the canvases that fly by. I notice something really weird: there's nothing I see that surprises me.

Now, that may seem normal considering she's my best friend. But the truth is that I barely know what Azilez was like as a little kid. It's not really something we've talked about. I'll make sure to do that once we're all done here, assuming we ever will be.

– Just as I thought. Another one.

– Another what? I look up and realize there's a gigantic, multi-colored door in the way.

– Let's see if it's like the last one.

– Wait, last what?

No answer. The Dark Spirit already took off and has started to try and get through this door. I say it a little louder. *– Get through the last what, Dark Spirit? Where did You see something like this?*

– Inside of Griff's body.

– YOU WENT THERE? He's OK now though, right?

– NO! He wanted you there!

– Huh?

– He said his neck didn't matter as much as seeing you first.

– Griff...

– Do you get it now? I wanted to do this as quickly as possible so we could get back to him! Call out for Azilez. She probably feels the same way.

– AZILEZ, OPEN THIS DOOR NOW!

– Huh...? Who's there?

– The one you fought for! The Dark Spirit and I are here to help you and Griff!

– Impossible. The one you're talking about is already close to dead.

– You underestimate me. I'm telling you, it's me.

– If it really is you, then what gift did you get me for my 11th birthday?

– Well...

– In great detail.

– I see why you chose that one. It was the first art kit I got you, once I realized how brilliant of an artist you are. In it, there were 5 different paint-brushes, each with different thicknesses. Also, it came with two sets of 15 water-color paints, two sets of 20 squeezable, regular-colored paints, a box of 20 white and black charcoal pencils, a set of 50 normal pencils, an eraser, a sharpener, and last but not least, a master brush. It's the brush that you carry around with you now.

– ...

– Well...?

Without a word, the invisible chains break, and the door flies open. There's Azilez, on the bland, purple floor. She's barely alive, but even so, she's so happy to see me that she tries crawling to me. With a broken back, however, that's close to impossible.

– V! AAAAHHHH!

– Don't move a muscle! I rush to her aid. *– DARK SPIRIT! HURRY!*

Realizing her fragile state, the Dark Spirit, without letting me even touch Azilez, blazes through her. Almost instantly, her entire body starts to rumble. Her back! It's being shifted back into place!

She instantly gets up and...slaps me really hard.

– OWWW!

– Never...ever...EVER...DO THAT TO ME AGAIN!

– Is it too late to say sorry for that?

– NO! WHAT? Of course not! You were possessed! I was only playing around!

– Tell that to my aching face…and, possibly, slightly fractured jawline.

– I got this.

– Thanks, Evil V.

– Ohhhh! Sorry! Didn't mean to hit you THAT hard! Before she can really do anything about it, though, Evil V works his magic once more and the aching instantly stops. *– Was that the Dark Spirit? Is it back?*

– Actually…no.

– WHAT? You can heal yourself now?

– Yes and no.

– What…?

– Remember the possessed version of me?

– What's that supposed to mean? She looks like she's ready to slap again.

– Calm down! Calm down! Turns out, it was the Devil controlling me.

– What's the point?

– The point is that I couldn't beat the Devil by myself in my condition, and I didn't have the Dark Spirit to help me at that time.

– So…?

– Say hello to the one who DID help me.

– Huh? Oh, uh…hello. I'm guessing being cooped up inside of my mind for almost 14 years would make Evil V awkward with anyone else besides me.

– What was that?

– That, Azilez, was the real Evil V.

– 'Sup?

Azilez looks down, almost in failure.

– How?

– How what?

– HOW IS THAT EVIL STILL INSIDE YOU? AFTER WHAT GRIFF AND I TRIED TO DO TO DESTROY IT!

– You haven't noticed yet?

– NOTICED WHAT?

– Azilez, calm down for a second. Do I look in any way possessed to you?

– What? I don't get it. Does that mean you're really evil? I don't want that...

– Whoa, hold on. That's not what it means.

– On the contrary, my dear. The Dark Spirit finally comes out of Azilez. –The evil is contained inside of V. He's controlling it. It's his to use however he chooses.

– Wait, I'm so confused...

– About what?

As if I don't know. I already know how she feels. She thinks that the evil inside me is the same one she tried to destroy.

– Why is V using evil for his own purposes? That's not right...

Wait, I was wrong? She understands? Hold on...oh. She's wondering how evil energy could ever be used for good.

– Azilez. Evil energy is just like good energy.

– NO IT'S NOT! EVIL IS EVIL, AND THAT'S THAT!

– AZILEZ!

– What?

She has a hint of fear in her voice. After all, she's never heard my voice combined with my evil half's.

– Remember how most people think that darkness immediately means bad?

– Well, yeah. But...!

– Let me finish. Evil ENERGY is different from evil INTENT. The evil energy is just ruthlessly powerful. Combine that with evil intent, and you have a recipe for disaster. But look at me now! Does it look like I would ever use this strength for anything ill-willed?

– ...

– Thinking?

– I...I'm not sure I fully understand yet. She fearlessly walks up to me and grabs my shoulder. *– But I see the real V in front of me. This concept is still a little hard for me to grasp. But, if you're here, that means it must not*

be all that bad.

    – Thanks, Azilez.

    – BUT THAT DOESN'T MEAN I DON'T HAVE MY EYE ON YOU!
She changes her facial expression to a super-serious one, and then breaks out laughing. This is how I know she's finally listening to me. I have one of my two friends back.

    – Well, I've got one more friend to save. Want to join me?

    – As if I wouldn't. Let's get Griff back!

    – V, WAIT!

    – Dark Spirit? What's up? Is it the Devil again?

    – Have you forgotten what I told you about bodies and their conscious-
ness?

    – You mean the part about 'if there's no soul inside a body, then prob-
lems occur'?

    – YES, that one!

    – But she's unconscious too.

    – WAS unconscious.

    – Oh…right. You healed her.

    – Exactly! She can't leave. She has to wake up.

    – Shoot! Is there no way around it?

    – If there were, I'd have told you about it by now.

    – Sorry, Azilez. I forgot about that.

    – No. She's going.

    – Who's there? DEVIL?

    – Ha. You could say that. Well, a she-devil if you wanna be more pre-
cise.

    – WHO'S THERE? Azilez is getting frustrated.

    – You don't know yourself, Azilez?

    – WHAT? Huh…?

It's as the voice says: it is Azilez. Well…evil her. Evil Azilez is un-leashed.

    – If you're here for V, you might as well forget…

    – I can fill in.

    – FOR WHAT?

– Listen to yourself, for once. I'm trying to help you go with V and save your little friend.

– You think I'll let you possess me?

– Silly girl, I've been inside of you forever.

– How…? What's going on? Why are you here?

– Azilez, it's OK.

– V…?

– This is like the evil form I showed you.

– How is that possible? I'm not evil!

This is my chance to show her!

– That's not what this means. Having this form unleashed means that you're growing stronger. The only way a form like this can be set free is if you commit a selfless act whilst in your evil form.

– Selfless…? Evil…? Are those even compatible?

I grab her by the shoulders and lift her up.

– If they aren't, then we'll MAKE them! You've just gotta believe you have the power to make them compatible!

Azilez takes a nice long look at Evil Azilez. The two stare at each other for a while. Eventually, Evil Azilez smiles. At that moment, Azilez realizes that it'll all work out. She finally understands what I was trying to tell her.

– Thanks, evil me. I'll do it!

– Good! GO! He doesn't have much time!

– She's right, V! Broken necks don't heal themselves!

Ah…good to see her back to normal.

– Good point! Let's go, Dark Spirit!

– Yes! Onward!

As I'm about to jump out and fly back to my body, I turn around one last time to give the evil version of my best friend some sage advice.

– Evil Azilez?

– Huh?

– Make sure her back stays intact. Avoid any and all Devils you see.

She chuckles and sends me off with my "V" sign.

I use one of the many conveniently placed rainbows to run outside of Azilez's body, while Azilez just uses her brush. Now, we're back into the swirling storm that is my body. – *Griff!! I'm coming!* I nervously take a look at his heart monitor to see if he's still alive. Barely, but he's still holding on. I look over, and see that the doctors are fighting over the last bar of Kit Kat inside of the vending machine.

– *Who hired these two?*

"So, let me get this straight." Erik is trying to comprehend what Vizor has told him about The Legend of V. "You're an alien-double of V that comes from a world that mirrors Earth called Treah?"

"Yup."

"The woman next to you is named Hazy, she's the daughter of Count Dracula, is 350 years old, lives underneath the Romanian province of Transylvania, and is your best friend?"

"That's right."

"AND the vampires are descendants of your people, the Omoh sapiens, and the two really don't like each other?"

"Fact."

"That's only covering you three! The two over here are the brothers of V and were KIDNAPPED by a possessed version of you for nearly a decade?"

"Well, maybe not that long…" Vizor tries to remember.

"A little less. 7-8 years maybe. I lost track after 5."

"I guess when you're just trying to survive, you lose track of time. But, these ten floating tablets called prophecies…is that story true? About a Great War? The creation of an Unbound Evil and a Light Spirit? The corrupting of the Light Spirit, thus turning it into the Dark Spirit?" Erik gets so excited that his mouth sort of runs away from his face.

"Slow down, dude!" The Speed Prophecy wants to answer all of his questions. "Yup! We were created by five, brave human soldiers from the Great War. Our purpose? Help V stop the Unbound Evil from destroying the entire universe!"

"Yes!"

"All right!"

"Wooohooo!" All of the prophecies get a little rowdy, except for the Prophecy of Wisdom.

"But then what are those five tablets?"

"The Shadow Prophecies? They're my set of prophecies."

"What's that mean?"

"The Solar Prophecies' rightful owner is V, right?"

"Yeah, oh! There's more than just one set? I wonder how many there are…"

"This is probably the last set."

"I don't know. There's no set of rules that outlaws more." Hazy adds.

"What do you know? You've barely even known about the legend."

"Says the one who has only known it for a mere 10 years."

"Hmph. You're right. There IS no rule that says there are only two sets."

"THEN THERE'S MORE!"

"Calm down. If there are, we have no idea about them, who they belong to, how they were created, and their locations."

"Oh bummer. You got me all hyped."

"Sorry about that."

"It's fine. One more question."

"Sure, wh–"

"HOW ARE YOU CARRYING THREE DIFFERENT COLORED FLAMES AND NOT BURNING?"

"This, my friend, is the power of the prophecies. All 10 of them can combine their strengths and grant a user incredible power. Having one set of prophecies grants the user something that's called an extreme form, but combine the two sets of prophecies together, and you get a chaos form. That's what you see in front of you, Chaos Vizor."

"That's awesome! I wonder how many applications this power has."

"I didn't even know the prophecies' power was this abundant." Drac adds on. "But Vizor did forget a small detail. Do you know what chaos is?"

"There's a lot of definitions for that."

"Well, the one I'm talking about is the power to link two distant powers together to make an even stronger power. Like light and dark, and good and evil."

"That sounds like a dangerous concept."

"In the wrong hands, yes, it's deadly. But, it can also be used to amplify extreme forms into pure extreme forms!"

"I don't think he gets it."

"I do a little. But once I see it, I'll marvel in it!"

– Since we're on the topic of prophecies and their owners…I wonder… lemme try this. V! Can you hear me?

– Vizor! Is that you? Such strength! I've never felt that before. I wonder how he got that much power.

– V, what's going on? Why've you stopped running?

– Don't you hear it?

– Hear what? We don't have time for falling dimes! Griff is worth more than minimum wage!

– No, no, no! It's Vizor!

– Vizor?

– Listen! I'm not exactly sure how I'm doing this, but I can talk to you guys!

– I got that much, buddy!

– Go! Keep running! Don't stop for me!

– How do you know we're running?

– I'm not sure. I'm not sure how I'm doing any of this! All I know is that I can sense you two, and it seems very helpful. That's not the point. Listen to me! I wanted to talk to you for a reason. I figured out why you're in a coma!

– What is it? I ask as I continue to run.

– There are two doors to your heart - one for each of your two friends. When you saw their states, they tightly shut, forbidding you to move forward unless they were safe. You need both of them to go back into your body to reopen them!

He can see the doors to my heart? I wonder what else he can see.

– Are you OK, V…?

– I'm fine. I just wanted you two at my side. You're like my brother and sister. I can't imagine my life without you two! I couldn't just live with the fact that I let the Devil possess me AND kill my friends. I needed to make sure they were safe. Without them…I don't even want to talk about that. *–Vizor, thanks! You saved us some trouble!*

– Don't mention it. I can't really go inside of that room. This is the most I could do.

– We'll take care of the rest. There! My hand generator!

– Hand generator?

– Let me explain…

I let Azilez know all about the wonders of healing with her evil form. I also tell her the story of how my hand generators were clogged, how the Devil was keeping me hostage inside of my own mind, and how Evil V broke free to help me.

– So you were your own prisoner inside your own mind?

– If that can even happen, yeah.

– I believe it can. With what we've been through, we can almost believe anything.

– Almost.

We exchange laughs. Now I wonder about the things I DON'T know about the Devil's, Unbound Evil's, Syzor's and the Hell Prophecy's plots. Who's the real mastermind out of all of them? I want to say the Devil, but I feel like It underestimates too many things. That'll probably backfire, right? I don't know the Devil enough to say that for certain yet. But at the same time, do I even want to know more about It? If I play too lightly with It, I'll be dead in no time.

At the same time, what's been the Unbound Evil's deal? It fought Vizor and me near the sun and just exploded out of nowhere! What's up with that? Did the Devil do that? There's too much to think about. I think I'll just let it play out and I'll adapt. The only difference now is that I'm more prepared with Evil V at my side.

– V! Watch out! To your right! Azilez warns me of an oncoming twister just in time for me to avoid it.

– Thanks!

– *How many more of these storms are there?*

– *Not too many more. I hope.* After a few more hurricanes, thunderbolts, and ground-shattering earthquakes, I spot my right hand's generator! Time to get to Griff's body! – *There it is! Jump into it!*

I take Azilez by her wrist and slide under the last barreling boulder and into the generator, which warps us through my fingertips into Griff's chest region.

– *What are we standing on? Is this a road? Azilez asks.*

– *I think I know what this is.*

– *What?*

– *As a little kid, Griff's favorite things in the world were cars. He'd do anything to get his hands on any toy car.*

– *Does he still have them?*

– *I think we have them stowed away somewhere, but look! There are two cars over there.*

– *I call the green one!*

– *That's fine. I wanted the blue one anyway.* We strap ourselves in, close the hoods, and before I prematurely floor it, I look for the narrow road like the Dark Spirit advised me to do in Azilez's body. – *That way!*

– C'mon! I'll race ya!

– I'd be insulted if you didn't!

We both hit the accelerator. In a matter of seconds, the cars reach speeds I didn't know were possible!

– *This is one insane engine! Azilez, what does your speedometer say?*

– *1000 mph!*

Yes! I'm 1001! I've got this race in the bag!

– *Whoa! Watch for the jump!*

– *I see it!* As we expect to be thrown onto the next part of the asphalt, we're launched instead into a black void, where all we're doing is steadily moving forward.

– *What's going on? Why is this part of Griff's body empty?*

– *I might know why.*

– *Huh?*

– *N-nothing.*

– V? AZILEZ?

– GRIFF! IS THAT YOU BUDDY?

– WHERE ARE YOU?

– I'M NOT ACTUALLY YELLING OUT. I PHYSICALLY JUST CAN'T. I'M SPEAKING TO YOU TELEPATHICALLY.

– ARE YOU USING THAT STRANGE POWER YOU HAVE AGAIN?

– YEAH. BUT, LOOK! THAT DOOR TO YOUR RIGHT LEADS TO ME.

– Door...? OH, THERE IT IS. I SEE IT!

– The door to his mind...is it shut, like Azilez's was? I wonder.

We fly through the door, and jump out of our cars and onto the floor below. This floor is much more hollow than the road we came from. Griff's door...it's wide open!

– V! The Dark Spirit! Please!

– On it! I run and grab his arm, then let the Dark Spirit flow through.

– Now, for the actual back in this body! The Dark Spirit flies out of him and nearly teleports to the shattered pieces of Griff's neck. It takes almost no time for It to put all of the pieces back together.

– Griff? SPEAK! Azilez's head pops out from behind mine.

– I'm OK! Griff props straight up almost like a stool, and he takes his backpack from the floor and carries it. *– No more doubts! Neither of you!*

– So I guess you heard what we said earlier?

– You bet.

– This power of yours intrigues me.

– Something else intrigues me, V.

– What's that?

– Why did you think we were dead? Also, why would you think you were responsible?

– I just didn't want you two dead, especially by my hands. The mere thought drove me to a coma I guess. I can't imagine my life without the two of you!

– And yet you didn't have enough faith for us to be alive.

– That's not…

– Listen, V. You wanted to save us, right?

– Yeah! Of course!

– So, why did you fall into a coma?

– Have you forgotten our normal lives this quickly? This goes beyond just this adventure. It goes to how much you two mean to me, and the thought that I was too weak to do anything about your situation.

– That's what I'm trying to say to you.

– Huh?

– NO. MORE. DOUBTS. These are the Devil's tricks: making you feel guilty for things you clearly didn't do. And look where it led you. To a coma.

– Griff, you shouldn't be so hard on him! He did come and save you after all.

– I'm just returning the favor. You think I'm trying to hurt him? The truth may hurt, but it'll help him in the long run. Besides, it's better than just senselessly slapping people into submission. Griff looks at Azilez. Nice shot, Griff. Way to lighten the mood.

– What's that supposed to mean? She blushes.

Did I really fall for the Devil's trap? And Griff knew all along? That guy…he's come a long way. I have a feeling this is only the beginning for him. Also, it's quite refreshing to see Azilez chase Griff around. I now know they're both OK, and that I'm still in reality. Well, sort of.

– Should we get going, guys?

– AS SOON AS I CLOBBER MR. SASSY-PANTS HERE!

Whilst chasing Griff, Azilez takes out her brush and materializes a rainbow hammer.

– A little help, V?

– Haha! You guys make me laugh.

– At least one of us is!

I run up behind Azilez and grab her by the arms, so she can't chase Griff anymore.

– LEMME AT HIM! LEMME AT HIM!

– Do you know a faster way out of here, Griff?

– I thought you'd never ask. It's my favorite car. Watch this! He unzips

one of the pockets on the left side of his backpack and takes a key out of it. With the click of a button, a bright red-orange car falls out of nowhere. This thing is a beauty! It has jet engines, two pairs of dual wings, three seats, and an awesome flame sticker on the side. – *If you guys thought the cars you rode in were fast, you ain't seen nothing yet!*

– *I don't like the sound of that.* Azilez tries not to remember the 1000 mph speedometer.

– *C'mon, Azilez. It's one more ride. How bad could it be?*

She reluctantly jumps into the middle of the three seats.

– *Make sure the ride goes smoothly, Griff.*

– *No promises. At all.* Without another word, he leaps into the driver's seat. I just shrug and fill in the last seat. Before the jet car can lift off, Azilez spawns a rider's helmet, armor, and a chocolate bar to melt her worries away.

– *Are you really that scared, Azilez?*

Shiver

– *And yet you're perfectly fine flying to the skies on a speeding rainbow?*

– *That's something I have control over.*

– *You're out of your mind.*

– *Yes. Fact. I'm in Griff's mind!*

– …

– *You had to be ready for that one, V.*

– *Nah. That was good, Azilez. High-five! SMACK!*

– *You guys ready?*

– *Yeah!*

No answer from Azilez. All we hear is her rapidly chomping at the chocolate bar.

– *BLAST OFF!* The jet engine ignites and we've almost reached light speed. We reach my body in a few seconds.

– *That's it?*

– *I told you guys you had nothing to worry about.*

– *No you didn't!*

Griff awkwardly laughs because he knows Azilez is right.

– *Anyway, these are V's two doors.*

The Dark Spirit picks up on something immediately.

– *Griff, do you feel that?*

– *Sure do. It's coming from over there. Behind the doors!*

– *Huh?*

– *What is…*Before I can finish, a giant, sturdy boy leaps from the area Griff designated. Oh Hellish nightmares, it's that kid that nearly beat me up in elementary school all those years ago! – *What are you doing here?*

– *I'm back for the remaining vertebrae you still have in tact!*

– *That's not happening!* Griff walks in front of me as a warning for the bully.

– *What going on? WHO IS THAT?*

– *That's the guy who nearly took my life when I was a kid!*

– *Vizor? This thing is too fat to be Vizor!*

– *Watch your mouth, sissy! I'll snap you next if I have to!*

– *Been there! Done that!* Azilez goes for her brush.

– *WHY DO YOU KEEP HIDING?*

– *Huh? What's that supposed to mean, Griff?*

– *YOU KNOW FULL WELL WHAT I'M TALKING ABOUT, DEVIL! NOW GET OUT OF THAT SHELL SO I CAN ACTUALLY SEE YOUR FACE!*

– *WHY WOULD I DO THAT?*

Griff's right. The Devil is inside of that monstrosity. The booming voice proves it. So, does that make the bully a monstrous monstrosity? Hmm…

– *Your Son takes after You nicely! It doesn't know when It's been beat!*

– *QUITE THE ARROGANT ONE YOU'VE BECOME, GRIFF! DO YOU PLAN TO SQUANDER YOUR POWER LIKE THAT?*

– *Shut up! I barely know myself! But with You here, I'll never have the chance to know myself because YOU'RE INSIDE MY BEST FRIEND!*

– *HE NEARLY KILLED YOU!*

– *YOU nearly killed them! I rebut. And nearly made me believe it!*

– *WELL IT DOESN'T MATTER NOW! ALL OF YOU ARE DEAD!* The bully puppet hammers the ground with his arm. The resulting fissures have giant, prickly rocks erupt out. The three of us transform into our pure extreme forms in time to dodge it. – *STAND STILL!*

– *That's kinda lame. Why would we do that?*

– *MAYBE YOU'LL ACTUALLY DO SOMETHING I TELL YOU FOR ONCE! YOU COULDN'T EVEN GET TREAH BACK!*

– *Do you honestly think we were trying to?* Griff is having a hard time imagining why the Devil didn't just do that Itself.

– *Remember, Griff? The whole chair thing?*

– *Oh yeah! I forgot about that.*

– *IT DOESN'T MATTER NOW! I'LL JUST DESTROY ALL OF YOU HERE! YOU WON'T EVEN SEE MY GREAT PLAN UNFOLD!*

– *We don't even want to know it!*

– *Well, we kinda do. Azilez thinks.*

– Shhhh!

– *AHAHAHAHAHAHAHAHA! YOU ENTERTAIN ME, AZILEZ! I'LL WIPE YOU OUT LAST!*

– *YOU'LL HAVE TO WIPE ME OUT BEFORE THOSE TWO IF YOU EVEN WANT TO TOUCH THEM!* Azilez holds her brush in the air and it sparkles. The bully, Griff, and I feel a vibration. In the horizon, we see a giant rainbow tsunami.

– *TASTE THE RAINBOW!*

– *OK!* The Devil literally opens the kid's mouth and swallows the entire wave. With one last hearty gulp, the tsunami vanishes into the bully's stomach acid. – *IT WOULD'VE TASTED BETTER IF IT WERE SKITTLES, BUT OH WELL!*

– *HOW?*

– *DO YOU NOT REALIZE WHAT IS IN FRONT OF YOU? HOW MANY TIMES ARE YOU GOING TO MAKE THAT MISTAKE?*

– *Uhhh…*

– *Hey, V.* Evil V whispers from inside of me. *We should help her out. I have an idea.*

– *What is it?*

– *Mind if I borrow the Dark Spirit?*

– *What for?*

– *To make the Devil shut up.*

– More specific?

– Fine! Do you know what you get when you mix dark and evil power?

–Uhh…no.

– Well, remember chaos?

– Is dark and evil another form of it?

– Bingo.

– Yeah! Go ahead. Borrow It!

– Ready, Dark Spirit?

– At your command!

– Brace yourself, V!

– I'm ready! The Dark Spirit and Evil V start to fuse inside of me. This is…awkward. I feel a pitch-black spiral swirling inside of me. Inside of it, nothing exists…emptiness…void.

Void V!

I feel my hair go out to the right, as Dark V's normally would. However, it takes a twist this time. The hair that would normally cover my right eye now expands so the core of my eye can be seen. What's in there? Darkness. Pitch black darkness. In the very center, though, if you look close enough, there's one white dot in the middle. In addition, my hands start to emit a blinding white mist. The rest of my body emits dark purple.

– ENOUGH.

– WHO WAS THAT?

– Why don't you look over and find out? My transformation is complete.

– WH…WHAT IS THAT?

– Shouldn't You know? You exist in this kind of state in Hell all the time: an existence that exists, yet doesn't at the same time - emptiness. VOID.

– WHAT'S THAT SUPPOSED TO MEAN?

– Exactly what it sounds like.

– GGGGGRRRRRRRRAAAHHHHHH! It tries to summon another wave of pointy stalactites to attack me. I've had just about enough of these little nuisances.

– Is this the only way you know how to attack?

I use the mist on my hands to pick up ALL of the newly summoned rocks and use them as bludgeons to knock the bully onto its back. – *Now LEAVE.* I pull off an attack I didn't even know was possible. I use my right eye and both of my hands as conduits to summon a black hole. It slowly moves toward the Devil. – *Tell me how THAT tastes.*

– *No! NOO! NNNNNNNNOOOOOOOOOOOOO!*

It can't get up and escape in time. The bully and the monster inside of him are captured inside of the hole's infinite gravity, and then, the black hole evaporates into nothingness.

– *Phew. I'm starting to grow tired of this whole 'possessed' thing.*

– *V? What is this new–?*

– *THAT WAS AWESOME! How'd you summon the black hole?*

– *The power of Void V.*

– *Void V?*

– *Yup. These two made it possible.* I reveal the two power sources.

– *WOW! Using your evil form with the Dark Spirit?*

– *That's pretty crafty, V.*

– *Ha. Thanks! Now then…the doors, you two. That's not something I can fix.*

– *Right!*

– *On it!*

They each walk to their respective doors. They reach out to touch them with the palms of their hands. Azilez's hand shakes a bit because she feels how cold the door is. It doesn't seem to bother Griff too much. Both doors open fully, and a giant light illuminates the room. Griff and Azilez are sent back to their bodies.

The three of us wake up, all in stable condition.

"BOB! Come quick! The patients have revived!" Phil munches on the last bite of the Kit Kat he took from the vending machine. As he talks, some of the crumbles trickle down his mouth onto the white floor.

Everyone outside, except Erik and the Solar Prophecies, hears that last part and face-plant the room's windows to see if it's true.

"V?"

"HE'S ALIVE!"

– I knew it. Good job, V. Vizor looks at me with a smile.

"Ow…" I sit up on the hospital bed, holding my head.

"That was the shortest lived coma I've ever seen!"

"Huh?" I'm still trying to grasp reality around me. "Azilez? Griff? You guys OK?"

"I think…" Azilez gets up, but lets out a sigh and goes back to sleep.

"That was some trip, guys." Griff nearly jumps out of bed.

"Save the celebration for later, Griff. This is only the beginning."

Chapter 31

Vampire's Vengeance

Griff and I get out of our beds and walk out.

"Azilez? You coming?"

"Give me a minute. I was just almost dead, after all."

"That's fair." Griff agrees. We open the door, and D leaps onto me before I can even take a step out the door.

"V! Thank goodness you're OK!"

"D, air…! Please!"

"C'mon. Be gentle, D. He was hospitalized only a half hour ago."

"V! My boy! You made it through!" Drac's arms and cape envelop every part of me, except my hair.

"I didn't even need to help him this time." Hazy pops out from behind Vizor. "No, but seriously, you're quite a trooper, V. Getting out of that coma in that short a time is commendable."

"Thanks, Ha–"

"But thank GOD that the only person that makes me feel sane anymore is still living!" Hazy's hug nearly crushes the soul that Azilez just got back.

"Come on! That's not true, my little one."

"Yeah. You still have me, right?" Vizor points at himself.

"How about Griff?" No one can tell if Azilez is saying that just to get Hazy off of her or to bestow some love on Griff. Well, considering Hazy just sucked all the love out of Azilez, it was probably just to get her off.

"Griff, you surprised me the most."

"Exactly why you went and tackled Azilez first, right?"

"Shut up. C'mon. You know I was just playing around. Isn't that right, Azilez?"

"Please… help…" She can't seem to get off the floor.

"C'mon. You know I was just playing around." Griff smiles and tries to mimic Hazy's voice.

"Hehe! That was cute."

"I couldn't quite understand the strength you displayed either, my boy," Drac says. "You got up quite fast."

"Wow! Thanks, Drac."

"Oh, yeah, by the way, you can't go out without this."

"My backpack!" Griff swipes at the tattered piece of fabric so quickly that he grabs the very air around it too.

"That…" Azilez re-gathers herself enough to stand up. "That doesn't count! Hazy nearly destroyed me."

"What was I gonna do? I thought you were dead. I needed to feel the love."

"No reason to kill me again!"

"You guys are no fun…"

"Wait a second." Azilez feels a disturbance in her back pocket. "WHERE IS MY BRUSH?"

"Calm down, calm down. I picked it up." Z reaches into his khakis and reveals the brush's tip.

"GIVE! GIVE! GIVE!" She runs over and takes it out of his pocket before he can.

"So you ready for the coming war, V?" Vizor asks as we begin to walk. Z and D follow from behind.

"Oh, yeah! I'm ready to go."

"Good. We'll definitely need you." Z puts his arm around me.

"So what's all THIS?" I point to Vizor's tri-colored hair.

"Oh, that's right. You haven't seen them yet. Behold: the Shadow Prophecies!" We stop walking momentarily. He steps aside so the five new tablets have enough room to fly forward.

"Wow! You found them! Where were they?"

"Get this: they were inside Treah's rings!"

"Huh. That's weird."

"What is?" Vizor looks at the prophecies with a sudden, dire stare.

"They're mute."

"Gee, you say that like it's a bad thing." Vizor glares at Solar Prophecies' Speed Prophecy.

"HEY! You watch it, mister!" It flies close to my side. "C'mon, you guys! Aren't you gonna welcome V back to life?"

It's no good. The other four Solar Prophecies and Erik are in a heated conversation. "What's wrong with them?"

"Let them finish, Speedy. Besides, it looks like they have Erik hypnotized. Or perhaps bored to death… I can't really tell."

"But still, I wonder why they don't talk."

"I'm not exactly sure either. And I command them."

"Can you speak with them telepathically?"

– Shadow Prophecies? Can you hear me?

– …

"Afraid not, V. They're thoughtless too."

"That's strange." Twirling my hair, I contemplate a reason. "Speedy? Do you know why only the Solar Prophecies talk?"

"No," it replies hesitantly.

"You sure? It didn't take you a while to think that through."

"V, remember. It doesn't think."

"Hey!"

"Haha! You're right."

"So, is this…?" I try to understand why Vizor's hair has three different colors.

"Oh, right!" Vizor slaps his forehead in remembrance. "You're gonna love this. This is the product when you combine your prophecies' powers with mine! The chaos form!"

"WOAH! So… Chaos Vizor?"

"That's right."

The Solar Prophecies finally finish their conversation with Erik.

When they turn to try and find the others, they air-flip at the sight of Azilez, Griff, and me.

"Oh, you guys made it out!" The Power Prophecy nearly runs into me.

"Well, this is a shocker! I thought you were long gone. Look at V getting the hang of his own body. Very well done," Wisdom adds.

"Aww, you guys." I look to the ground and twiddle my right foot.

Suddenly, the other two prophecies huddle around me and ask questions as if they're paparazzi. I try to make out each individual question, but then the building unexpectedly shakes.

"What was that?" Griff looks up.

Another rumble.

"Who's there?" D grips his pickaxe tighter.

"Everyone! They're coming! Come! We have a war to win!"

With one horribly unitized battle cry, we fly out of the hole in the hospital's roof.

We land in between an army of angry citizens and an actual army. The entire traffic flow of San Francisco has been halted. You can hear all of the angry, blaring car horns ordering the giant crowd to move.

"For real? Right in the middle of the road?"

"I'm gonna miss my 5:00!"

"Why do aliens love this city so much?"

"Quiet! All of you!" One of the two army leaders shows himself. His flaming-red hair, solemn expression, and commanding, blue eyes cause the furious San Franciscans to quiet down.

Here's the odd part though: it's not the Omoh sapien army we're facing. It's an army of vampires.

Hazy's eyes pop. How can I blame her? She thought she and Drac were the only ones left. And now It looks like her entire race is standing against her. She notices the two vampires in front of her. "Dante? Myra?"

"Huh? Who are you?" Myra raises one of her glaringly sliver eyebrows and stands next to Dante.

"Come now!" Both excited and confused, Drac lands on the pavement next to his daughter. "We're so happy to see you! We thought all the vampires were eliminated. You don't remember Hazy? Do you at least remember me?"

We hear a faint whisper among the two. It's a little hard to catch exactly what they're saying because both are wearing very thick, furry jackets. Dante's is blood-red, and Myra's is dark-blue.

"You don't ring any bells either. Sorry, kiddies, but end of line for all of you."

"No…"

"HAHAHAHAHAHA! What an awkward reunion! I love it!" Out from behind the army, the Hell Prophecy reveals itself.

"Finally came back from orbit, did you?" Vizor smirks.

"You don't scare me, Vizor. Not even with the energies of BOTH prophecies. I have far more tools at my disposal than you do!"

"Quality over quantity, buddy. These guys are all I need."

"Aw! That's cute, Vizor!" Azilez preemptively shouts out. "But wait a second. What did the Hell Prophecy mean by power of 'both' prophecies? Did you combine the two or something?"

"That's exactly what I did."

Griff and Azilez exchange glances.

"Wait a second… Another form of chaos?" Griff puts his hand on the side of his head.

"Yes. Exactly."

"No way!"

"That's a neat experiment, Vizor."

"HELLO? Army in front of you. Remember? The whole 'end of the line' thing?" Myra tries to remind us of our peril.

"Wait your turn. I'll kill you next."

"NO! Don't!" Hazy puts her hands out and stands against us.

"Huh? What do you think you're doing?" Vizor crosses his arms. "Get out of the way."

"I won't let you! I finally have a chance to bring them all back?"

Dante sharpens his right fang with his fingernail. "Do you know what she's going on about?"

"Your guess is as good as mine, Dante."

"I don't think you get it, Hazy."

"No, you don't."

"The Hell Prophecy has them possessed."

"Huh? Possessed?" Dante feels too proud to just accept that. "I'm in complete control! Watch! Go, everyone! Destroy these misfits!"

"Aaaaaaahhhhhhh!"

"Dante…? Myra…?"

"Stand back, Hazy! You too, Drac! Drac?" Z looks around as he sporadically summons golf balls to slam into the vampires. But as he turns around, a group of them are in his face. "Golf balls, anyone?" The group of vampires dog-piles on top of him. In the middle of all of the dust, fists, and fangs, Z explodes into his extreme form. "C'mon, every-one! These vampires aren't gonna fight themselves!"

"Fact." Vizor clenches his fist and flies next to Z.

"Right behind you, D!" Azilez summons one of her hoverboards.

"Where are Drac and Griff though?"

"Grrrrrrraaaahhh!" Slowly turning around with slightly con-cerned looks, we find Drac in his dragon form, chasing the Hell Prophecy across the bay.

"Woooooohoooooo!" A sonic boom fills the air as a rocket car takes to the skies. Its pilot? Griff.

"Where'd you get that, buddy?" I ask.

"You know how Azilez can materialize rainbows?"

"Yeah? Did she do it for you?"

"Yup!"

"It suits you!"

"Thanks! Let's get 'em!" Griff tries to come in range of the army, but is afraid he'll burn the civilians in the process. Definitely something he doesn't want to do.

"Vizor, do me a favor and move all of these people somewhere."

"On it!"

"Ha, please! Like one guy's gonna carry… aaaahhhh!"

Vizor uses the same purple sphere he used to kidnap my family to transfer the crowd to safety. How ironic.

"Get me down from here!"

"You're welcome." Vizor takes it as a "thank you".

"Oh, no, you don't!" Dante nearly pummels Vizor, but he evades in time. "Come at me."

"Don't need to tell me twice." Vizor can't use his hands to fight. Despite that, his kicks seem to be enough to fend off Dante's swift bites. "What is all of this energy?"

"I already told you." Vizor winds up one last kick. "You're possessed."

"What's that got to do with–?" BANG! One colossal kick to the chest, and Dante meteors into the San Francisco Bay.

"From my closest companions to enemies…" Hazy hears the giant kick from atop the Ghirardelli building.

"Grrraaahhh!" Drac's cry sounds urgent. Hazy turns to see the Hell Prophecy pinning Drac to a small beach.

"Daddy?" Hazy yells out. He doesn't seem to hear her. From where she is, no one can hear her. "What am I doing?" She looks at her hands. After taking a few deep breaths, she realizes: "If I want my friends back" — she takes a look at her dad — "I have to fight for them!" She jumps off the building and molds herself into a dragon. Unlike Drac's dragon form, Hazy's form is much more petite. Instead of the rough, tough, and scaly dragon skin, her exterior is made of a slick silver lining, with blades on her arms for close combat. With no time to spare, she jets forward. By the time it notices her, the Hell Prophecy can't do anything about it. The blade is already on it. "You like Hell? I'll send you back there!"

"Well, now. My little girl. Now a dragon!"

"I have to do something. I can't just let the Hell Prophecy do what it wants with our kin."

Drac gives her a smile of approval, but the gratification is premature. The Hell Prophecy materializes a hand and drags Hazy down into the depths of the bay.

"My girl!" Drac dives, head first.

Vizor gently places his purple orb near a cow farm in Central California. "Stay here. If you don't want to get killed."

"Where are we? My family is worried sick right about now!"

Vizor simply rolls his eyes and leaves, knowing he has more important matters to attend to. He flies back to the bay, looking for the Hell Prophecy. He picks up a sign of Hazy and Drac in the bay's floor.

"You are going down! To the ground!"

"We're in the ground!"

"That's quite the mouth on you, Hazy."

"Vizor?"

"Must you eavesdrop on me at all times, Vizor?" The Hell Prophecy is out to kill him.

Diving into the water, he rebuts: "Well, when it involves the fate of Hazy and Drac's people, then yes."

"You are a pain."

"Funny. V said the same thing at one point. Now he's my friend."

"I wouldn't dream of that."

"'Cause your dreams are nightmares in Hell!" Vizor flies around the prophecy so quickly that he creates a waterspout. Expecting it, the Hell Prophecy flies out of the water.

"Ha, too slow!"

"Take two."

"Huh?" The waterspout expands into a giant whirlpool with enough force to keep it still. "No!"

"Oh! I have a better idea!" Vizor dives into the bay.

"Where are you going?" Vizor flies out of the water with Hazy and Drac. They make sure to position themselves so that they don't miss the Hell Prophecy. "Oh…"

"You might feel possessed after this." Vizor cracks his knuckles. The three charge into the one rock. They exert such force that as the Hell Prophecy hits the bottom of the bay, the very air of San Francisco shakes.

"That's it. It's done."

"Look!" Drac uses one of his giant fingers to point at the rest of the vampire army. All of them are released from their mental prisons.

Dante climbs out of the bay coughing up water. Hazy reverts back to her regular form and rushes for him.

"Dante!"

"H… Hazy?"

Hazy holds him tight, but she makes sure not to hug him as hard as she had hugged Azilez. "Oh, Dante. You're back!" A tear runs down Dante's jacket from Hazy's face.

"Where am I? This doesn't look like Transylvania. Or did the humans get to it?"

"No. Quite the opposite actually." Z, D, Griff, Azilez, and I all fly down to where Hazy, Dante, Vizor, and Drac are. "They helped me save you."

"Really? I'm confused. My head hurts. And my chest," Dante says as Vizor starts to whistle.

Near the rest of the collapsed army, Myra is lying down. Drac changes back to his standard form and runs to her aid. "Do you remember me now?"

She turns her head and smiles. "How can I forget? Drac?"

"Yes! They really are back!"

"All right! Everything's OK then!" Azilez jumps up and down like she used to in fifth grade.

Just then, the Solar and Shadow Prophecies show up, and they… fly right past me? They all rush to Vizor, who is looking down into the bay.

"Huh? What's up, guys?"

– *You can't feel it, V? The Dark Spirit's voice sounds frightened.*

– *Oh. Now I do.*

– *It's coming.*

– *The Hell Prophecy? I expected that.*

– *No, V. You still haven't caught on?*

I don't know what the Dark Spirit is referring to, but this mystery energy creates the biggest earthquake San Francisco has ever seen. And that's saying something, considering this city is known for its massive earthquakes. This particular tremor is so catastrophic that the buildings aren't just falling apart; they're flying across the bay.

"No! It's still alive!" Hazy turns around, flaring with rage.

"YOU FOOLS. I'M NEITHER ALIVE NOR DEAD. I JUST AM."

"What was that?" Azilez holds D like a stuffed teddy bear.

Griff, Vizor, and the prophecies are staring into the bay. "How? I thought It couldn't leave Its chair…"

"What was that, Griff?" Azilez tries to hear him over the earthquake.

"YOU HAVE STALLED FOR LONG ENOUGH! VIZOR! V! GRIFF! AZILEZ! Z! D! HAZY! DRAC! ALL OF YOU!"

The bay's water turns bright red, and the Hell Prophecy, with three cracks in it, surfaces. Upon returning, its wounds heal. A giant red ring appears under it. "I NEVER THOUGHT I'D SEE THE DAY." Volcanoes and stalactites replace the destroyed buildings.

"No!"

"OH, YES. YOU ASKED FOR THIS!" The tips of a molten-red chair pop out of the ring, then the back frame, then the base. From the depths of Hell, the Devil makes Its grand debut on Earth.

"HAHAHAHAHAHAHA!"

We would all cower in fear, but…

"Uh, Devil?"

"HUH? WHERE ARE YOU?"

"You're facing the wrong way…" Azilez slaps her forehead.

"HMM?" The Devil tilts Its head around. "OH. GIVE ME A SEC." It uses the red ring to lift and turn the chair around.

"HAHAHAHA!"

"Oh, brother…"

"We're in for it now, guys. This is it!" Hazy clenches her right fist.

Chapter 32

The Devil's Playthings

"**I** CAN'T BELIEVE YOU ALL DRAGGED ME UP HERE."

"Technically, we didn't." Azilez's timing is as sharp as ever.

"THIS IS STARTING TO GET ANNOYING RATHER THAN HU-MOUROUS." The Devil holds Its head. "SLAVES, GET DOWN HERE!"

The Devil's echo destroys the remaining glass on the toppled buildings. We have to close our ears just so it doesn't destroy those too.

A cloud of reflecting light becomes visible in the newly formed blood-red atmosphere. Syzor, Eliza, and Pippin all come down first, and the rest of the army follows.

"Your Dastardliness, we have no sign of Vizor on Treah any-where."

"It's like he vanished."

"We checked every single crevice."

"Except for the one in your heads." Vizor walks into the army's view.

"What did you just–?"

"That's quite the light show." Syzor takes out his hair blades and cuts Pippin off.

"Don't get any funny ideas now. You might hurt yourself."

"Please. Remember who you're talking to."

"I'd advise you to do the same." Vizor trailblazes black flames until he rams into Syzor.

"Hey! Cheap shot." Eliza takes out her brush and fires a quick crystal at Vizor.

He grabs it out of midair, turns around to make sure Eliza can look at his face, and munches on it.

"Ugh… disgusting."

Eliza takes a step back, just to get away from Vizor's menacing eyes.

Pippin tries to conk Vizor with his blades, but upon impact with the flames coming from Vizor's body, the blades melt.

"How?"

"Don't you know?" Vizor grabs him by his shirt collar. "I'm the chosen one." From a distance, I give him a thumbs up. He winks back at me. "Let your friends know. That way THIS won't happen to them." Vizor throws Pippin into the air. On his way back down, Pippin receives a firm kick to the stomach, which hurls him into Eliza and Syzor. "You're next." Vizor points at the Devil.

"BWAHAHAHAHAHA! VERY NICE. VERY NICE INDEED." The Devil claps Its hands and stomps Its feet for Vizor, causing another earthquake in the process. "ALTHOUGH IT DOESN'T LOOK LIKE YOUR KIND IS DONE WITH YOU JUST YET."

"Huh?"

– V! Eliza's after Hazy! She's behind you, underground.

– I see her.

In the nick of time, I claw Eliza out of the ground and throw her at Vizor. Instantly, the Omoh sapien army charges at me.

"They gotta get through us first." Griff steps up.

"No way out for you guys." Drac transforms into his dragon form once more and takes to the skies.

"I'm with Griff! V, leave 'em to us." Azilez is raring to go.

"You go and deal with their Master." Hazy holds her arms out, triggering her dragon transformation.

"We're always here for you!" D holds his pickaxe like a sword.

"I got this one, brah." Z turns around and gives me a little smirk.

"Don't call me that again." I slap myself on the forehead.

"OK, bro."

Much better.

All of their bravery is still not enough to halt the army. They still want my head on their blades, but then…

Vizor flies in front of the other six. The Omoh sapiens transform from lion-hearted warriors into cats in a cradle. Vizor does nothing but stare at them.

"WHAT ARE YOU DOING? HE'S RIGHT IN FRONT OF YOU! KILL HIM!"

No response. All of them just sit there with wide eyes. Some even get teary-eyed.

"Is this truly what we're capable of?" Syzor walks up.

– UH-OH. THEY'RE CATCHING ON…

"This power… It's unlike anything I've ever imagined." Something clicks in Eliza's mind. I feel she's starting to have a better understanding of the power of chaos energy.

"Does everyone get it now?"

"I do!" Pippin prematurely smiles and throws his right hand in the air, thinking he is now a master of the element.

Vizor turns around and stares into his eyes. Pippin's smile fades away and he intently focuses on Vizor's eyes. He even drools a little bit… Eww.

"I SAID KILL HIM!" The Devil pounds Its fist onto Its chair, causing a volcano to erupt behind It. And still no response.

– You feel it too, Dark Spirit?

– It's incredible! I never knew there were locks inside the Omoh sapiens' minds.

– I don't think that's it.

– What do you mean?

– I think they were designed that way.

– Designed? Wait a second!

The Dark Spirit looks at the Devil from inside me. It sees how nervous It has become.

– Of course! If the Devil let the Omoh sapiens use that kind of power, imagine the collateral damage. A bunch of wild savages with near-limitless

power… Unfathomable. That's why the Shadow Prophecies were hidden. The Devil designed the Omoh sapiens in such a way that they thought they were powerful, but they weren't even close to true power.

– Ha! That's funny. It sounds like you're describing humans more than aliens.

"This is chaos energy, everybody. The power of V's Solar Prophecies combined with these Shadow Prophecies — two distant energies coming together to form something even more powerful. That's chaos. It's not measured by the limit of your strength, but rather…"

"NO! DON'T!"

"The limit of your mind!"

In that instant, all of the chains inside the Omoh sapien race break. Their minds are set free. Now they can find their own paths and strengths.

"ENOUGH!" The Devil presses a big red button on the side of Its chair, and, almost instantly, the chains fly back onto every alien's mind. They struggle within themselves. They pound their heads in an attempt to break free, but it's no use. The Omoh sapiens' hair blades start to point outward like a bull's horns, and their eyes bleed red like rivers. The Devil has complete control of them. "NOW FOR THE MAIN EVENT!" One final set of metaphorical chains is sent out to Vizor. He merely smiles and stands there, waiting for them to come. Not a good idea. The Devil is not anything to mess with. Before the chains get to Vizor, I use the Dark Spirit's energy to kick them into the stratosphere.

"Not gonna happen!" I stand firm, with my right foot on a small rock.

"LOOKS LIKE YOUR FRIEND SPARED YOU SOME PAIN, VIZOR."

"Ha. I could've tanked–"

"Vizor, no. Not this time."

"V?"

"Trust me, I know." Vizor now realizes what I'm talking about, takes a deep breath, and crosses his arms.

"Right. Sorry. I guess I'm starting to think I'm invincible."

"Don't! Especially not now. Bad time to get cocky. We are dealing with one of the strongest, if not THE strongest, evil force in the universe."

"All right. I get it now. Thanks for bringing me back to reality."

"Reality?" I smile and turn my head, looking at the tri-colored alien in front of me. Apparently, I'm in reality.

"Hahahahaha!" Both of us start to laugh.

"YOU THINK THIS IS FUNNY?" The Devil's scream sends both of us careening into a blown-apart Ghirardelli factory. The shattered sign is a glaring reminder of I'm fighting for.

"We're gonna need help."

Vizor shakes off the excess debris on his head. "Agreed."

"Let's show this freak show what we're made of!" We fly out of the remains of the building. I look back one last time.

– *This city will be safe again… I promise.*

– *Eventually,* the Dark Spirit adds.

We return to the scene of the bloodthirsty aliens and our six friends fighting them off.

"Look at yourself! Snap out of it!" Azilez uses a rainbow hammer to block Eliza's onslaught of blade attacks.

"I HAVE NO SELF." She doesn't let up.

"Die, Griff! My shameless copy! Hiiiyyyaaa!"

"I'm not even sure if he's possessed or not. He's not much of a threat either way." Griff closes the hood of his rocket car and uses the thruster engines to knock Pippin into the pavement.

"Azilez, Griff, Z, D, Drac, and Hazy." Vizor uses his chaos powers to make his voice echo so it gets heard. The six of them fly into the sky to where Vizor and I are. "It's time."

"Time for what? Fighting? We were in the middle of that! C'mon!" Azilez signals Vizor to follow her.

"No! That's not what I meant." Vizor holds his hand out.

Before he can say more though: "GRRAAHH!" With a sneeze-like motion, the Devil spews fireballs from Its mouth at us. The fire rate grows into that of a machine gun.

"I got it. This time, I'm sure." Vizor takes out his hair blades, dips them in the flames around his body, and uses them to deflect the rapid shots back at the Devil. Realizing that the smaller fireballs aren't as effective, the Devil charges up a sphere the size of the city. Vizor spins his blades around, preparing to deflect this one last shot. On impact, he seems to be doing fine, but the fireball begins to get the best of him. He needs help.

"Nrrgh!" Using my pure extreme form, I push with him. Then Griff. Then Hazy. Then Drac. Then Z. Then D. And, lastly, Azilez. The energies of the seven pure extreme forms and one chaos form are enough to bounce back the shot into the Devil's open mouth. It falls back, with Its chair, into the Pacific Ocean. It creates a tsunami so big that Japan might actually feel the splash It makes.

"Quick! While It's down, gather everyone! Let me bestow this strength upon you." Vizor closes his eyes and puts both his hands up like a conductor in front of a symphony orchestra. Here it comes… the evolution of the extreme forms, unique to all of us: chaos!

"I'm ready!" Griff jumps out of his rocket car and gets bright-orange eyes and pure-white hair. At the back of his head, a giant amount of orange-colored energy shoots out like his jet car's engine. His eyes turn a light yellow.

"Behind every rainbow, there's a storm front!" Azilez changes drastically. Her entire outfit swaps. Her leather jacket turns into a three-layer blue dress with puffs of white fur on its rims. Her paintbrush extends into a long golden staff with a giant diamond in the middle. Her right eye maintains her normal brown, but her left gets a new gold hue. Her hair maintains its color but changes texture. It becomes smooth and glossy, as though she's about to perform in a Broadway production.

"This is for Dante and Myra." Hazy reverts back to her normal state. Her hair strands are half black and half silver. Even though she isn't a dragon anymore, her arm blades stay on her elbows. While in her chaos state, she has them, regardless of what shape or animal she is. Her left eye maintains her extreme form's pink color, but her right gains a new, dark red.

"I'll get the vampires up and running again!" Drac hides in his cape, and comes out with slight differences. First, the inside of his cape no longer looks like space; it looks like a black hole. His eyes are the only ones to have the same color: a bright, creamy blue. His hair color becomes exactly the same as Hazy's. Glistening mini spikes grow on the outsides of his cape.

"This is for putting V in a coma!" D transforms into a deadly sage of nature. If Mother Nature ever had a son, it'd be Chaos D. His eyes become a bright, sunflower yellow, and the area around his right eye gets a tattoo shaped like blowing leaves. His pickaxe morphs into a ten-foot-long medieval pendulum. His hair flies around like crazy, and it even spews out green leaves.

"I'm taking you to the links!" Z's hair flies like D's and gets a rusty-red color. About 20 golf balls fly around him like electrons around a nucleus. The shield will smack any enemy that comes too close. Z's eyes become the color of his club: silver, with patches of dark green.

"The legend lives and grows, Devil. You won't bring us down! Nothing will!" My hair transitions to every color imaginable. If you try naming them all in your lifetime, you'd probably run out of time. My hands steam white smog like they're about to explode, my right eye becomes a bright scarlet red, and my left eye takes on Dark V's eye color.

Oh, boy, some serious stuff's about to go down, isn't it? Lock and load, people. This'll be a wild ride.

Chapter 33

Uninvited Guests

"YOU ALL ACTUALLY HURT ME." The Devil reattaches Its jaw into the correct place. "I NEVER IMAGINED IT'D COME TO THIS. EIGHT NUISANCES VERSUS THE DEVIL." It clicks another button on Its chair, causing it to levitate, giving It full 360-degree control of Its chair. It can virtually see any attack that comes Its way.

"Make that number nine." On the shore of one of the many beaches of San Francisco, Dante punches the ground to help himself get up.

"No, stay." Hazy becomes protective.

"How can I?" Dante smiles. "The lives of everyone here depend on this fight. I will NOT back down now!"

"I can't stay down either, little Hazy." Myra helps Dante up. "The Omoh sapiens, the humans, the vampires… all of us! All of our existences depend on taking down this Monstrosity. No matter how tattered we look, we're still fighting with you."

"But…"

"No objections allowed."

"Just be careful."

"PLEASE! I'M NOT HERE TO WATCH YOU GUYS MAKE UP. I'M HERE TO DESTROY WHAT GOD AND I HAVE CREATED. AFTER THAT, I WILL DESTROY THE UNBOUND TRAITOR FOR GOOD."

"So You're after It too? If that's the case, why are we fighting?"

"YOU THINK I'LL HAVE A PROBLEM GETTING TO THAT PA-THETIC LITTLE HINDRANCE AFTER I KILL YOU?"

– *Will It?*

– *The Devil should be able to sense where the Unbound Evil is. As long as It is in this universe.*

– *So then it's weird that the Devil hasn't destroyed the Unbound–*

– *NO MORE OF THAT, YOU TWO.*

"So it's true then! It's not that You HAVEN'T destroyed the Unbound Evil yet; it's that You CAN'T."

"YOU QUESTION MY ABILITY TO DESTROY? THE VERY THING I'M KNOWN FOR?"

Hmm… now that I think about that, does it matter? Who cares if I question It? What matters is that the Devil tried to stop the conversation between the Dark Spirit and me. That says a lot. It's afraid!

"Yes, I do. You truly don't know where the real Unbound Evil is hiding!"

"YES, IT'S TRUE. THE MAIN REASON I'M TERRORIZING EVERY-THING HERE IS TO LURE THE REAL UNBOUND EVIL TO ME. IT SEEMS IMPOSSIBLE TO FATHOM, BUT IT LOOKS LIKE THE UNBOUND EVIL IS NOT IN THE UNIVERSE ANYMORE. IT'S LIKE IT VANISHED."

"Ha! You're off Your game, Master." A voice echoes from beyond the crimson clouds. Everyone looks to see where the voice has come from. Except Vizor. He seems to be angrier now.

"Vizor? You know who that was, don't you?"

"How can I not know the voice of MY OWN LITTLE BROTHER?" Heads turn to gaze at Vizor. Out from the clouds, X descends. He has black, straight hair, golden hair blades, a green cape, but, most shocking-ly, he wears a blood-red shirt with a white circle and a black swastika in the center. That looks familiar. That's not what I think it is, is it?

"No, you didn't!" Griff senses their presence. The stench of the worst Earthly evil known: the Nazis.

"What can I say? I need an army of my own!"

Vizor is not having any of X's games. He grabs him by the shirt collar. "FOOL! You think you can control something like–"

"Time for some fun!"

"Stay down." Vizor kicks X down into the bay from a few thousand feet in the air. He doesn't resist at all and obeys Vizor's order.

With the clouds still open, the blitzkrieg follows their leader into the sky zone where Hazy, Drac, Griff, Azilez, Z, D, Vizor, and I are. At the helm of the few thousand people is Adolf, the man with the largest murder count in human history.

"So this is America? Looks like I already visited. HAHAHA!"

– *It's here. You feel It, Griff?*

– *How can I not? It's practically right in front of us.*

– *HOW CLEVER. The Devil decides to actually join our conversation* instead of disrupting it.

– *So Treah was Its hiding spot?*

"Adolf, the most horrendous man I've heard of, is actually floating in front of me?" Azilez grasps the gravity of the situation. "Wait a second. You killed yourself! You're not Adolf."

"Foolish little girl!" The little shrub of hair on Adolf's philtrum scrunches. "Have you forgotten about the freezing mechanism the Omoh sapiens invented? I've been hidden in there ever since I 'killed myself'."

"So you never really killed yourself?"

"That's not all the historians got wrong, Azilez." Griff intently stares into Adolf's eyes.

"Huh?"

"The Unbound Evil is inside this 'man'."

"AND HAS BEEN FOR A LONG TIME." When the Devil reaches out to grab the Nazi leader, a giant purple shock sends Its hand back into the chair.

"Fool. I have pets, once more. You think I'm going to fight you all? I'll just have them do it for me."

"I TAUGHT IT WELL…" the Devil tries to make Itself feel better at the worst possible time.

"Really? That's all You can say? I don't think You realize how powerful this man is."

"AND I DON'T THINK YOU REALIZE HOW DUMB YOU SOUND."

"What does that mean?"

"V, Adolf isn't human," Griff says.

"Wait, then that makes him an Omoh sapien!" That'd explain a lot, actually. No wonder he enjoyed devouring so many innocent souls.

"Exactly."

"I DON'T CARE WHAT RACE ADOLF IS FROM. I JUST CARE ABOUT THAT WRETCHED SPIRIT INSIDE HIM."

This'll definitely work. The Devil's mind is vulnerable right now. If I irritate it enough, It'll be revved up to fight the Unbound Evil alongside us.

"It did absorb You the last time You fought It."

"SILENCE! I WON'T FALL FOR THIS TRICKERY. I'M THE MASTER OF PRANKSTERS. I DO NOT SIMPLY GET PRANKED. NOW, GIVE ME YOUR ENERGIES AND I'LL DESTROY THIS MISFIT ONCE AND FOR ALL."

"We can fight It TOGETHER, but there's no way I'm giving You this power, Devil. I think the rest of us can agree." I turn back to make sure I have everyone else's approval.

"WRONG ANSWER."

"Well, there was never a right one…" Azilez comes in at the worst possible time, once more.

"Blitzkrieg, march!" The soldiers behind Adolf walk on air. They all hold different types of weapons. Some have pistols. Some have grenades. Some wear gas masks and have very colorful tubes in their hands. Some even have swords.

"Vizor! You take the Nazis with Hazy, Drac, and Z. The rest of us will handle the Devil."

"Sounds good."

"That won't be necessary, everyone."

"WHAT NOW?" The Devil pounds the side of Its chair in frustration.

"Hold on… It's Electrox!"

"What? Really?" I rush to Griff's side. "And it has brought reinforcements!" The citizens of Zaptropolis are a group of magnet people led by their king, Electrox the Third. They all have lightning rods at the top of their magnet bodies, making their lightning strikes more accurate.

"Electrox!"

"V. Griff. I came as soon as I could rally up all of my men. We're at your command!"

"Hey, Electrox, don't be so quick to give them ALL the authority." A man sitting on an electrically powered hoverboard flies next to Electrox. It's the FBI agent we met on our last adventure, Melok.

"You're commander of the magnet people too?"

"Well… co-commander, yes. It looks like you have your hands full. Which do you want us to tackle first: the Devil or the Nazi army?"

"The blitzkrieg. That'll help."

"You heard him! Go, men!" Melok puts on some gloves and pulls out a metal pole from the pocket on his hoverboard. Electrox charges it up and Melok looks like he's holding a bolt of lightning.

"Ahhhhhhhh!"

"You two again. Looks like you can't get enough of Me! If it's death you want, it's death you'll get. Attack them, men!"

"Thanks, guys!"

"Don't thank us just yet, V. Now, get your head in the game." With that, Melok takes off.

"Hey, guys," Vizor says to Hazy, Drac, and Z. "Let's go help V, now."

"Can we pick up two more on the way?" Hazy's referring to Dante and Myra.

"Sure. C'mon." Vizor puts his arm around Hazy. We all regroup and fly toward the sand where Dante and Myra stand.

"So, Hazy, Drac… I'm sorry for all of my trouble." Dante kicks the sand around.

"As long as you're back now, that's all that matters." Drac smiles at the two of them.

"Wow, how flashy you look, count."

"This is the power of the humans and the Omoh sapiens combined."

"Really now? I never knew that was possible."

Drac turns around and looks at Vizor. "Neither did I."

"TIME TO END THIS." The Devil slams both of Its fists on the sides of Its grand throne. The shockwave sends all of us rocketing into the sky and close to the Devil. "THIS POWER WILL BE MINE. AND I WILL DESTROY THE UNBOUND EVIL. BY MYSELF."

"Try us." Vizor smirks.

This is it. There are ten of us standing against a Devil and Its army of mindless drones: the entire Omoh sapien race.

Chapter 34

The Thirst for Power

Syzor charges headlong, pointing his hair blades at us. Pippin follows behind him.

Vizor enlarges the flames on his head and dive-flips onto the two reckless Omoh sapiens, sending them off to the bay. Coincidentally, at the same time, X emerges from the sea.

"What just happened...?" He holds his head. After he surfaces, Pippin and Syzor land on X, toppling him into the bay again.

"Two down. About a few hundred million to go." Vizor cools his flames down back to normal size.

"RIGHT YOU ARE, METTLING FOOL. YOU'LL NEVER HAVE THE STRENGTH TO TAKE OUT ALL OF THEM."

"We don't have to." Azilez flies forward. "All we've gotta do is hammer YOU!"

"That's just the problem, Azilez," Griff says. "It's got an entire race of aliens as a shield!

— *There's a way to lure them all away, V. You want to try it?*

— *How so?* I ask Vizor.

— *Any great surge of energy will lure them like moths to a flame.*

Before I can respond, the entire Omoh sapien race dog-piles us. Z and D use a combination of golf balls, golf clubs, the pendulum, and trees to slow down as many as they can, but they can stop only so many.

"Time for some bling!" Azilez twirls her staff around to create several rainbow hands that scoop up whole groups of aliens at a time.

The Devil doesn't like that, of course, so It tries to swipe away the staff from her. Azilez holds the staff close to her chest to create a shield that protects her from the Devil's attempt to strip her of her power.

"You can't just take someone else's strength for Your own! That's something THEY taught me." She points to Griff and me.

"HOW ADORABLE." The Devil blows another fireball at us. Griff uses his newly acquired jet-engine hair and burns it to nothing. He then flies up to the Devil's hand, turns around, and uses his scorching hair to burn Its arm. Surprisingly, the flames on Griff are enough to actually hurt the Lord of Flames. The flames don't last very long, and the Devil's hand seems fine, but It's starting to worry.

"WHAT? NNNGGHH! HOW CAN YOU WORTHLESS TRASH BE ENOUGH TO ACTUALLY HARM ME? I CAN'T REMEMBER THE LAST TIME I FELT PAIN LIKE THAT!"

"Get with it, cross bones." Hazy rushes with her arm blades into the Devil's left arm. She is easily blown away. But she won't give up that easily anymore. After a swift recovery, she tries again. And again. And again. And again…

"STOP THIS WORTHLESS FARCE. IT WON'T LEAD TO ANY-THING GOOD."

"Right You are!" Drac comes in from behind the Devil and lights the top of Its head on fire with his mouth's flamethrower.

"MORE FIRE? AND, AGAIN, WHY THE PAIN?"

Something different happens with this flame. Once it hits the Devil, the Omoh sapiens freeze, seemingly trying to fight the mind-control mechanism in their heads.

"So that's it!" Azilez points her staff to the Devil's burning head. She fires a rainbow at it, keeping the flame enclosed, and thus burning longer. The Devil tries to tear the rainbow off Its head, but It can't grab what It can't comprehend.

"AHHH! THAT'S IT!" The Devil's eyes become pure-white, and all the Omoh sapiens except Vizor dissolve into blue sand. The giant sandstorm closes in on the Devil. When It comes out of Its blue shell, Its horns grow massive, bulging caps. It obtains two swords that look like they are made from Its spine, and a full set of scaly, red dragon armor. Yet

It still can't walk out of Its chair. "NOW THEN…"

"Stay strong, guys. We've got… umph!" A black figure with a shotgun in his hand tackles me. The blow sends me into the streets that were once San Francisco.

"V!" Azilez tries flying toward me.

"No." Vizor holds his hand out, not letting Azilez go any further. She raises an eyebrow. "I'll help V. You guys need to stop Devil-zilla. At the very least, stall it."

"Huh? Why stall?"

"Trust him, Azilez." Griff looks in their direction. "Go, Vizor."

Vizor gives a faint smile and flies off.

"Do you know something I don't, Griff?"

"V and he are the keys to ending this entire thing. They need to be with each other to unlock both prophecies' full power."

"I guess." She slumps a little.

"Hey, c'mon. Don't feel like that. We have another battle to fight. For them. For this city. For the entire universe."

"Well, when you put it like that…" She regains her composure and flicks her staff. Griff nudges her shoulder. They fly to help the other four already fighting the Devil.

Meanwhile… "Oww! What was that?"

"V!"

"Vizor?"

"Adolf!" The Nazi leader is standing in front of me with ten of those black-suited men. "What is this?" I give him a scowl.

"Come now! Don't be so distasteful." Adolf reveals his eyes from under his hat.

– There is no question. The Unbound Evil is inside him.

"Let's NOT focus on that slithering worm for a few seconds and let's talk to the man in front of you instead!" Adolf angrily points at himself.

"You know the 'It'?" Vizor lands next to me.

"Know the Unbound Evil? It offered to help me during the time of my cleansing."

"The Holocaust…" I whisper.

"Huh?"

"Holocaust, Vizor. It was the greatest mass killing in all of human history. Eleven million people were slaughtered by Germany in the name of 'cleansing' Europe. This man was the dictator of Germany at the time. His name is Adolf."

"Thanks for the summary, chosen one."

"So you do know about my legacy."

"Well, of course! How could I not? It's the very aspect of history I studied while becoming ruler of Germany."

"Whoa, whoa, whoa, whoa. Stop there. You studied my legacy to become the genocidal tyrant of Germany? *My* legacy is what inspired you to KILL?"

"My, my. Watch your tongue, V. Let's not confuse my methods with my noble goal."

"NOBLE? Are you out of your mind?"

"My goal was to make the world free from impurities. You and I: we aren't much different. We both strive for the same thing, a cleaner world. One where justice and peace of mind exist. Don't you want that? Come, V! I want you to join me."

"NEVER! You and I are NOTHING alike! You mistake me, Adolf."

"Oh? Do I now?" He tilts his head up and crosses his arms, then breaks into sarcastic, malicious laughter. "Together, we'll cleanse the world!"

"NO! I know my history well, Adolf. I know you didn't even want to lead Germany! You felt inclined to because you thought you were the 'chosen one'. But you aren't. You became a pawn to society and forced these people into submission. Well, I've got bad news for you, Adolf. Our goals are NOT the same."

"They aren't? If you're not trying to make a pure world, then what are you trying to do with this whole legacy of yours?"

"Do you realize how boring that would be?" My voice takes on Evil V's tone.

The black-suited guards point their weapons up. "Now, now, now, V. You wouldn't want to get a bullet through your head, would you?"

In silence and with my eyes closed, I walk toward him.

"Burn in Hell, V!" Adolf's guards shoot at only me. Vizor doesn't even try to get me out of there because he knows Adolf's weapons can't harm me.

"Been there, done that." I open my eyes and channel the power of Evil V. It spreads into my eyes, making them white again. And those two, soul-eating red dots stare into Adolf's eyes. All of the shots that his guards fire bounce off my body as if they were tennis balls.

"Keep firing, you worthless lot! It's one guy!"

"STOP!" Vizor's voice echoes through the broken buildings. The black-suited men look at him, ready to fire. Vizor isn't phased. He takes a step forward. "You aren't like him, Adolf. You might have been a long time ago. But now you aren't. It's because of the fake arsenal in front of you, fighting for you. V, I think I'm starting to understand now. That man is what happens when people like you are taken up by things like the Devil, things like the Unbound Evil. They're unable to control the evil within them. Evil takes over the very essence of who they are. The decent part of them is lost — molded, rusted, transformed into a rotten core. They become evil and nothing else. You: you are V, powerful and complete. Nothing and no one can get you down anymore. Not the Devil, not the Unbound Evil, and not society."

That last word surprises me: society — the very thing I'm fighting for.

"Let me put it in words you might understand, Adolf." I continue to stare at him. "Your own cowardice will be your death. You cower when your weapons cannot kill something. Because now they're all you have, and in the future they're all you'll ever be. And my goal? It's to change the world, with all I am. Unlike you, I fully embrace who I am, and am not caught up in things that don't matter — such as being a dictator, a soulless monarch. Think about that for a second. Do you honestly think society can rank who you are? And let that be satisfying? You'll die an honest death as a lying man."

"What are you saying?"

Vizor stomps toward Adolf. The men aim and fire. The bullets bounce off him too, and some are even consumed in his flames.

"What the…" Adolf can't believe that the weapons and tools he had once used to destroy lives can't even scratch them anymore. This realization makes his eyes widen. The mass killings… the death camps… the gas chambers… the many lives he silenced for the "purity of mankind": all mistakes that he's about to pay for. Yet he still has an evil smile plastered on his face. It's almost like he's physically sick. Vizor plows through the ten defenders and pounds Adolf in the chest, causing him to fall.

"Here's your second mistake, Adolf. LOOK AROUND!" Vizor becomes passionate. "This is what men like you bring to the world. Let's say you got what you wanted. THEN WHAT? Nothing remains! Everything is gone. And it's all…" — Vizor reaches for Adolf's head — "your fault." Vizor's hand touches Adolf's forehead. A giant black tornado flies through his skull and out into the sky. In the aftermath, Adolf lies dead as the life force has left him.

Vizor looks back and finds me stationary.

"OK, V. You can stop being creepy now."

As soon as we smile at each other, a giant gong bell fills the air. It sounds like a grand church bell: so soothing, so soft, as the sound waves hit your ears. Or so we think. The sound is so great, it forces Vizor and me to fall down.

"What's–"

Another one.

"!"

Another one.

"…"

And another one.

Vizor and I now lie on the ground, with our chaos forms subsided, unconscious.

Chapter 35

The Bad Guys Won?

Normally, I would never have expected to be beaten that quickly. It doesn't make sense to me. How can a bell sound drain our power? The power of friendship? The power of companionship?

An unknown amount of time passes, and I finally wake up, barely having enough energy to stand.

– *Dark Spirit?*

– *Nrrg…huh? What'd I miss?*

– *I wish I could answer that. It seems Vizor's not even up yet.*

– *Then this situation is most grave, V. Who knows what could've changed?*

At first, I lightly tap Vizor with my big toe. When I see he's not responding, I grab him and shake his entire body.

"Ahh! Who? What? When? Where?" He jumps up, paranoid. He goes for his hair blades, but when he notices that it's just me standing in front of him, he calms down. "What's going on, V? Everything is still."

"It seems like the battle has finished." The Dark Spirit jumps out of me.

"Well…" Vizor grabs the sharp end of his right hair blade. "What of the others?"

That's when my eyes pop. If they, too, have heard this bell sound, then… "I just woke up. I couldn't tell you."

"Then let's not waste any more time than we already have." Vizor takes out his blades.

"OK then." I solemnly nod. We attempt to fly, but face-plant onto the pavement after jumping only about a foot high.

"Ow." I would've said that louder if there weren't any asphalt in my mouth.

"Heh. Klutz." Vizor temporarily catches himself by sticking his hair blades into the street. But his lack of strength makes him release his grip, and he falls chest-first onto the ruined street. "Why are we so weak?" Vizor gets frustrated.

"I'm not exactly sure how this is possible, but I've never heard a bell sound like that in My existence."

"So you can't even clarify for us?" There goes my idea of the Dark Spirit trying to make us feel better.

"C'mon, V. Even if we can't fly, we've still got our feet."

"Right…" I'm still trying to imagine how our power could've been stripped from us just by a bell sound. As I'm running, I'm shaking just thinking about it. There's no power great enough to shatter the bonds of my friendships, right? There's no way!

"Uh-oh. It's worse than I imagined." We finally get a view of the Devil's chair. Lying limply at the gravel floor of its base is everyone who had bravely fought with us.

Vizor and I look at each other, and know that this is a point of no return. Something big is going to happen soon, if it hasn't happened already. We rush to our friends' side.

"Z? D? Griff? Azilez?" I find all of them piled on top of each other.

"Hazy? Drac? Dante? Myra?" Vizor looks to the bays of the city. He finds the magnet people and Melok scattered throughout one specific area. Everyone seems lifeless. Even the Devil is slumping in Its chair. And the worst part of all: both sets of prophecies are missing.

"Griff? Griff! Wake up!" I shake him like I did Vizor, but it doesn't work this time. "Azilez, get up!" I get frustrated when she also doesn't wake up. I punch the soil, almost hitting Griff in the process.

"NOW… URGH… IS NOT THE TIME." The Devil grabs the left arm of Its chair with Its right arm, readjusting Its balance so It can sit straight again. Despite this, It is still dizzy. "THERE IS LITTLE TIME, YOU TWO. IN BRIEF, THE UNBOUND EVIL COLLECTED ALL OF THE

PROPHECY ENERGY PRESENT AND IS NOW MAKING ITS WAY TO THE SUN. LIKELY TO DESTROY EVERYTHING."

"How was It able to just take the energy? You know something, don't You? Something You don't want to tell-"

"IT'S SOMETHING THAT NO ONE KNOWS EXCEPT FOR GOD AND ME. SOMETHING NO MORTAL IS TO EVER KNOW."

"Huh? A divine secret?"

"SURE. LET'S GO WITH THAT. ANYWAY, THE HEAVEN PROPHECY AND HELL PROPHECY ARE UNIQUE. WHEN CLAPPED TOGETHER, THE FORCE RESONATING BETWEEN THE TWO DRAINS ALL ENERGY FROM ALL LIFE FORMS IN THE AREA. I'M AMAZED THAT YOU TWO EVEN SURVIVED."

I'm just dumbfounded that something like that even exists. If it's something that the Devil and God knew about, why didn't They take away the prophecies' abilities to drain all that power? I know this isn't exactly the greatest time to be wondering, but still…

"So that was the bell sound? The clapping of the two?"

"YES."

"What about everyone else?" I ask, shaking in nervous anticipation of what I might hear.

"THEIR FATES… ARE UNDECIDED."

"That's not like You to say that." Vizor raises an eyebrow, grabbing his chest as he gasps for air, out of exhaustion.

"LOOK, I'M USUALLY NOT THIS GENEROUS, BUT ALL WORLDS ARE AT STAKE HERE. I NEVER THOUGHT I'D EVER HAVE TO GIVE THIS TO ANYONE, BUT…"

"But what?" The Devil is a hot mess right now, both literally and metaphorically. I never thought I'd ever see It this out of sync.

"YOU TWO… YOU HAVE A BOND THAT SURPASSES ALMOST ANYTHING I'VE EVER SEEN. TO SHOW LOVE AND COMPASSION TOWARD VIZOR THE WAY YOU DID, V… AND MY EYES GAZE UPON ALL OF CREATION. DON'T EXPECT TO GET A COMPLIMENT LIKE THAT EVER AGAIN."

I have to ask that question now. It's buzzing in my head. "But hold on. If You knew You could drain the prophecies' energies, why didn't You just do that? Instead, You fought us."

"TWO REASONS. FIRSTLY, DO YOU THINK I'D REVEAL A SECRET AS WELL-KEPT AS THAT TO A CIVILIZED AREA? AND SECONDLY, EVEN IF I WANTED TO, I COULDN'T. I DIDN'T EVEN KNOW THAT THE PROPHECY OF HEAVEN AND THE PROPHECY OF HELL COULD ABSORB THE OTHER PROPHECIES' ENERGIES. I ONLY THOUGHT THEY COULD NULLIFY THEM. YOU KNOW, CANCEL THEM OUT. IT WAS AT THE MOMENT THE UNBOUND EVIL DRAINED ALL ENERGY WITH THOSE TWO PROPHECIES THAT I DECIDED THAT THIS IS A MOST GRAVE SITUATION."

I'm not even sure what to think anymore. Two rocks and a slithering freak took the power of friendship, the unbreakable entity, from all of us, and now the Devil is being nice to Vizor and me?

"GRRRGG!" The Devil grabs Its hip like there is a thorn there. When It yanks away, Vizor and I lay our eyes upon a sword-like object. After tearing that thing off Its hip, It grows even weaker than It already was.

"HERE... YOU... GO. THE UNBOUND EVIL IS WAITING..." the Devil says, shivering.

"What is this?"

"YOUR FRIENDSHIP... WILL GUIDE... YOU..."

"What?"

It's too late. The Devil's chair falls into the hole it had come from, and the Earth closes in on itself like a giant zipper. As I hold the red, glowing blade in my hand, the Devil's last words ring in my head:

– *YOUR FRIENDSHIP... WILL GUIDE... YOU...*

"V, you heard It. The Unbound Evil is waiting for us."

"Did you not just listen?" I turn around, revealing Void V's eyes.

"How? I thought the energy was drained."

"It told us to believe in our friends. IT. The DEVIL. It has no friends. It has only enemies. Evil, supposedly, longs merely for power. And you know what? That doesn't really matter right now... What the Devil just exemplified here..." — I close my eyes — "is that chaos exists in everyone!" I thrust the sword into the air. The red light grows exponentially, and the red mist soon turns into bright flames. A flame of life, a shimmer of hope, and FRIENDS THAT NEVER QUIT! The fire envelops every living being in the area. Everyone slowly starts to get up, all eyes flowing with life.

Griff gets up, wobbling around. "Where am I?"

"GRIFF!" I grab him and lift him off his feet. I spin him around a few times because I'm just that happy to see he's all right. (In hindsight, that wasn't the best idea, because when I put him back down, he fell down again from dizziness).

"Hazy! Drac!" Still a tad confused, Vizor helps the two get their footing. Hazy nearly slips, but turns into a bat to catch herself. As she reverts back to her normal self, Vizor and she exchange high fives. Drac looks at the two, crosses his arms, and nods in delight.

"Are you all right, Myra?"

"I feel like I've just woken up from falling down a flight of stairs, so... eh."

"You two are OK!" Vizor is still taking all this in.

"Of course we are. What'd you expect?"

"Hey, I was worried. You are my friends after all."

"I wouldn't say that." Dante sarcastically smirks. Vizor and he share a laugh.

"Azilez! Z! D! Everyone's OK!" I throw my hands up in excitement, careful to not hit anyone with the base of the sword that the Devil gave me. D jumps on me. So does Azilez. Z is a little smarter and refrains from putting more weight on me. Strangely, it doesn't bother me. I feel much better now, and, from the look of things, so does Vizor. Our breathing is stable again, and we aren't falling over anymore.

Despite the happy atmosphere, and the now clear sky over the remains of San Francisco, Vizor looks to the sun and remembers that the final battle is still upon us.

Chapter 36

Limitless Power

"There isn't a whole lot of time, everyone." Vizor turns so everyone can see him. "And sadly, there are also a lot of unanswered questions, but the Unbound Evil is headed to the sun to try and destroy everything, again. We have to stop It."

"Everyone still on board?" I stand next to Vizor.

"I'm all for it."

"Count me in!"

"Wouldn't miss it."

"Let's go, now!"

"All right, good. Then let's–"

"WAIT!" From the other side of the bay, Melok calls out to us. "We'll help you guys out too!"

"If you need a power jolt, just ask." Electrox chimes in.

"Thanks, guys. But I think we have all the power we need," I reply. "Could you guys actually hold the fort for us? Maybe start rebuilding the city? And getting everyone back here too?"

"Sure thing." Melok happily complies. Electrox and its followers float behind Melok into the rubble of San Francisco.

"Now then!" Let's see if the Devil's weapon really works. "Everyone, place your hand on this sword."

Without wasting any time, everyone trots over. Once the final hand touches the sword, a red light beams from the tip of the weapon and shimmers onto everyone. Almost instantly, everyone's chaos forms are brought back. Dante and Myra even get in on the action. Looks like I was right. There is nothing in this world, or out of it, that can ever quell friendship.

"Out yonder, everyone. The sun awaits!" Z points to the ball of fire in the sky. Everyone jumps up, and, before we know it, we're out of the Earth's atmosphere. Bad news though: we have company.

"Hello again, V!"

I look behind me, and, with the Dark Spirit's power, spy Adolf's soul tailgating me.

"Oh, of all times. Z, help me out!"

"Huh? Sure."

Midflight, Adolf summons ninja swastika stars and throws them at Z and me.

"Three iron? Or four wood?"

"I'd go with the four. Get that extra height, you know?"

"Good call." Z uses his power to materialize a golf bag, and pulls out the four wood. "Go above me and distract him. I'll get a good swing that way."

"Will do." I go high and charge up power like I'm about to attack. This grabs Adolf's attention, giving Z enough time for one good power shot.

"Now!" When the lights from my hands fizzle, Adolf is confused. Realizing that there's a third person, he looks at Z, only to find a ninja star on his forehead and a Titleist golf ball on his nose.

"EEEAAAHHH!" Adolf holds his nose in pain.

"Time for a cheap shot." Z raises his four wood in the air and throws it at Adolf. PING! The resulting impact causes Adolf's spirit to hurl back toward Earth. The four wood returns to Z like a boomerang.

"Nice!" I give him a "V" sign.

"Good thing I got a practice shot in after a few days."

"Well, get ready. We're about to get to the real deal."

We fly until the sun is in our faces. Behind it, there are 12 floating tablets and a giant, dark-purple sea serpent with arms and deformed wings.

"AHAHAHAHAHA! It's good to be back!"

"So, back at Your old game again? It'll only end like last time."

"We'll see. Oh, yes, we will…"

– *Caution, V. It does have 12 prophecies.*

– *I'm aware. Thanks.*

"Where's your grand speech this time, chosen one? Something like 'your ways are mad.' Or… hmm…'Your evil ways are over.' Make this interesting for Me. What? Nothing?"

"I'll just let my actions do my talking for me."

"Ohohohohoho! Yes! This is what I mean. Make it interesting. It'll make destroying this worthless universe all the sweeter."

Right, It wants to destroy our universe and build one in Its image.

"You bore me, Unbound Evil."

"Oh, is that so, Vizor?"

"This isn't Your root. Haven't you learned anything? V's right. This WILL end like last time."

"Ahahaha! But that's where you're WRONG." With that last word booming, It claps the Heaven Prophecy and Hell Prophecy together again. Hazy, Drac, Dante, and Myra start tumbling in confusion, Z's golf bag and four wood disappear, D's pendulum gives off static electricity, and Griff's hair and Azilez's staff explode. "HA! How's that for learning?"

"You want learning? Here's your next lesson." I hold up the Devil's weapon in the air again. Everyone's powers revert back to normal, almost as if nothing has happened to them at all.

"That thing… What is it?"

"Even if I knew, you really think I'd tell You?"

"I can feel its essence, fool. The Devil gave that to you." The Unbound Evil's nose scrunches.

"Wow. Looks like It did learn after all." Vizor sounds a little surprised.

"Regardless. I don't really care how much power you have. It PALES in comparison to what I have now! Wither in fear, you roaches!"

The 12 prophecies light up and gather around the sun. The Unbound Evil flies into its core.

"Uh-oh! Guys, we have to stop…" Before Griff can even finish,

KABLOOEY! A giant ring of fire is exuded from the sun, twisting and turning us into each other. The Unbound Evil comes out looking much different. Its head turns bright red, It grows two more sets of eagle's wings, and Its chest, spine, and head grow black stalactites.

"It doesn't stop there either. COME HERE, MY CHAMPION!" The evil's cry soars throughout the cosmos, loudly enough to be heard by "the champion".

"You rang?" Fear runs through my forehead as I hear the eerily familiar voice of Adolf.

"Ah, yes, indeed I did. Why don't you come on over and fuse with me so we can WIPE THIS BUNCH OFF THE FACE OF EXISTENCE?"

"I like the way You think!"

"How 'bout NO?" Azilez flies forward and straight-up smacks Adolf's spirit with her staff. "Do you guys have cement for feet? MOVE! We can't just watch It get stronger!"

Everyone silently agrees and disperses.

"Try exploding Your way out of this!" Vizor uses his hair as a conduit to summon a triangle of flames and shoots It. He goes for the stalactites.

Turns out, the Unbound Evil has gotten MUCH stronger. Not only does Vizor's projectile not hurt It, but the spikes somehow knock it back at him. "Good riddance."

"You can say that again." Hazy charges headlong at the Unbound Evil's wings. With one giant flap, the wings not only send Hazy back, but everyone behind her starts tumbling aimlessly.

"Are you serious? Ugh! This is NOT the resistance I expected from you guys. Looks like there's no more power to absorb. You guys are useless to Me. Shoo, shoo!" It turns to face the only two that are left standing, Vizor and me. "Now, if you'd be so kind to give Me that glowing sword. You can just skedaddle along back to the hole you call home." A little frightened by Its new powers, I retaliate by smacking Its hand with the sword. "Good to see there's still some fight left in you two. Maybe that explosion was a good idea after all…"

Vizor and I exchange puzzled looks. Then we remember the encounter we had with It here last time. The time when we forced It out of Drac and fought It here.

"Oh, yeah, that. Wait, that explosion was planned?"

"I saw no use in fighting you then. It would've been a waste of time and power. So I made that much weaker version of Me return to what you see in front of you…"

"To give Yourself more power when the big fight came around?"

"Good to see that there's at least two beings with some sense left in them. However, I'll have to strip that from you too."

"Never!"

"Oh, I'm afraid what you have to say doesn't matter at this point, V. You see, I've already won."

"No! You've still got us two to get past."

"Then how's a cosmic bomb for you?"

"Wait. What?"

No more words are spoken. The Unbound Evil merely flies up into the giant ring of prophecies and causes the sun to explode. Everyone gets knocked into different directions.

"V!" Vizor reaches out for my hand. I quickly grab it. That moment, when his hand touches mine, reminds me of some of the Devil's words:

– YOU TWO… YOU HAVE A BOND THAT SURPASSES ALMOST ANYTHING I'VE EVER SEEN.

I'm not exactly sure how, but when I grab Vizor's hand, the blade in my other hand violently reacts with a giant red glow. This time, however, the glow includes hues of blue as well. Within seconds, the blue-and-red light is twice as big as the Unbound Evil. Since I'm having trouble holding on to the blade and Vizor at the same time, I'm not noticing what the glow is doing: it's absorbing the energy released by the sun-sized nuke. After the explosion subsides, the fabric of space-time pulls itself back together. As the stars and the constellations re-gather, I see them all glowing like they're smiling upon Vizor and me. It's as if we're in a universe-sized gladiator cage match to the death and the entire crowd is rooting for our victory. The sword absorbs the last bit of energy, and then returns to normal.

Yet after all that, Vizor's hand is still in mine. "Are you OK?" I ask.

"Yes. Thanks for saving the entire universe from exploding!"

Due to the amount of force I had to exert just to hold the blade and Vizor at the same time during that giant explosion, my chaos form subsides and I pass out, dropping the blade from my hand. Vizor immediately picks up the blade and me.

"N... nnnnn... nnnnnnnnn... NNNNNNNNNNNNN-NAAAAAAAAAAGGGGGGHHHHHHHHH! GIVE ME THAT BLADE, NOW!" The blade summons a giant energy shield that the Unbound Evil runs into, causing It to ricochet. "IF I CAN'T HAVE THAT BLADE, THEN NO ONE CAN." It reveals Adolf's spirit and the 12 prophecies, once more. With another clap of the Heaven Prophecy and the Hell Prophecy, Adolf's life force completely fizzles, as does any of the Solar and Shadow Prophecies' remaining energy. It drains so much of their power that the prophecies' colors subside. They become lifeless, ordinary stones. "TREMBLE BEFORE THE NEW RULER OF THE UNIVERSE! PURE CHAOS EVIL!"

– *Pure Chaos…?*

– *Nnn… ahhhhh!*

– *Dark Spirit? Wait… What?*

As existence itself shakes, the Dark Spirit flies out of me and into the Unbound Evil. "I'M GOING TO HAVE TO BORROW THAT, IF YOU DON'T MIND. ON SECOND THOUGHT, I DON'T CARE WHAT YOU MIND. I NEED THAT DARK SPIRIT FOR THE PURE CHAOS TRANS-FORMATION, AND MY DECREE IS ABSOLUTE. AFTER ALL, I AM THE NEW SUPREME BEING OF THIS UNIVERSE."

– *Hold on… God! I'll just consult…"*

"LOOKING FOR THIS?" A surge of electrifying light fills the black void of space and envelops the Unbound Evil.

"V, I'm sorry. The light cannot stop It now…" With those final words, the Devil sucks the light through Its mouth like It is drinking a giant glass of milk with a bendy straw.

The Unbound Evil continues to grow until all of Its joints spew out colossal elephant tusks. It grows three sets of dragon's wings, and grows three tails, each with a separate head on the tip. "I AM COM-PLETE!"

– *Heaven Prophecy? Hell Prophecy? You're still there, right?* Vizor tries to get to them.

– *Of course we are. Why do you ask?*

– *Why are you just sitting there? Stop It!*

– *…*

– *Do SOMETHING!*

– *…*

– *Really? At a time that we need help the most?*

– *…*

– *Some friends you two are.* Vizor's eyes pop after he says that.

– *Friends… friends. I think I now get what V was trying to tell me back on Earth. He sacrificed his chaos form, just to save me from flying into space. He could've chosen to save only himself and fight the Devil as he is "destined to", but chooses friends over that. Friends ARE THE KEY!* The blade the Devil bestowed upon us shines with a black and white wave of light. With one sword thrust into the air, the blade telepathically finds Griff, Azilez, Z, D, Dante, Myra, Hazy, and Drac. It brings them all back to the scene of the fight. Despite the fact that their chaos forms have been drained multiple times, the blade gives them the power to transform once more. Except for Vizor and me.

"SO YOU GOT YOUR CHAOS FORMS BACK AGAIN? IT MEANS NOTHING! I'LL JUST WIPE THEM OUT AGAIN."

"I'm not done!"

"HUH?"

"Time for the ultimate chaos transformation! THE TRANSFOR-MATION OF SOULS!"

"WHAT ARE YOU SAYING? THERE'S NO SPIRITUAL ENERGY FOR YOU TO COMBINE WITH!"

"Wrong. It's been in front of me this whole time! Now, using this blade's energy, I fuse V's spirit with mine!"

"WHAT?"

The blade levitates on its own, and Vizor's body breaks down into a blue, gloppy energy. Mine does the same, except the energy's color is red. The two blobs of energy meet at the point of the sword, and the resulting flash of purple light forces the Unbound Evil to cover Its eyes. When our energies collide, a single body is formed. It has a white, fluffy Afro, a pair of Devil's wings with several hair blades attached to the top of them, my big, brown eyes, and Vizor's devilishly good-looking smile. When the body finishes materializing, the Devil's sword gently falls into the body's right hand.

"WHAT IS THAT?"

"The physical hope of friendship's true power. The bane of all greedy and power-hungry evil. The final solution... to THREATS LIKE YOU."

"And what is this being's name, if I may ask?" Griff is really curious. So is everyone else, but they're a little speechless after seeing Vizor and me combine.

"Vexus. Chaos Vexus."

C h a p t e r   3 7

The Fires of Friendship

I t seems that in the course of this adventure, Vizor has really started to figure out who he is and who his real friends are. He came from a planet filled with power-hungry murderers who wanted to try and kill me. Now look at him: he's literally a part of me. And I'm a part of him.

"WHOOOHOOO! Let's dance." Unable to contain her excitement, Azilez fires a volley of homing rainbows.

"Finally, something interesting!" The Unbound Evil, or rather Pure Chaos Evil, easily sidesteps to avoid the attack. Or at least the initial part of the attack.

"C'mon…" Azilez lifts her staff, and the homing shots fly back at the Pure Chaos Evil. Not expecting it, the evil's back is bombarded with all eight shots.

"Daddy! Let's help her out."

"I couldn't agree more." Bursting into their dragon forms, Hazy and Drac charge at the Unbound Evil.

"Hmph. I've never seen her so brave." Dante rushes after them. Myra shrugs and follows behind him.

– I like the look of this, V.

– Why?

– We greatly outnumber the Pure Chaos Evil. If everyone keeps up the pressure, we can deliver fatal blows.

– Sounds reckless, but it has to work.

After we finish our internal self-dialogue, Z and D fly above the Pure Chaos Evil, and throw every projectile in their arsenal at It. This forces It to constantly be on the move.

Since the evil is distracted by all the attacks hitting It at once, It doesn't even pay attention to Vexus, thus giving him the prime opportunity for a massive sword swing.

"GRRRGGG!"

"I'm not through with You." Vexus jumps off the Pure Chaos Evil and detaches all of the hair blades on his wings, sending them into the evil.

"So many misfits, so little time." It tries to flap Its wings again, but Hazy and Myra hold down two of the three left wings. Dante and Drac hold down two of the three right wings. As a result, the Pure Chaos Evil can only flap two wings. Its attempt to shake off the vampires fails. "Fine! Have it your way, everyone. I'll just…" It reveals the Hell Prophecy and the Heaven Prophecy and collides them, again. This time, nothing happens. We keep fighting, without disturbance.

"HOW?"

"This power wasn't born of the prophecies, Evil." Vexus hovers in front of the Pure Chaos Evil. "It was born of our friendship with everyone: Griff, Azilez, Hazy, Drac, Dante, Myra, Vizor, V, and even the prophecies. And, like last time, you can't take what you can't comprehend."

"OF COURSE I CAN. WATCH ME!" It tries to grab Vexus, but he easily flies to avoid the evil's slow reach. It cannot focus on Vexus while being distracted by everyone. "GET OFF ME!"

"Why should we? This is actually kind of fun." Hazy chuckles.

"I'm with her," Azilez adds.

"Hey, wait. Where's Griff?" Vexus' head wanders.

"Here I am!" Griff launches from under the Pure Chaos Evil. He rams into Its jaw with such force that a dentist probably couldn't fix the tooth damage.

– *C'mon, you tools, do something!*

"They won't, Pure Chaos Evil."

"And why not? They're mine to command."

That's actually a good question. If those prophecies aren't going to help us, shouldn't they be helping the Pure Chaos Evil? Why do those prophecies really love to do nothing? Not only that, they're consciously not doing anything. I can still sense their energies, but their thoughts suddenly just blew away. So what gives?

Despite what these two prophecies are doing, it changes nothing. This evil still wants all of the power It can gather. And to what avail?

"You know, I'm not even sure myself. Those two prophecies are a mystery," Vexus replies. "All I know is that Your power is going to turn against You." Vexus body slams the evil, sending the Heaven Prophecy and the Hell Prophecy into the air. He grabs both of them and claps. The Pure Chaos Evil's power bursts out like a balloon that just popped. As the energy is about to scatter away, Vexus absorbs it in his hands. "Everyone, gather around!" He throws the evil's power into the Devil's sword, which glows red again. "Get ready to fire your most powerful attack."

"You… will never… truly… defeat Me!"

"Never TRULY? I don't care how long it takes," Vexus begins, "but I will find Your root. And when I do, this'll happen!" He fires a giant, celestial comet from the blade; Azilez shoots out a giant rainbow; Z strikes a giant golf ball; D materializes and launches a Redwood Tree; Hazy and Drac cough out huge fireballs; Griff turns around and uses his hair as a flamethrower; Dante fires a white laser from his hand; and Myra fires a blue laser. Midway between the Unbound Evil and us, all of the attacks combine into a super-charged finisher. KAAAABOOOOOOOM-MMMMMM!

Sparks and ashes spew in every direction. Black fog corrodes the air as the evil's own power betrays It.

"NOOOOOOOOOOOOOOOOOO! I WAS SOOOOOOOOO CLOOOOOOOOOOOOSSEEEE!"

In the final explosion, a profusion of colors and flashing lights replaces the prior grim atmosphere. It almost looks like a new star is being born right in front of our eyes.

After the lovely fireworks display, It explodes, once more, into nothingness. The day is saved, and the battle is won. Vexus splits into Vizor and me. The Devil's sword disappears.

C h a p t e r   3 8

O-moh-ternal Instinct

Huff… puff… it's finally over. I don't know how we did it, but the Unbound Evil has been thwarted once more. I believe this calls for a victory dance!

"Oh, yeah! Go, V! Go, V! Uh-huh, uh-huh, uh-huh. Whoo!" Even though my tattered body barely allows it, I breakdance in midair.

"HEY! No celebrating! Not without me anyway." Azilez spawns a rainbow hoverboard, sits on it, and flies in endless circles.

"This means we can go home now, right?" D holds his giant, death-inducing pendulum like it's a baby rattle.

"I'd say so." Z tries to balance his golf club on his pinky finger.

Amidst the festivities, Vizor and Griff remain in a secluded space with stern faces. I wonder why. "Hey, guys. What's up? Join the party!"

"The celebrations are premature, V." Vizor looks into the distance. "The Unbound Evil is still upon us." No sooner these words are uttered than everyone falls silent and turns to the direction Vizor is staring at.

"I don't feel anything, Vizor."

– *Try harder, V.*

– *Not you too, Dark Spirit. I thought it was finally time we went home and all–*

– *Believe me, I want to as well. But Vizor is right: the Unbound Evil IS still here.*

– *Grrr… where is It? I'll tear It to shreds!*

– *V! Calm down. We don't want another Evil V mishap.*

Can you blame me though? I'm sick of this Thing! One second

I think the world is saved, and then It just has to come in and ruin it, again! To be fair, what else should I have expected? … Oh. That. I guess that never crossed my mind.

"Hello, mother." Vizor crosses his arms and examines the floating female figure in front of him. She's a towering figure, with purple hair blades, forest-green hair, and a fiendish grin that's the stuff of nightmares.

"So you've finally returned, have you? Why would you, anyway? You couldn't even destroy V like you were supposed to. Go flaunt your disgraceful face to some other galaxy or something."

"Good to see you too. Now, if you don't mind handing over the evil there?"

"Why should I? With it, I can finally destroy everything the Omoh sapiens fear and return them to their glory days."

"Mother, please. You know as well as I do that 'glory' isn't a word that describes our people."

"That's because you took it from us, m'darling. I'll be taking it back now, thank you." She throws her hair blades like a boomerang and slices Vizor's face. On their way back, the blades head straight for the Shadow Prophecies. Everyone tries dog-piling onto the tablets so that the blades just pass them, but when Vizor's mom widens her eyes, a purple shockwave temporarily paralyzes everyone and drains their chaos forms. As the paralysis wears off, everyone lies around helplessly.

"Wa… was that the evil's power?"

"Yes, Vizor."

"How? How is it not overtaking you?"

"M'darling. Did you really think I didn't know how to control the Unbound Evil? I, the queen of the Omoh sapiens? You're just as laughable as your father."

"But the Unbound Evil–"

"Enough. I don't have time to explain it to you. Instead, why don't I just show you how I control Its power? Hmm?"

"I…"

"Excellent choice, m'darling." She locks Vizor and herself in a giant purple sphere, the same that Vizor had used to take my family seven years ago.

"I… can't… fight." Vizor attempts to go into his chaos form but can't, as his energy is completely drained.

"Just as I suspected. Now everything will go according to plan."

"What do you want… mother?"

"You, out of my sight."

"But why?"

"Figure it out. You've been doing it all week, no?"

"I don't want to kill you, mother. But if you continue to drag me down like this. Grnk!"

"Ha. You can barely stand. Kill me? The Unbound Evil's bountiful energy fuels me. It's everywhere."

"We just killed It!" I wake up, nearly in my evil form. The mist is spewing out of my hands, but I make sure the beast stays contained.

"Think about it, o' great chosen one. Do you really think you're killing the evil every time It blows up?"

"Huh? Of course! What else could It be doing?"

"Such a narrow-minded fool you are. Well, to make a long story short, It's transferring Its energy to Its core."

– *Its core?* The Dark Spirit begins connecting the dots. – *Oh, dear.*

– *What now?*

– *If what she says is true, V, then the Unbound Evil has been powering up this way for a long, LONG time. There's no telling how powerful Its core could be!*

All this time? And we never knew? It was slipping Its energy right under our noses? Not only that, but the Adolf situation. How many copies of Itself did It splatter throughout history? It could feed off past evils, present evils, hell, probably future evils to boot. Anything's possible with that wiggly slime ball!

"That's not all It's transferring. It's also transferring the prophecies' energies which you all exert in your so-called 'final attacks'. I guess what the humans say is true. You do get out what you put in."

"… Ugh. How could we miss this?"

"Because you're m'darling. And m'darling is an idiot. Time for your purification period. But don't fret. Your helpless friends will join you."

"NEVER!" Azilez musters enough strength for one last blurt.

"You have no choice, I'm afraid. All fates within this one-hundred-foot radius are sealed."

"Got that right, mother."

"Vi… Vizor?"

Vizor's mom is confused as to how her son's eye color has changed so quickly. And how he's suddenly standing up again. Seems she only uses evil to gain power, not to understand it. Big mistake.

"Seems you've been out of the fray for too long. I'm not your child, I'm not an Omoh sapien, and I'm not just some chosen one. I'm Vizor, and THIS is a part of who I am."

"Me too." Griff stands tall, in his evil form.

"What the–?"

"Me three." Azilez stands… not as tall but still in her evil form.

Everyone rises in evil forms, standing in unity with Vizor. Well, everyone except…"And lastly, me." I open my eyes, and the white typhoons with red centers reveal themselves. Combining the last of our remaining strengths, we knock down the force field containing Vizor.

"Game over, mother. It's ten against one."

"But you forget that one has your finishing blow at Its disposal." She holds her hair blades out like a cannon and shoots out our own finishing blow against us. "Die! All of you! Stains upon the Omoh sapiens."

"Drop dead, lady." Vizor stops calling her "mother".

"What the hell? How aren't you all dead? You're taking tons of chaos energy to the face? You can flinch or something!"

"We can, but why should we? Stains upon the Omoh sapien race? News flash: they're all gone! None of them are left. There's nothing left for you. See, these guys have taught me something really important. It's not about finding evil to gain power; it's about finding power to understand evil! The Omoh sapiens aren't special because evil is a part of everything in the universe. Everyone has to accept the fact, at one point or another, that evil will come catching up to them. It seems to me that you made the same mistake everyone else on Treah did, and, for that, you'll perish by the very power you try to control. Ready, guys? ONE LAST TIME!"

"One! Last! Time!"

We all place our hands out, remaining entirely stationary. Within seconds, the beam that was firing at us is now firing in the other direction with amplified evil energy.

"Reveal to us the evil inside you! The heart of the Omoh sapiens!"

"Never! I'd never help the likes of you!"

"Well, it's like a certain someone once told me: you have no choice."

"Grrrr!"

"Hey, lady! One more thing! Whenever you meet the Unbound Evil at Its core, tell It something for me. Tell It that no matter how much power It sucks up in Its oversized vacuum, It'll never be as strong as us. Tell It that no amount of artificial power can match what we have. And tell It that we'll be waiting… and we'll be ready!"

"NOOOOOOOOOOOOOOO! AAAAAAAHHHHHHH!" The giant white beam overtakes Vizor's mother, revealing to us the primal form of the unconscious evil inside.

"I'll take That to go." Vizor absorbs the Unbound Evil into his body — rather akin to the way I absorb the Dark Spirit into my body.

With that, the entire Omoh sapien race is now extinct.

Chapter 39

The Dust Settles

Whew… what a week it's been. I don't know about everyone else, but, boy, am I exhausted! Once we get back home, I'm going to take a few weeks off. I can't go on another adventure in the state I'm in.

No, seriously, look at me. Transforming in and out of my chaos form has done a number on me. I feel bruised all over, and my bones feel like they can break at any moment.

In fact, I feel really light-headed…

"V? V!" Vizor realizes I've passed out.

"What's wrong with him?" Griff catches on.

"He looks fine to me." Hazy thinks about biting me again.

– V? Do you need my assistance? You know I'm here for you.

– Just take me home.

– You don't want healing?

– Please. Home.

– OK. If it's what you want. The Dark Spirit becomes a visible phoenix. It uses Its claws to grab my shirt and fly back to Earth.

"Dark Spirit? What are you doing? Heal him!" Drac points out my poor physical state.

"That's not what he wants."

"What does he want?" Myra asks.

"Home."

Griff and Azilez look at each other and smile. Z and D smile and nod.

"I think I understand." Griff steps up. "In fact, I'm with the guy.

He misses his home. He has put so much strain on himself on account of these adventures that the only medicine for him is home."

"Home sounds nice! I'll make some food for us to eat. It's on me!" Oh, goodie, Azilez is as good a cook as she is an artist. She likes cooking so much that she always wants to cook her own birthday cakes, and Candice has to stop her.

"I bet he misses Smash and SpongeBob too." D revels in the thought of TV.

"I miss playing real golf." Z examines his driver.

"Well, there's a place that has all of that and more, everyone," Griff says.

"Let me guess: home?"

"Don't be such a buzzkill, Dante." Myra shoves him a little.

"At any rate," Vizor breaks up the two, "home is that-a-way."

"Are you sure you're pointed at the right planet?" Z has the look of a "smart aleck".

"You know, that's a good question, Z." Vizor is blind to Z's sarcasm. "Thinking about it, I have no reason to go back to Treah. There's no one else there. All of my friends live on Earth now. So my home is where my friends are."

Z actually smiles this time. "Well, then, I hope you're good at golf."

"What's 'golf?'"

"Blasphemy. Oh, we're gonna have tons of fun with you when we get back. Come on, everyone!" Z seems the most anxious to get back now.

"Hold it! What about these things?" Myra picks up the Solar Prophecies.

"And these?" Dante holds the Shadow Prophecies.

"I'll take yours, Myra." Griff stuffs the lifeless stones inside his bag.

"And I'll take those." Vizor doesn't have a case to hold his prophecies, and they can't float, so he ends up carrying them all.

Eventually, the Dark Spirit makes it back to San Francisco, where all of the magnet people are rebuilding the city. The first thing It notices is that the magnet beings are trying to replicate the old-fashioned feel of San Francisco. That seems to give some of them trouble since they're so used to technological advancements.

"Oh, dear. Where's the tree house?" The Dark Spirit thinks out loud.

"What seems to be the trouble?" Electrox reveals itself.

"I was wondering if V's tree house was anywhere around here."

"You're in luck. It happens to be the first thing we rebuilt. My orders."

The Dark Spirit flies behind Electrox, and the two make it back to my street. It looks just like I remember it before I left for this whack trip. At the front, there wait my mom and dad; Griff's parents; and Azilez's mom, Candice, who looks MAD.

"Here you go, V. This is what you wanted." The Dark Spirit gently places me on the soft grass and reenters my body. My parents kneel to my side when they see me unconscious.

"Quick, get him inside," my mom nearly orders my dad.

"Hey, I missed him as much as you did."

"GET HIM INSIDE."

"Yes, ma'am." My dad's voice becomes shrill.

"Where's everyone else?" Griff's mom is concerned for her son.

The Dark Spirit exits my body to go and ease her mind. "They're all still coming. Nothing bad happened. It's just that V passed out suddenly. We needed to get him home first."

"WELL, WHENEVER MY GIRL GETS HERE, SHE'S NEVER GOING OUT OF THE HOUSE AGAIN." Candice looks like she can pull her hair out at any moment.

"Ma'am, with all due respect, your daughter was vital in this journey for everyone. She's gone through a lot, and is even planning to cook when she gets home…"

"Oh, she's planning on cooking? Well, why didn't you just say so? No trouble at all for her then. In fact, I might be in for some trouble if I eat too many of her cookies again."

The Dark Spirit has a hard time keeping up with her fluctuating personalities. "Can I see you two for a quick moment?" It goes off to the side with Griff's parents.

"Is she always like this?" It tries to sound as calm as possible, but still comes off as worried.

"Oh, all the time. It's nothing to be afraid of."

"She just takes a lot of getting used to," Griff's dad chimes in.

"Home sweet home, I guess. Thank you for the reassurance."

"No problem. Same price."

"What price?" The Dark Spirit jerks Its head around, paranoid. Griff's parents share a hearty laugh. The sad part is, the Dark Spirit actually thinks there's a price. It still can't shift gears into relaxation mode. The Dark Spirit eventually shrugs it off and finds my body again.

"There you all are!" Candice runs up to Azilez, and gives her a nice, big hug.

"Mom!"

Griff finds his parents as well.

"Mom! Dad!"

My two best friends reunite with their families, and Z and D run into the tree house to look for our parents.

"Mama?"

"Baba?"

"In V's room," Kal replies. The two make haste and run to the very top of the tree house. There, they start panting.

"Lara, you have this from here, yes?"

"Of course. Go help Z and D."

"With pleasure." Kal carries D in his right arm, and hugs Z with his left.

"I really missed all of you. It's great to have you back. No more adventures for a few weeks, OK?"

"Got it."

"Yes, papa bear."

The three stay silent for a few minutes and revel in each other's company.

"Now then… you two STINK."

"I call showering first."

"In your dreams, Z."

They race down, each determined to get into the shower before the other. They even trip each other, using their pickaxes and golf clubs.

"They do realize that there's more than one shower in this giant tree house, right?"

"Give them a day or two to simmer back into their normal lives. They did just save the universe after all."

Back outside the tree house, Myra opens up. "So what do we do now?"

"I guess the first thing is to round up all of the vampires again."

"Did someone say 'vampires'?" A floating magnet with a construction helmet overhears their conversation.

"Yes, over here." Hazy waves.

"We have gathered all of your kind in one convenient location. Would you like to take them back home? Our king has given you permission to do so."

"Wow. You guys work fast."

"It is what we do best."

"You heard it. This way."

Dante, Myra, and Drac all rush over to Hazy's side. Vizor shrugs and follows behind.

They're all led to a port near Pier 33. There, a boat is docked, waiting to be boarded. The five trot onto the vessel, and a magnet with a sailor's hat starts driving. After a nice, soothing boat ride across the San Francisco Bay, the group lands on Alcatraz Island.

They're taken into the main lobby. The magnet guards enter a ten-number PIN, and the floor goes underground. In this secret, gigantic underground area, all of the vampires are sound asleep.

"Again, you guys work fast."

"What can we say? It's what we're programmed to do."

– *Programmed? They were programmed? Who made them?* Vizor thinks to himself.

"You want to wake them up, daddy?"

"It'd be an honor, my sweet Hazy." With one giant breath, Drac lets out a dragon's roar and makes the entire vampire clan jump. Since they're all underground, they hit their heads on the solid concrete above them. "Good day, everyone! My little Hazy, Dante, Myra, and I have returned to take you home!"

"HOOOOORRAAAAAYYYYYY!"

"YEAH!"

"THE PRINCE OF DARKNESS IS BACK!"

"I CAN'T WAIT!"

"TRANYSLVANIA, HERE WE COME!"

"But what about the sun? We'll never survive in that harsh, icky sunlight!"

"Icky? Harsh? No, no, no. Far from it, my dear friends! Pay close attention." Drac waves his cape around, producing sun-colored dust. The particles gently sift onto everyone in the room and give the entire vampire race a taste of the sun. "No words." Drac throws his hands in the air before everyone starts noisily stirring chaos. "If you liked what you just felt, then come with me. Back home." Drac flies out of the hole in the ground. Hazy follows. Then Dante. Then Myra. As soon as Vizor is about to leave, he turns around to look at the vampires. The immediate disdain is almost palpable. Being the son of the hated Omoh sapien king, how can the vampires not feel this way? All they know is Vizor's reputation. Despite that, Vizor only smiles at them, turns around, and leaves.

Confused, they transform into bats and fly out of the hole, only to find Hazy, Drac, Dante, and Myra all happily flying with their Omoh sapien friend, Vizor. They start to cheer again, and with smiles on all faces, the vampire train is headed to Transylvania.

Chapter 40

Peace of Mind

A few hours pass, and everyone, except Vizor, is settled back into the tree house. Azilez is preparing a big feast for everyone. She's wearing an apron that says "Kiss the Chef!" Everyone else is talking at the dinner table.

"I'm NEVER leaving here." Candice is breaking out into tears of happiness.

– *Not sure if this is a good thing or a bad thing.* Griff looks a tad worried.

"It's only temporary, you know." My dad tries to get that across to her.

"SILENCE."

– *Jeez. What is with all the women today?* My dad isn't having the best time coping with the new guest.

"So, Z, do you want to go play golf after this?"

"Are you for real? I'm hibernating after this."

"I thought you were excited to show Vizor what golf is."

"Well, uh… he's not here. So…"

An hour later, the families sit around the dinner table to enjoy the sumptuous meal. Even Vizor is back, and everyone is eager to show their new alien friend what they like to do on Earth.

"Wanna play video games with me, Vizor?"

"Uh–"

"Of course he doesn't! He wants to practice painting with me."

"What he really wants is to see my toy car collection."

"Well, I'd–"

"He wants to be my new intern."

"He's going to go to the store with me to pick out his new room's floor design and color."

– I wish I were sleeping like V is…

I feel bad for the guy. I'm going to throw him a bone.

– Dark Spirit?

– Yes?

– Do you want to help Vizor through this family ordeal?

– Definitely.

Out of my body It goes and heads into Vizor's ears, so he becomes temporarily deaf.

– What the–?

– You're welcome, Vizor.

– Oh. Thanks, Dark Spirit. Thanks, V.

– Finally I can go to sleep, knowing Vizor isn't in torment.

Come to think of it, that's what this entire adventure's been about: trying to get Vizor back on his own two feet again. Or, rather, for the first time. The more I think about it, the more I realize that the guy never really had a life back on his home planet to begin with. All he had was Hazy. That one friendship has branched into several, and the whole universe is at his fingertips now, thanks to the awesome new power we've acquired.

– Hehehehe! I'm going to get the jump on V this time. He won't even see it coming without that putrid Dark Spirit. Adolf's spirit somehow survived the Unbound Evil and is back to haunt me.

As it turns out, I don't need the Dark Spirit to detect spirits anymore. Evil V has got me covered.

– IF YOU GO ONE STEP CLOSER, I SWEAR I'M GONNA–!

Realizing that evil me means business, Adolf steps back. *– On second thought… RUN!*

– That's what I thought you said.

Oh, yeah. That happened too. The evil natures of my best friends and me were revealed. As it turns out, we've got bad guys inside our minds, but that doesn't exactly make us bad guys. In fact, we are more powerful and complete than ever. All we had to do was control and embrace the chaos within us.

Speaking of embracing, it's time I embrace this pillow under my head. I close my eyes and fall asleep, with my red doll in hand.

I dream about our adventure, starting from the very beginning — that is to say, the moment Azilez was possessed. At the end of it all, I still find myself in the dream, but there's only white space now. After some time, Griff, Azilez, Z, D, and Vizor join me in the white space. What's about to happen? I'm not exactly sure, but I can tell it'll be something I wouldn't want to miss. That's because, as we all know, the best adventures are those that take place inside us.